ALSO BY K. L. ABRAHAMSON

Phoebe Clay Mysteries
Through Dark Water
Beneath Malabar Nets
Within Angkor Shadows

The Detektiv Kazakov Mysteries
After Yekaterina
Mareson's Arrow
The Tsarina's Mask
Ivan's Wolf

The Aung and Yamin Fantasy Mystery Series
Death By Effigy
A Death in Passing
Death in Umber

"Chan." At a stoplight Phoebe leaned forward and managed to catch his attention. "There's someone following us. A yellow motorcycle has been behind us since the temple."

He flipped up his visor, his expression grim. "I see him. That's why I pass truck. I lose him." A huge grin, and he flipped his visor down. "Hold tight," he called.

She did as told and braced herself as the light changed. The motorcycle taxi raced off the mark, dodging through traffic more swiftly than she'd thought possible or ever wanted to go.

They roared down the street, barely making a tight, left-hand corner and accelerated down the road, whipping past bicycles so close Phoebe swore she could have wiped people's noses. At the next corner the light changed, but he roared through anyway, barely missing an orange-robed monk who stepped off the curb.

They were going to have such bad karma if Chan wasn't careful. She glanced back. The yellow motorcycle was a good way behind, probably slowed by the heavier traffic on the main road. But Chan was taking them onto less trafficked streets and the yellow motorcycle was catching up. Clearly the motorcycle taxi was no match in power or speed.

Chan must have seen, for he took a corner so sharply that Phoebe screamed. The motorcycle taxi cab went up on two wheels and the metal roof squealed as it scraped along a building wall. Then the cab crashed down to level and her head smacked into the metal crossbar on the ceiling. She bit her tongue. They were in a narrow lane sided by tall brick walls. Broken glass gleamed at the tops in the late afternoon sun.

Tasting blood, the motorcycle taxi's engine roaring in her already ringing ears, she closed her eyes and wished for the whole thing to be over. And then suddenly Chan stood on the motorcycle taxi brakes. She held on tight as the vehicle swung hard right through a gate. Chan was off before the vehicle stopped rolling and shoving shut a solid gate. Then he ran back and shut the motorbike off, shushing her queries with a finger to his lips.

"My house. It safe. But must be very quiet. He can still hear us."

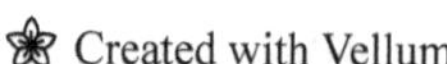 Created with Vellum

WITHIN ANGKOR SHADOWS

K.L. ABRAHAMSON

1

————————

Along the Mekong River, the overloaded barges chugged black smoke into the crystal blue sky, their gunnels mere feet above the river's sullen surface. Last night's rain had cleared the yellow haze, and so far, the morning was still relatively cool—not the sweltering heat that made sweat spring out on skin the moment you stepped from an air-conditioned room.

The barges sent water washing up over the muddy banks, rocking the small boats drawn up on shore with their faded green, blue, and red paint. Though this was Cambodia, the fishermen were Vietnamese, and they lived on the small craft. During the day, they sold their catch in the market south of Phnom Penh's palace. This early, however, as the sun burned a gold band onto the water, the more industrious fishermen tossed circular nets out above the water with a mesmerizing soft whir and splash.

Phoebe Clay stood on the ferry dock watching the slow rise and fall of the fishermen's boats and the magical bloom of the nets, like blossoms opening over the gilded water. Alice would be astounded. Her camera would be clicking like mad.

The thought brought a sad smile to her face. Alice was no doubt in school back home in Canada, her days and evenings filled with extracurricular activities her mother, Becca, planned. Safe activities, Phoebe was sure.

Around her the rumble of the barges and overfilled cargo ships were overtaken by the call of the ferry crew to the waiting passengers. Time to go aboard. Time to leave Phnom Penh and the slowly fading capital of the country, and head farther away from civilization to Angkor Wat, the temple complex that was one of the wonders of the world.

She shouldered "Stoney," her backpack, inhaled the mud-scented, moist air and, for the hundredth time since arriving in Cambodia three days before, turned to say something to Becca and Alice. They had returned home from India a few weeks ago and left Phoebe to fend for herself until, Becca said, Phoebe came to her senses and stopped putting herself in danger.

The unfair statement still made her angry.

And sad.

It wasn't like she went looking for danger to get into.

Sighing, she brushed her fingers through her short blonde hair. On the river waited the ferry that wasn't much more than an extra-large cabin cruiser with an extra-large indoor passenger cabin and virtually no deck space. That was disappointing given she'd envisioned sitting in a deck chair in the shade and watching the countryside go by. But on this ferry, the only open area looked like it was the open prow that would be ungodly hot with not a stitch of shade…

She was already starting to sweat and it was only seven thirty in the morning. God help her at noon. She'd thought Kochi, India, was hot and humid, but at least it had the breeze off the Arabian Sea to cool it down. So far, Cambodia in September was a sultry place of seemingly stagnant river and still air—and rain. Lots of rain and it wasn't even monsoon season yet. These were just the "little rains" she'd been told as she waded the streets of Bangkok while she waited for her visa to Cambodia to come through.

It had poured two of the three days she'd been in Phnom Penh so that she hadn't done any of the sightseeing she'd planned. Instead she'd hunkered down in her room, only stepping out in search of new accommodation after the rain began to run down the inside wall of the first room in her low-cost lodging. Thankfully she'd found a better place to stay and had sat in her room watching the wall of monsoon water fill the streets and overwhelm roof gutters. Maybe it was Becca and Alice's absence—Alice was up for anything—but Phoebe had braved the downpour only enough to buy a plastic poncho and food before retreating to her room. Beyond that, a break in the rain had allowed her to visit the Royal Palace and find the flower market, both of which Alice and Becca would have enjoyed.

Looking back at the city strung along the river, she shook her head at what she might have missed. If she was honest with herself, she was a little nervous about this trip alone. She'd never done solo travel in such a foreign country. England and France, yes. Even in India, the people spoke English, while here, beyond native Khmer, French was the second language. On the other hand, the Vietnam war and tourism had increased the number of English speakers big time.

She joined the line of tourists and locals behind a father holding his daughter's hand. The local man wore a plain, white shirt and chino trousers gone soft with age, while the girl wore a blue sarong like so many women seemed to wear, and a chaste, white blouse with lace at the collar. The girl could have been as young as twelve or as old sixteen. Maybe older. Phoebe couldn't be sure given how young most Cambodians appeared, and this girl was so delicately boned, the word fairy came to mind—certainly something magical. Certainly her youth and refined build brought home Phoebe's fifty-five years and made her solid, five-foot-six build feel decidedly moose-like. The girl had black hair twisted up behind her head and a blue plastic flower clipped above her left ear. Fly-away strands framed her smooth forehead and almond eyes that seemed almost too large for her delicate skull. The girl smiled up at Phoebe until her father noticed, then her long lashes veiled her gaze. He nodded at Phoebe and tugged the girl closer to him as if he considered Phoebe a threat.

Frowning, she made the long step over the river to the gunnels of the white cabined river ferry and then had to decide whether to follow father and daughter into the cabin that filled most of the ferry's length and breadth. Inside there would be air conditioning, but inside she'd be confined to peering out what looked like perilously grimy windows. The alternative was to edge around the cabin to the prow of the ship. A few young people had already done so and had staked out spots to suntan while watching the scenery go by.

A good place to get a sunburn, Becca would say. Alice would roll her eyes.

Phoebe grinned at the image and edged away from the door. If she was in Cambodia for an adventure, she might as well go whole hog; and she seriously was *not* going to miss her family. She'd promised herself that when she booked this trip. Wobbling along the narrow cabin edge before stepping down into the railed prow, she then found free deck space at the railing and settled onto the warm metal with Stoney at her side. The prow space wasn't large. The wedge-shaped area could hold perhaps ten people all seated on the floor. There were eight people seated here now. Most of the youngsters had taken up positions in front of the cabin so they could use it as a backrest, but that didn't allow the best view. Phoebe's position almost under the flag on the prow seemed like it would provide a better vantage. From her day pack she claimed her hat, sunscreen, sarong, and a large bottle of water. She'd save the oranges and rolls of cookies and crackers for later, in case food at the planned stop for lunch was inedible.

"Looks like you're all prepared," said a male voice with a faint British accent.

She glanced back at the cabin. Against the peeling white paint of the pilot's cabin, between two groups of long-legged, tanned, twenty-something tourists, sat an older man in worn sandals, cream-colored trousers, and long-sleeved shirt rolled up over his forearms. He wore a broad-brimmed hat that shadowed his eyes, but his widemouth was smiling from within a few days' worth of gray-blond beard.

"Trying to be," she said and slapped her Canuck's hockey team ball cap on her head. Two could play at hiding their eyes.

"Been to Angkor before?" he asked.

She shook her head, wondering where this was leading. It wasn't as if she didn't have *tourist* emblazoned all over her. She'd heard enough horror stories about the things that could happen if you took up with strangers. Becca had made sure of it. She still sent Phoebe links to newspaper articles even though she hadn't responded to any of Phoebe's emails.

The stranger leaned forward and stuck out his hand. "Trevor Morgan. Trev to my friends. I live in Siem Reap. I manage a nonprofit there."

On shore, the last of the tourists came aboard and the ropes tethering the ferry were cast off. Out in the channel, a fisherman hauled in his net and shifted his small wooden boat out of the ferry's path.

She considered his hand. Long fingers. Clean nails and skin. His movement had released the faint scent of laundry soap and she caught a glimpse of two piercing blue eyes under his hat brim. Could someone with eyes like that, who made sure his clothes were clean, be that bad? Besides, he was sitting on his fanny on the prow of the boat, just like any tourist.

She accepted his hand even as a small part of her said, "If you wanted to bilk a tourist, what better place to meet them?"

Of course, if he was out to bilk someone, he was going to be terribly disappointed in Phoebe Clay. She was traveling on a very strict budget.

"Phoebe Clay," she said. "And yes, to answer your question, I'm one of the tourist hordes headed to Angkor." His grip was surprisingly cool and dry compared to her sweaty palm. The rumble of the ferry engines vibrated up through her seat as the vessel left the dock behind. She turned to look upriver as they started to move and a blessed breeze ruffled her hair and lifted the sweat from her skin.

"From the States?" Trev asked.

"Nope." She glanced back at him and tapped the flag patch Alice had carefully sewn to Stoney before they'd all left Canada. "Vancouver. You?"

"London. But that was a dim and distant time ago. I've been in-country for the past fifteen years."

"No wonder you're not sweating! You're almost a native!"

He chuckled and slid his bum forward beside her at the prow. "I fear that will never happen. The Khmer people have been through a trauma that someone who hasn't survived with them will never know. I think the entire country is dealing with PTSD."

Just what she needed to hear, given she'd been dealing with the condition since the school shooting that had led to her forced retirement. She glanced sideways at Trevor. "You a counselor or something?"

He shrugged and stuck his legs through the ferry rails to her left so his feet dangled down the side of the boat and turned toward her. "Sometimes it comes with the job. You see things, you know? Luckily the internet gives you access to all kinds of expertise. I've got experts in Australia and London who come to visit now and again. They triage people and give me and my staff the direction about how to best help."

"Interesting. So what do you do, then?"

"Like I said, I manage a nonprofit. There's a lot of us NGO types here helping the country rebuild."

On shore, the city fell behind, but there were still plenty of buildings and the spires of new temples under construction. Gold spires stuck up out of the trees. Here and there, white temples caught the sun. Alice would be like a kid on this ride. She couldn't imagine Becca not enjoying it either.

Phoebe tilted her head back and basked in the wind streaming over her face. Her white blouse fluttered around her and so did her pant legs.

"A lot of temples and buildings were destroyed during Pol Pot's regime. A lot of people were killed. A lot," Trevor said.

Even though she'd read about it before coming to Cambodia, his bald statement sort of put a damper on the bliss she was seeking from the fact she was here adventuring on her own. In fact she still was reading about the reign of terror of the Khmer Rouge, where nothing like modern medicine was allowed, anyone with any education was killed, and the entire population was basically enslaved.

"It's tragic on so many levels," Trev continued. "Historic Cambodia was the source of much of the rich cultural traditions found throughout Southeast Asia. The fusion with French culture during colonial days led to a vibrant second cultural tradition. The Khmer Rouge wiped all that out. Today I see a lot of people who don't know and don't care about their history or traditions—only about the money they can make."

"That's so sad," she said

"The Khmer Rouge thought the Chinese didn't go far enough with their cultural revolution." He shook his head. "Anything vaguely educated, cultured, or capitalistic had to go."

"Back home, Canadians are struggling to deal with the cultural genocide of our First Nations people. In schools, we're even teaching First Nations history so our Aboriginal students learn to be proud of who they are. We're seeing higher graduation rates for Aboriginal kids." She could imagine how the lack of tradition would leave youth anchorless and with little guidance to help them live their lives.

"Let me guess. You're a teacher," Trev said. Beyond him, the broad river had widened further and there were more small fishing boats along the shores, and overloaded barges and steamers passing up and down river. An egret lifted from the edge of water in a flash of white.

"Guilty as charged. At least I was… for twenty-eight years. Some things stay with you for a long time."

Beneath the brim of his hat, Trevor's brows rose. His blue eyes were studying her. "But you left?"

For a moment her throat tightened and she swallowed back the loss. The school shooting had apparently been the beginning of the end of so much she'd thought would be forever. Her career. Her relationship with her sister and niece.

"I—retired." Hopefully that would put an end to his prying. This level of sharing was simply too much. Maybe Trev Morgan felt comfortable divulging all his secrets, but she did not.

A slight sound turned her around to see the young girl she'd seen earlier swiftly traverse the narrow walkway from the cabin door to the space over the prow. She stepped down into the crowded space to pick her way over outstretched legs to where Phoebe sat. She glanced at Trev, folded her legs under her, and sat behind and between them as if she had something to say and something to prove. The sunlight caught on the flowered clip in her hair.

"H—hello," she said in a soft voice barely audible over the ferry's engines and the wind. Those long lashes still demurely veiled her eyes as if she had secrets to preserve. "You are American? From America?"

Phoebe shook her head. "Afraid not. I'm from Canada." When the girl looked confused, Phoebe pointed at the flag on Stoney. "Not America, but we are right next door to them."

Of course the girl wouldn't understand. Since Phoebe had arrived in Asia, it seemed few people understood where Canada was—if they'd even heard of the country.

Trev said something Phoebe didn't understand and then looked at her. "I translated for you."

"What is your name?" Phoebe asked. On the shore, tall stands of bamboo swayed over stilted houses while water buffalo wallowed at the river edge or chewed their cud on shore.

"Sokha," she said and tapped her breast. "My name is Sokha, Aunty." She said it with a flourish as if proud of her English. She didn't even have any accent.

Phoebe pointed at herself. "Phoebe. My name is Phoebe and this is Trev."

"Trev?"

"Exactly," he nodded and smiled.

"Are you traveling with your father?" Phoebe asked.

Sokha looked at her blankly until Trev translated. Then she solemnly shook her head and they conversed in what must be Khmer.

"She says he's her uncle, but I'm not sure. She doesn't seem to want to talk about him or where she's going."

A little flutter of concern ran through Phoebe, but she tamped it down. Becca always said she went looking for trouble. Here was proof it wasn't so. The girl's business was no business of hers.

As if on cue, a male voice called Sokha's name. Her uncle stood in the cabin doorway, one foot on the narrow pathway to the prow.

The girl turned to Trev and spoke some more as she shook her head. She looked unhappy, but then climbed gracefully to her feet, smoothed her sarong, and nodded goodbye before picking her way over the tourists to join her uncle. He nodded once more in Phoebe's direction, but caught Sokha's upper arm and seemed to haul her down into the cabin. Or maybe he was just steadying her and Phoebe was misreading given she'd already decided she didn't much like the man after the way he had acted on the dock. They disappeared inside and the door closed behind them.

Phoebe sat there a moment, a knot of concern in her stomach, but she couldn't say why. She turned back to Trev. "You think everything's okay?"

He frowned, apparently surprised at her concern. He shook his head. "Probably. People here can be pretty relaxed about their kids—or else they aren't. Parents love their kids a lot, but they can be pretty demanding of obedience. I wonder what drew her out to talk to us?"

"You'd think she'd be attracted to all the youngsters. They're clearly more fun." And a girl between the age of thirteen and sixteen is pretty sure to be attracted to kids just a smidgen older.

As if to prove her point, from behind them came a burst of laughter from one of the groups of young people.

She and Trev Morgan talked casually as the river narrowed and the scenery became more rural. The sun lifted and the air filled with the murky scent of muddy river water. A haze made the distances soft, but the landscape that flowed away from the river was mostly flat. Farms and fields with ramshackle stilted houses built on the riverbank.

"I imagine it floods here," she said. "That's why the stilted houses."

"That's one of the reasons, but even houses not prone to flooding are often built on stilts. A lot of household life takes place in the shadows under the houses. It's cooler there. But once a year, during the monsoons, the deluge out of the Tonle Sap will flood a lot of the landscape—more so since logging took out most of the jungle. Not as much flooding here as around the Tonle Sap, but let us just say that stilts are prudent."

The air heated and the breeze couldn't stop the sweat running down Phoebe's back. The river split into two broad channels and they left the main river. At noon they pulled into a floating restaurant that stood off-shore from a small village and passengers were free to disembark into the restaurant for a thirty-minute break. There were more covered boats like the Vietnamese boats she'd seen in Phnom Penh—long and shallow-drafted—but these were larger with curved, half-moon walls and ceiling forming living quarters. Women cooked in open areas on the sterns of the boats. Children leapt from the sides into the murky water and splashed about. One boy leaned out a boat's window and held out a huge snake. Phoebe recoiled.

"Is that a pet?"

"Maybe. Or they plan to eat it. In Cambodia, everything is fair game. There's a town north of here that specializes in deep-fried tarantulas. They're not bad actually."

She looked at him in horror until he burst out laughing—a good, hardy laugh. "You really haven't done a lot of traveling in less developed countries, have you?"

"Tarantulas?"

"Yup. Nice big crispy ones on a stick."

In self defense, she pulled out a package of crackers and offered Trev one. "This is about as crispy as I want."

After they left the restaurant, the river broadened out into a wide lake that seemed to stretch on forever. Here and there, small, treed islands stuck up from the water, some with small farmsteads on them. Here the water was the same blue as the sky, with shimmering reflections of puffy clouds, so for a moment she felt disoriented except for the rumble of the deck under her.

Becca would love this. She'd always had a weakness for the water.

"Tonle Sap Lake. Those islands you see are actually hilltops. The monsoons have flooded the lake. Twice a year, the river changes direction due to the volume of water. In between, thousands of acres of rice fields are under water. The river hasn't even changed direction yet, but the rains have come early."

A small, gas-powered boat passed them hauling a second boat full of tree branches. A man steered the first boat past them. With him was a young girl who met Phoebe's gaze and held it as they passed by. She was perhaps the same age as Sokha—maybe fifteen—with the same long dark hair coiled up behind her head and the same sad expression. That was the thing about Cambodia. She might not have been out and about a lot in Phnom Penh due to the rain, but the shopkeepers and even the manager of the second guesthouse had all seemed to have an air of sadness around them. As if the whole country was grieving.

She understood about grief.

Sighing, she looked out over the water and let herself just "be," caught between the vast sky and the shimmering expanse of water as she steadied her breathing. The wind ruffled her hair and she took her hat off to let the sun drink her sweat. She closed her eyes against the glare and inhaled the ferry's diesel and the scent of the lake. Overhead, the Cambodian flag on the prow flapped and slapped in the wind.

These were the experiences she wanted. Things that took her out of her comfort zone. Things that were totally foreign. Surely it would be easier to set aside her history and the shooting in a place this unfamiliar. She could be someone else. Become someone unfamiliar to herself.

Maybe that had been the issue in Kochi. Sure, she'd been in a foreign country far different from Canada, but she'd been with Becca and Alice. She'd brought "her" country with her by traveling with them. On her own, she wouldn't have to take care of them.

"Water hyacinth," Trev said beside her.

She opened her eyes and glanced at him. He was leaning his arms on the railing, peering out at the lake much as she had been. He noticed her noticing him.

"Beautiful, isn't it."

"It looks pristine. Untouched. Not even much garbage." She lifted her chin at a pop can floating on the water.

"Unfortunately, you're wrong. There are a lot of problems including garbage. It's just that the currents run the garbage together under the trees so you don't see it here. And there's rampant overfishing, not to mention the environmental disaster that's water hyacinth."

He motioned to an undulating patch of green they were nearing.

Spikes of lush purple flowers bloomed above the tangle of green leaves.

"It's everywhere. It clogs waterways. It kills endemic plants and lowers the oxygen content in the water. Eventually, if it's allowed to spread, there won't be any fish for fishing. An entire way of life will be destroyed and people will starve. Damn stuff is everywhere in Southeast Asia. Should never have been introduced."

"Let me guess: because it looked pretty?"

He shook his head. "Of course. There are people trying to save the fish stocks in the lake, but they are fighting an uphill battle. I don't envy them. Dealing with the government doesn't make anything easy and there are always people in opposition to progress."

He stared out at the water as if considering the effort of those others—or maybe his own attempts to deal with that same government. Should she ask him about it? She looked back at the lake. No, asking about his problems might pull her back into her problem-solving mode and hadn't Becca said that was at the heart of her issues—always rushing in to save people…

It was some world where you weren't supposed to help people.

She turned back to Trev. "Sounds like you've run into the government, too."

"It's nothing, really. The same as when I did embassy work years ago. Just red tape and general interference when a foreign nonprofit is involved. And you've always got officials and others demanding to be paid off. The usual business."

"So that's what you do? Pay off corrupt officials?"

He gave her a sheepish smile and looked back to the lake. "If it gets the job done, yeah. It's our dirty little secret. We're building something here. Changing communities. We're doing good work and I'm not allowing some bugger with a bit of authority, or someone who sees us as a rival, to stop us." He spoke passionately with his hands. His work was important to him—whatever it was. Once she'd felt that way about teaching…

"What are you smiling at," he asked.

"You. You care about what you do. A lot. I'm not exactly sure what a foreign NGO does in Cambodia, but given what you've said, I think maybe the Cambodian people are lucky to have you on their side."

"Well, thanks, I guess. Kind of you to say, I'm not doing this alone. I'm just the manager. There's a whole Board of Directors that I have to answer to, but what we're trying to do is build for the future. Give them the opportunities and jobs and skills so that they won't need outsiders like me anymore. That's what I want to see, the Cambodian people celebrating their culture and their pride."

Regardless of her vow to remain uninvolved, her curiosity got the better of her. "That sounds like a tall order. How do you do that?"

An hour later, after Trevor regaled her with talk of working with specific villages to build businesses, construct schools, and raise international funds, and she talked about being a school teacher, they came to a floating town. The ferry had ploughed through channels cut through acres of hyacinth-covered water to reach the village of boats seemingly trapped between the undulating hyacinth invader and a man-made, gravel-and-stone jetty. The ferry eased into shore and plank gangways were laid from the deck onto gravel. Then the cabin passengers stumbled out onto the land. Phoebe scrambled to her feet with the others from the prow and hefted Stoney onto her back to follow behind.

Without the boat's movement, the sun was a heavy hammer on her head. The humidity made it worse so her body was immediately covered with a sheen of sweat. Her shirt clung to her and her capris had racing stripe lines of sweat down the front of her legs. After wobbling across to land, she picked her way up the loose gravel and rock of the steep-sided jetty. At the top of the jetty, a few passenger vans and a line of motorcycles and motorcycle taxis waited in a parking area to take the passengers into town.

Along with most of the local people on the ferry, Trev headed over to the motorcycles. Then he turned back and returned to Phoebe, who had just found what seemed to be a shuttle van into town. She hoped. The driver had nodded when she'd said Siem Reap and had taken her money, so she had to figure that was a good sign.

"Here's my card," Trev said. He handed her a green card with the name *Cambodia Prosperous* scrolled in a darker green across the top. His title was managing director. "I realize I don't even know how long you're here for, but maybe we could meet for a drink while you're in town. It can be lonely here on your own."

Someone important. She was a little surprised.

"Thanks. I'll see how things go. No firm plans here, you know. I'm just going with the flow." She grinned, accepted the card, and stuck it in her day pack. She wasn't really here to have drinks with strange men.

On the other hand, wasn't that part of the whole idea of adventure? Meet new people? Talk about new things? Things that matter? With people who didn't know her history?

Trev patted her shoulder. "Enjoy your stay in Siem Reap—and enjoy Angkor!" With a wave he went back to the motorcycles that were quickly being taken by Cambodians. He climbed aboard the back of one and the bike roared past her as she climbed into the van.

She settled in a seat in the back and wished she hadn't. The air was close and the smeary window beside her wouldn't open. She fanned her face and spotted Sokha and her uncle. They were standing with another man in a crisp navy suit at the open rear door of a dark blue Audi sedan, which was a surprise given the worn state of the uncle's clothing. Sokha looked like she was studying the toes of her shoes, until suit man caught her chin and tilted her face up to him. They stood like that a moment as if Sokha was being inspected, and then he released her. And smiled. The two men spoke and then the suit man caught Sokha's arm and urged her toward the rear seat of the car. Sokha hesitated and said something, but the man waved her in impatiently.

Then uncle spoke to suit man before the man in the navy suit climbed inside the sedan beside Sokha. Uncle walked away to one of the motorcycles and climbed on the back. The car and the motorcycle both pulled away from the parking area.

Phoebe craned around in her seat to watch them go. Something about the whole experience with Sokha left her uneasy. The uncle certainly wasn't in any way affectionate to Sokha. And what uncle basically hands their niece over to someone who, judging by Sokha's reaction, was a stranger, or certainly someone she appeared to be afraid of?

A heavy clot of anxiety formed in her stomach and she could almost see Becca shake her head and throw up her hands.

2

———————

The sun's heat made the waiting van an oven and Phoebe was slowly basting in her own juices. Sweat rolled down her chest and back. Sweat poured from her scalp and she must have looked a total mess, because she sure felt like one.

She peered out the window at the narrow jetty and the single lane road at the top that led away from the broad expanse of Tonle Sap Lake. Heat radiated off the water in humid waves. The pavement glimmered. Sokha had gone along that road and Phoebe was going that way, too. Regardless of what Becca thought, maybe Phoebe could find the girl, make sure she was okay.

But then maybe she was only dealing with her own overactive imagination. Maybe the suit man wasn't a stranger to Sokha. Maybe he was just someone Sokha was shy with. Or something.

She thought about that as an older couple climbed into the van and the driver ran the van door shut before climbing in the cab. The vehicle was a furnace until he turned on the engine and started toward town. He touched a button and a blast of chill air ran over her skin. In a few minutes, Phoebe was shivering.

Nope. She shook her head. She'd been a school teacher long enough to know when a kid was scared and that was how Sokha had looked to her. But her uncle had literally done nothing, regardless of her reservations about getting in the car. *If* the man traveling with her was even her uncle.

God, had she just been witness to a child abduction? Or a child sold into slavery? She'd heard stories about Southeast Asian children sold into international sex rings.

She sat forward in her seat, hoping to catch a glimpse of the motorcycle or the dark sedan, but there was no sign of them.

The road ran along the top of a wide, raised, dirt ridge between vast expanses of water. Stilted houses and small stalls of produce crowded to either side of the pavement and people walked and rode bicycles along the roadsides as they did their morning marketing. Out on the water she glimpsed between the buildings, trees poked their heads out of the water. Of course. These were rice fields flooded because of the monsoons. How strangely beautiful it was, boats floating on their blue reflections amongst the clouds over what would be land in a few months' time.

But the serenity of the scenery couldn't dispel her worry for Sokha. Just what fate had befallen the girl?

The busy stilted town fell behind them and the road finally left the water behind. Men drove oxen to plough rice fields that were as yet unflooded. Trees shaded the road. Bougainvillea strung splashes of pink, purple, or white over stone walls. A small river ran under the road, but its sides and the trees around it were clotted with garbage that gave truth to what Trev had told her. Ramshackle shacks of corrugated metal sat along the road. And then suddenly they were on a busy street in a small city. Motorcycles, motorcycle taxis—basically a rickshaw-type cab tethered to a motorcycle—and cars vied for the road. The van turned in at a bougainvillea-bedecked gate and ran along a circular driveway through expansive gardens to a lovely, three-story hotel with palm trees framing the doorway. A porter ran outside to open the van door. The couple climbed out, paid the driver, and the porter took their bags and whisked them inside.

From the look of the place, it was a little too upscale for Phoebe's budget, so she sank back in her seat a little concerned because the sun was getting lower in the sky and she didn't want to be dropped somewhere after dark.

"Where we go?" the driver asked again. She'd told him when she first got into the car.

"The Blue Lotus Guesthouse." She'd found and booked the place on line and just prayed that it was as nice as the pictures. Certainly her first hotel in Phnom Penh hadn't lived up to the advertising, what with the wet walls and the sugar ants she'd had to endure in the bed. *That* hadn't been in the advertisement.

The driver looked hesitant for a fraction of a second and then steered them out of the circular driveway to the street. At the next stoplight, he rolled down his window and spoke to the motorcycle taxi driver idling beside them. The motorcycle taxi driver spoke and gestured and when the light turned, he sped off. Her driver proceeded at a more sedate pace and drove her back through the main center of business into what looked like an old part of the city. The buildings were mostly two-story with an old, art deco feel, though most showed signs of needing repairs and paint to deal with the stains left behind by the monsoon rains. Long shadows were stretching across the street when she spotted what looked like a coffee shop and a restaurant, both with signs in English. That seemed hopeful that this was a safe part of the town. There were local people hurrying about their last business of the day and even a few monks striding down the road and riding on the backs of motorcycles just like she'd seen in Phnom Penh. That made her feel marginally better, too.

Then the van turned into a shadowy lane between two buildings. Her heart sank. Back home, this was barely wide enough to be a back lane. She stiffened in her seat. Where was she being taken? Her concern lessened as the "lane" widened out so that small kiosks and shops lined the shadowy street, with what looked like two-and three-story apartment buildings in the back. She caught a sign that said restaurant and another that said Buddha Home Guesthouse. Both establishments looked neat and clean.

Then the van pulled over and the driver glanced back at her. "Blue Lotus?"

She nodded and he climbed out of the vehicle, coming around to open her door and retrieve Stoney from the back. She accepted the pack and felt it press on her spine, then turned to consider where he'd brought her.

The Blue Lotus was built of large wooden timbers stained dark with time or pollution, she wasn't sure which. The main floor was an open lobby built on two levels, the lower of which held comfortable looking lounge chairs and coffee tables and the higher one with an efficient-looking desk and computer with an equally efficient-looking woman seated behind the desk. The woman rose when she saw Phoebe and came out into the street to greet her and the driver.

"You are Phoebe Clay?" The woman asked. Her voice was firm and fit the way she had her long dark hair twisted up in a neat bundle behind her head and the crisply ironed blouse and skirt she wore. How she looked so cool and professional in this heat was a wonder, considering how the sweat was running down Phoebe's body and her "guaranteed wrinkle free" shirt and capris hung on her like limp rags.

"I am. I booked a room, but I'd like to see it before I agree to stay." After her experience in Phnom Penh, she wasn't taking any chances with wet walls or sugar ants for bed partners. "Would you wait for me, please?" she asked the driver.

When he agreed, she followed the woman into and across the lobby to a set of broad stairs that must lead up to room levels. That was good for security, right?

"Is there someone in the lobby at all times?" she asked.

"Of course. I am Jorani. I hope you will like our rooms. We have very many and have taken great care."

"Are you a new guesthouse?"

"We are under new management. It is much better now."

Which sort of indicated that the place wasn't that great before. She'd reserve judgement until she saw the room.

On the second floor, the woman paused. She looked at Phoebe's pack. "Perhaps the second floor would be better."

Phoebe shrugged but Stoney *was* living up to his name. "Let's look."

Jorani unlocked a room door and stepped back to allow Phoebe to pass. It was a large room with high ceilings compared to both the pocket-sized rooms she'd stayed in, in Phnom Penh. Clean tile floors spread between two twin beds, a desk against one wall and a wall of louvered windows and a door. Individual ceiling fans hung above each bed and another door gave onto a pristine white bathroom complete with shower and western toilet.

Jorani crossed the room and open the louvers and door onto a small balcony that overlooked the street. It was perfect, but…

"Are the rooms upstairs the same?"

Jorani nodded. "Except the balcony receives more sun."

Which meant that the room got more sun and was, possibly, hotter.

"Then I think I'll take this room." She dumped her pack off her shoulder in relief. "Should I come back down with you to register?"

Jorani shook her head. "You settle in and I will see you later. I will tell your driver that you are staying. You have paid him?" When Phoebe nodded, Jorani turned on the ceiling fans and left down the stairs.

Phoebe unloaded Stoney onto one of the beds, choosing the one closer to the bathroom to sleep in. Then she stripped out of her sweaty clothes, had a shower, and washed out her sweaty clothes, hanging them on a clothesline she strung on the balcony. In twenty minutes she felt like a new woman, and with her passport and money belt, she headed down the stairs to the lobby, registered, and paid for the room for five days—she wasn't sure how long it would take for her to see Angkor because she really wasn't sure just how big the temple complex was. Just as the sun went down and all the shadows turned deep blue, she headed out the door for the restaurant she'd seen down the block.

The only diner in the bamboo-walled restaurant, under tiki lamp lighting, Phoebe had a dinner of rice and Cambodian pumpkin that was like a cross between a custard and soup. It was rather good, both sweet and savory in each bite. She was pleased that, even alone, she felt safe, contrary to what Becca had suggested would happen. But then maybe this was just the same running into danger that Becca had complained about. Either way, Becca would likely like the food in Cambodia because there were lots of vegetables, and Alice would just be thrilled at the adventure.

She ordered a cup of tea and they brought her a red rose teabag and a cup of tepid water that wasn't so good. She took a few sips and gave up, paid, and left the restaurant. It was fully dark.

After the lights of the restaurant, she felt momentarily blind and stood in the restaurant doorway waiting for her eyes to adjust. The street was unlit, though streetlights glowed at the end where her van had turned down the lane. In the other direction, there was a glow of dim lights, but also the movement of people. When she'd made her reservations at the Blue Lotus, their website had said they were near a market. That was likely what she was seeing.

It had been a long day on the ferry, but it was barely seven o'clock and really she'd only been sitting, though the sun had been draining. She decided to take a stroll to settle her dinner and get the lay of the land. She headed back past the Blue Lotus, stopping long enough to ask Jorani to make arrangements for a guide and driver to take her to Angkor the next day. Then she headed down the narrow gravel street, careful of the water-filled potholes. So there had been rain here recently, just like in Phnom Penh. The air was cooler after dark. Houselights glowed dimly from courtyards and she heard voices and laughter. The scent of hot oil and rice water permeated the humid air. From behind a closed gate, she heard a child's soft sobbing and male voices.

Sokha's face sprang into her head and she paused for a moment. No, Sokha was gone to whatever her life was.

She kept going, the equivalent of two city blocks, to the other end of the street where it ended at a cross street. This street was broader, though not paved like the street at the other end of the Blue Lotus's narrow lane. This one looked like in daytime it would have a variety of shops, but now the shops were closed and small booths had opened along the street, strung with colored lights to hold back the dark. Along her side of the street, tourist vans and motorcycle taxis waited for their passengers to return.

Checking her landmarks so that she could find her way back to the guesthouse, Phoebe turned right down the street. It looked like she was at one end of the string of booths. There were only a few people around and the booths displayed unusual things like dried frogs and snakes. Remembering Trev's story of deep-fried tarantulas, she hurried past toward the more crowded areas where the street widened out to a well-lit square.

Knobby-kneed, geriatric male tourists in white shorts and t-shirts emblazoned with Angkor Wat temples strolled between the kiosks with their wives resplendent in capris or skirts and floral blouses. They pawed displays of t-shirts and jewelry that, when she checked over a woman's shoulder, looked suspiciously like the silver jewelry she'd seen in India. There were miniature paintings of Angkor and rice farmers, and others selling wood carvings, woven baskets, and even small shadow puppets.

The shadow puppets drew her and she stopped at the kiosk as the vendor held up the small, dark brown, carved-leather figures between a lantern and a sheet strung up as a screen in what was almost an impromptu puppet show. The small puppets were on sticks that he manipulated so that a troupe of figures banded together and walked across a landscape, led by a sly-looking little monkey figure. Fabulous trees sprang up, carved of the same leather. "Very good. Very good puppets," sing-songed the vendor while his wife collected money from the enchanted tourists.

Phoebe was close to parting with some of her money herself—after all, Alice would be enchanted and a little leather puppet wasn't going to add much weight to Stoney-the-pack—when she heard her name called.

She swung around searching for a familiar face, then spotted an arm waving from a kiosk down the street a bit. Feeling a little regret at leaving the puppets behind, she aimed for the waving arm and recognized Trev standing behind the counter. A sign behind him said *Cambodia Prosperous.*

"Phoebe! I didn't expect to see you here your first night in town. I thought you'd be sleeping off all that sun you got today." Trev grinned.

He wore a different, slightly wrinkled, white, raw cotton shirt and white trousers, but his broad-brimmed hat had disappeared allowing thick, wavy gray hair to stick out charmingly over his ears.

His sharp blue gaze once more made her uncomfortable as if she'd done something wrong.

She shrugged it off and nodded. "I probably should be. It was a long day, but I thought I'd go for a walk after dinner and then I found this market. So here I am. What are you doing here?"

"Would you believe working?" He motioned at the kiosk. Its interior walls were filled with photographs. Some were gorgeous art images of monks in the ruins of Angkor, but others were humbler in nature, documenting the construction of a school, bridges being built, children in school uniforms, and people with shiny new bicycles. "These," he pointed at the art images, "I sell to support myself, and these," he motioned to the images of the school, bridges, and so on, "are to raise donations by showing what *Cambodia Prosperous* can do. These are shots of the work we do with individual villages to help them improve their infrastructure and education and to ensure that they have land tenure. The people who live there agree to do the work and we chip in the expertise and equipment and sometimes supplies needed to get a project done. We hope that tourists to Angkor will want to help the local people help themselves. Some even return to Cambodia to volunteer. So far we've got fifteen villages we're working with." He tapped a package of art cards that miniaturized some of the images on the kiosk walls and she picked up a package.

"These should be in galleries."

He nodded. "They are. Here in Siem Reap."

"So you live on the proceeds and use all your donations for the Cambodian people."

He tipped his head. "As it should be. We let the village decide what the project should be and then they work to complete it. Within villages, individual families can also work extra to earn bicycles. The bikes open the world to the people. They can get to jobs or get produce to market."

She glanced over her shoulder at the puppet kiosk. She'd really liked the monkey figure, but now more tourists were crowding around and the monkey would most likely be sold. Besides, here was a better use for her few dollars. Art cards wouldn't weigh much more than the monkey puppet and Becca would love them.

"Those puppets really caught your interest," Trev said. "Let me tell you a little secret. There's a place I know run by orphans for their own welfare. They carve the puppets this guy is selling, but they also sell them themselves so all the money goes to the orphans—not to this—this showman." He shook his head, clearly disgusted at someone making a profit off of children's efforts.

"What's it called and where is it? I'm hiring a driver and guide to show me to Angkor. Maybe I could go by there."

He gave her the information and she noted it in her phone.

When she was done, she tapped the packet of art cards. "So how much are they?"

When he told her twenty US dollars, she fished money out of the cotton travel safe she wore around her neck and gave the cash to him. "So you doing good business tonight?"

He shook his head. "The older tourists mostly avoid me like the plague. They don't like to feel uncomfortable with their wealth and it's the discomfort that usually makes people give."

She frowned. "That's a cynical view of the world."

He sighed and shook his head. "It's just the result of years of observation."

A shout back the way Phoebe had come disturbed their conversation. A woman screamed. She sounded young. Down the dimly lit street, a commotion brought the tourists around Phoebe to a standstill and vendors out of their kiosks.

A flood of people from near the commotion pushed into the brightly lit square. They shoved tourists aside in their rush to get past. People plowed into kiosks and one collapsed. Tourists flooded away as they scrambled for parked tour vans. A heavy-set gray-haired man plowed into Phoebe and sent her staggering against Trev's shoulder. He steadied her so she didn't fall.

"What's going on?" she shouted over the growing clamor.

"Don't know." He went to shield her from more people, but his gaze was on the commotion. Phoebe stepped around him. A woman had screamed. Clearly, someone needed help.

She dodged away from Trev and into the surge of people, elbowing her way through. The initial press of people gradually dispersed and she pushed through those that remained. When things happened, most people were only good at running away. As a teacher she'd found that her skill was running into situations to stop bad things from happening. It had been that skill that had helped her save students during the school shooting. Unfortunately, she hadn't run in deep enough to stop Rick Hanes from killing in the first place.

The well-lit area fell behind her, and so did the dispersing crowd. She was back amongst the strange displays she's seen when she first arrived. Ahead, a clot of people milled as if they weren't quite sure what to do. As she approached, the figures parted to reveal a prone figure on the gravel roadway.

It lay sprawled, presumably as it had fallen. Phoebe stopped. Hadn't she seen enough dead bodies to last a lifetime? Hadn't she and her sister and niece almost died as a result of the *last* body?

But there was something familiar about this body. Something that drew her so she couldn't look away.

Male, clearly, by the short hair and barrel chest. Worn trousers. A light-colored shirt that had a growing dark stain on the front from what appeared to be a vicious knife wound, though there was no weapon in sight.

The heat of the night suddenly dispersed and she was left with a chill that brought gooseflesh to her skin. She stepped forward until she stood over the body. Yes. It was him.

Sokha's uncle stared blindly up at her.

A blue flowered hair clip lay abandoned next to his hand.

3

The slight night breeze chilled Phoebe's skin. The excited voices of onlookers seemed to bounce off her ears as she knelt beside Uncle and checked his carotid pulse. Nothing, though his flesh was still warm, as if life was still leaking away with his blood.

Shaking her head, she stood, the voices, the shouts from down the street finally sinking in. People pressed around her and the press brought the heat slamming into her and made it hard to breathe. The night seemed copper-scented with blood, and something warm and wet was on her left hand. When she looked, her hand was bloody and, turning back to the body, her hand print was clear in a red pool beside the dead man.

"He's dead," she said to no one in particular. She felt strange and distant and disoriented at the same time. Maybe her long day and too much sun was catching up to her, or maybe it was coming across a body again…

No one seemed to be listening. In fact, no one seemed to be doing anything other than standing there talking.

She shook herself. "Has anyone called the police?" She scanned the crowd—mostly men. A lone woman in a green-flowered sarong by one of the kiosks. She was gray-haired, black-eyed, and she briefly met

Phoebe's gaze, then faded back into the shadows behind a kiosk that displayed dead framed butterflies.

Phoebe scanned the crowd again and glanced down at the body. The plastic floral hair clip looked exactly like the one Sokha had worn in her hair, but there was no sign of her, and Phoebe couldn't imagine the girl she'd met stabbing anyone. But there had been that scream…

"Phoebe, are you okay?"

She looked up at the familiar voice as Trev pushed through the crowd to her side.

"I'm fine. Definitely better than him." She pointed to the body. "Recognize him?"

Trev glanced at the downed figure, expressionless. "The girl's uncle."

Phoebe nodded again and felt like a bobble-head figure because words seemed a little beyond her and that was strange, given she'd dealt with this sort of thing before. Beyond the crowd and the buildings, a siren whined closer.

"Where's Sokha? Isn't that her hair clip?" She nodded at the flower by the man's hand like the single flower people sometimes left at gravesites back home. "I don't see her around, and if she's his niece, she has to be told."

She caught the arm of the man next to her. "Have you seen a young girl of perhaps fifteen? Her name is Sokha. She was with this man earlier today."

The man shook his head and hurried away to disappear into the crowd. As the siren came closer, people dispersed down the street until only a few kiosk vendors remained and she and Trev. The vendors rushed to lock up and left like the others.

"Phoebe, we should go." He caught her clean hand and swung her around to him. "You don't want to be here when the police arrive. It's one thing to call the tourist police about a theft. It's another thing entirely to get caught in something like this. Do you understand?"

For a moment she didn't. Then she held up her hand. Bloodied as it was, she could easily become a suspect. She nodded and let him lead her back to his kiosk. He had clearly shuttered the front before coming after her. Now he took her in back and used a bottle of water to wash away the worst of the blood.

When he was done, he nodded. "That's got most of it." His blue gaze met hers. "You look like you could seriously use a drink, though."

She nodded. Something that would burn through the fog she was feeling would be good.

Trev checked his watch. "The bars will be heating up about now, but I think it's still early enough we can find a quiet corner. Come on."

He led her down the street away from the murder scene to a motorcycle parked against a building. "My ride. You game?"

She wasn't. In fact, motorcycles terrified her, but she climbed on behind him anyway. An adventure, right? That was what she was looking for. Well, this one looked like it dropped her in another murder investigation. But she didn't need to get involved. It was none of her business who killed Uncle.

But Sokha? What had happened to her? Was she all alone in Siem Reap? There had been the man whose car she rode in…

The ride was entirely too intimate clinging to Trev's warm body. She was too aware of how sweaty she was. It was a relief when the ride wasn't long, only down a few streets. She thought she recognized the main thoroughfare she'd been on before her shuttle van turned down the narrow lane to the Blue Lotus. He pulled in, in front of an establishment with a Union Jack-colored sign that read *Trafalgar Pub.*

"Trafalgar Pub in Siem Reap?" she said, scanning the faded art deco style façade with its pealing cream paint.

Trev shrugged. "It's as good as it gets in this area and doesn't get the same party animals some of the other places deal with. A couple from Kent started the place seven years ago, but they've since moved back to the old country. A lovely local woman runs the place now."

He led her inside to a dark, smoky establishment of heavy dark wood and small wall sconces, many of which were missing a portion of the sconces so just the bare bulbs glared light into the room. Yellowing photos of the English countryside adorned three of the walls, but a large mural of Angkor Wat adorned the back of the tall bar. Small tables were scattered around the room, most of them filled by westerners, mostly male, who had the jaded air of people who were here for the long haul, not just passing through as tourists. A few of the men raised a hand to Trev as he led her to a table given privacy by low half walls that showed the dents and scuffs of past patrons. The tabletop was covered with the water stains of previous misuse.

They settled themselves into hard-backed chairs and she tried not to cough at the cigarette smoke. The shock of the murder was wearing off. She could have a drink in a local bar without gasping for air or otherwise being a prima donna.

A slim Cambodian woman came to the table. "What you like?"

Trev grinned up at her. "Samphy, meet Phoebe. Samphy runs the Trafalgar and runs it well. She was married to another Englishman for a while—a buddy of mine who's gone back to jolly ol' England. Phoebe, I ran into on the ferry today. She needs a drink because she's just seen her first body. I'm suggesting a good scotch whiskey."

Samphy nodded her hello and then left them, leaving Phoebe feeling a tad uncomfortable though she wasn't sure why. Maybe she didn't feel she knew him well enough to be introduced to his friend's ex-wife?

But then again, they'd just seen a dead body and escaped the police together…

"It's not, you know." Phoebe shook her head and looked around the room. It seemed so normal. Then she turned back to Trev. "My first body. I seem to be around a lot when a body turns up." She waited to see what he would do or say.

He sat back in his chair and seemed to reappraise her. "A woman with a past, then, are you?"

She rolled her eyes. "We all have pasts, especially when you reach our age. You have the dirty little secret of paying off governments. I have a dead body or two." There. She'd made light of it, but there was a part of her still worried about Sokha. Should she go to the police about her and explain her concerns?

Samphy brought them both a generous shot of whiskey. The glasses sat on the table between them, but Trev was clearly still sizing her up.

"Dead bodies, plural I might add, is a wee bit more of a past than paying off a corrupt government official or two. At least in the circles I travel in. Care to tell me more?"

Tell him? His gaze was intense, as if he was trying to assess just who she was. She had no reason to tell him. But what did it matter if he knew?

"I came to Cambodia from Southern India. I was there on a tour with my sister and niece. While we were there, our guide was murdered. My niece and I found the body."

Trev picked up his drink and sipped. He nodded, but his blue gaze still waited. "That's one body."

"I was out kayaking once and found a body on a beach." Why did this feel like a confession when she'd done nothing wrong? Why did she feel like she was revealing too much of herself?

"Is that it?"

Phoebe shook her head and grabbed her glass. Her hand shook as she raised it to her lips. She took a deep gulp that burned down her throat. "I told you I was a teacher. What I didn't say was that one of my students decided to bring a gun to school. Students were killed." The horrific image of the two innocent students gunned down and the bloodied body of Rick Hames. If she'd only been able to stop him. If she'd only done more.

But she had done more than anyone else. She'd *tried…*

She squeezed her eyes shut to stop the recriminations from taking over her brain as they'd done before. She had to forgive herself if she was ever going to have a life. She had to move on. Taking a deep breath, she took another sip of her drink and concentrated on the deep peaty flavor and the burn.

"Nice scotch. Just what I need at the moment." She opened her eyes and found Trev looking at her. The searching intensity had been replaced with concern.

"Holy mother of God, that must have been hard. And every body must bring it all back."

At least he got that. A recurring nightmare.

She nodded and allowed herself to relax back in her chair. Maybe the scotch was helping. "It doesn't help, that's for sure. I'm traveling for a change of scenery, but so far the places are different but I keep finding myself in similar situations." Or putting herself there, Becca would say. Running in, when she should be running away. Well, today she'd run away, so Becca would be proud of her.

Except she wasn't particularly proud of herself.

"You're thinking about something," Trev said as he finished his drink and waved Samphy over. He nodded down at her drink that was almost empty. She'd drunk it faster than usual and felt the heat and lethargy seeping into her limbs. "I was thinking about a gin and tonic. Perfect for the heat. You interested?"

She was, but… "I thought mixing alcohols wasn't a good idea."

"After our evening, I think we deserve it." He looked up at Samphy. "Two G and T, with extra lime, please, sweetheart."

Still deadpan, Samphy returned to the bar and poured their drinks.

"She doesn't smile much, does she? Or is it just seeing you? Or me?"

Trev choked out a laugh, but then sobered. "When I first met Samphy, she was this laughing bride. But marriage seemed to turn her into the serious woman you see now. Unfortunately, it didn't get any better when Michael left her and went back to Britain. He left her with a heap of money troubles with the bar. I helped bale her out, and under her management the place found its footing again, but the laughing girl still hasn't returned." He waved expansively around the bar.

Phoebe's gaze snuck to the woman deftly making their drinks. She was petite and pretty with lovely almond eyes, but frown lines had made nests around her mouth and eyes. Still, Phoebe could see the beauty that must have once attracted men like Trev's friend. Samphy headed in their direction, two drinks on a tray.

Trev turned back to Phoebe and picked up his drink. It left a wet ring to join the others on the table, concentric rings of interlocking history brought together at this table. "So I asked you what you were thinking about. I'd asked you about the bodies and you got this faraway look in your eyes."

Samphy deposited their fresh drinks on the table and removed the two empty glasses.

Phoebe picked up her G and T, and cool condensation ran down her fingers. She sipped, and tart lime and the bitter flavor of the tonic melded on her tongue as the bubbles got up her nose.

"Mmm. Good." She placed the cool drink against her cheek. "I was thinking about Sokha. I'm worried about her. Did you see her at the ferry? When we got off, she and her uncle met another man in a dark blue sedan. Sokha looked—I don't know—uncomfortable? Afraid? But her uncle sent her off with the man in the car while he followed on a motorcycle. The whole time Sokha was with him, she kept her head bowed."

"It could just be respect for whoever he was." Trev leaned forward over the table. "You've gotta realize this is a different culture, Phoebe. Young people respect their elders."

"This wasn't like that." She shook her head. "At least I think not. I know kids and this wasn't respect. This was—well—maybe dread? Like someone expecting punishment, maybe. And yet her uncle sent her off with that guy. And then her uncle turns up dead! So where's Sokha? Left with a man she's seriously afraid of?"

She could tell her voice was rising, but she hadn't realized how much until she caught people turning to her from the other tables. The cigarette smoke coiled through the sconce light and suddenly she was exhausted and she didn't want her drink. She'd probably had more than she should as it was. The heat was turning to numbness in her limbs.

She shut her mouth and felt herself sway in her chair. "I think... I think I need to get back to my guesthouse and think things through."

She slid back from the table and stumbled up to standing. Swayed. God, she was half-drunk after one drink—well, make that two. Trev stood and steadied her. "That's probably a good idea. Have a good night's sleep. Things will look better in the morning. I always find they do."

She glanced up at him, nodded away his platitude, but allowed him to walk her out the tavern door. His motorcycle waited and she wasn't too sure she wouldn't fall off, so she wrapped her arms around his chest as he started the engine.

"Where to?" he asked over the rumble.

"The Blue Lotus Guesthouse."

"Nice place. Recently refurbished." He eased away from the curb and seemed to take extra care as he wound around corners and then down a narrow street she recognized as her own. At the end of the street, the flash of blue and red lights showed the police were still at the murder scene. He pulled in at the front of her guesthouse and she stumbled off.

"Thanks for an interesting evening," she called as she climbed the stairs into the lobby.

"I could say the same to you, Phoebe Clay!"

She waved back at him and then crossed unsteadily to the stairs to her room. A young Cambodian man sat behind the registration desk and seemed to swallow either a smile or disapproval at her state. Trev gunned his motorcycle engine and then headed back the way they'd come, probably avoiding whatever the police were doing at the other end of the street.

Interesting, indeed.

4

————

The morning sunlight crept in through the louvered windows placing intimidating black bars across the room's floor and rear wall as if Phoebe woke in a jail cell. The slatted openings first allowed in the sound of doves cooing, then voices calling and, finally, the increasingly frequent—and annoying—roar of motorcycle engines. The overhead fan buffeted already too-heated air around the room, but at least it cooled the sweat on her skin. She lay, sheets manacled around her legs, feeling a tad ashamed that she hadn't done more for the dead man and Sokha last night and at having gone to a bar with a stranger.

Not that anything had happened with Trev Morgan.

And the body had nothing to do with the bar. At least she hoped not. Becca would say she was foolhardy staying in a place like the Blue Lotus instead of some upscale hotel where there were security guards to protect you. Becca would also disapprove of Phoebe walking off her dinner instead of going immediately back to her room. And of course Becca would disapprove of Phoebe running toward the commotion instead of away and then—of all things—going to a bar with almost a complete stranger.

Thinking about it, she had to wonder that the two of them were even sisters, they were so different in temperament. How had she never recognized Becca's disapproval until the events in India? The more Phoebe thought about it, the more it became clear: Becca really was a stick-in-the-mud. She would leave a girl like Sokha in dangerous circumstance.

No wonder she rarely left home. Heck, it was a wonder she wasn't a shut-in. She'd been protective as heck of Alice until Phoebe had urged her to cut the girl some slack. But now? After all the things that had happened, she could imagine Alice being practically suffocated by her mother.

Which was why Alice and Phoebe got on so well. Phoebe understood the importance of some risk-taking for young people's development. And if you still took risks as you grew older—well, wasn't that how great accomplishments and great art occurred?

No, Becca's way definitely wasn't the way Phoebe chose to live her life.

With that decided, Phoebe kicked off the sheets and swung up on the side of the bed. Clearly she wasn't used to drinking because there was a definite unpleasant pulse behind her eyes, but nothing she couldn't deal with.

She used the facilities and showered, washed out the clothes she'd worn—and sweated in—the night before, and pulled on the wrinkle-free shirt and capris that she'd washed out when she arrived in the hotel. Then she headed downstairs in search of breakfast.

Stepping outside the room was like stepping into a sauna. Where the sun caught her on the stairs it was almost burning hot, and the humidity immediately dampened her clothes. She'd arranged to have the guide and driver meet her at nine and it was only eight now, so she nodded good morning to Jorani, the desk clerk, and headed down the road toward the restaurant she'd frequented the night before.

Of course it wasn't open.

Feeling Becca frowning over her shoulder, she ventured to the end of the lane and spotted what looked like a café across the street and down a block. Thankfully, there wasn't much traffic so she ducked across the street and followed her hunch.

The Café Camboge was a hole-in-the-wall, with its doorway filling the front of a curved corner of the weather-stained, faded blue, art deco building. Its entrance was three steps up from street level and the interior held only three white bistro tables and a small glass display counter in back. The place looked pristine clean with white walls and floor all scrubbed clean and a picture of monks at Angkor Wat that looked suspiciously like the ones Trev had been selling last night. The man, apparently, got around. Or his photographs did.

A man with a past, too. Embassy work, he'd said, but she couldn't picture him behind a desk.

She climbed the three steps following the scent of coffee—and not just any coffee, either. This was espresso, strong and acrid in her nose.

The glass-fronted display that was part of the counter showed stacks of mango-cardamom scones and pineapple and cashew, or cinnamon cashew muffins, and even bagels. Phoebe's mouth watered as she looked up at the coffee menu printed on a board above the cashier, a young Cambodian woman perhaps in her late teens, wearing jeans and a t-shirt.

"Is that right?" She motioned at the sign. "I'd love an extra-large café latte, a scone, and a cinnamon-cashew muffin, please."

The young woman smiled. "Let me guess. You're off to Angkor today for a tour and you want to fill up before you go."

Phoebe considered. "More or less. I've hired a driver and guide for the day. I have a five-day pass, so I'll decide from today. I might decide to ride a bike there on my own the other days."

The cashier eyed her up and down. "Just remember the heat. It's worse as the day progresses."

As if Phoebe didn't have what it took to peddle through a few ruins.

Well. She'd reserve judgment.

The cashier worked the espresso machine behind the counter as if she knew what she was doing and Phoebe settled at one of the tables, reveling in the fact that contrary to her sister's dismal assessment, she'd managed just fine in Cambodia so far. The only downside had been the murder and, worse, the missing girl.

The cashier brought her the latte, scone, and muffin and Phoebe thanked her, then sipped her coffee wondering where Sokha might be. The girl had seemed so vulnerable and now she could be on her own in Siem Reap. In a country like Cambodia, had the girl ever traveled out of her home town? If she hadn't, she could be totally on her own and potentially in the hands of someone who was not her friend.

"Do you not like the muffin?" The young woman's quiet voice disturbed Phoebe's thoughts. She looked down at her plate. She'd basically shredded it into small pieces, but didn't even remember tasting it. The scone lay untouched.

She sampled a few of the muffin crumbs, then ate a few more. The cinnamon was sharp and sweet, the cashews surprisingly crunchy. "Actually, it's marvelous. I've just got things on my mind." She smiled an apology at the girl. "Sort of made a mess, didn't I?"

The young woman didn't say anything.

Phoebe shifted in her chair to face the counter. "Listen, I came up on the ferry yesterday, and while I was traveling, I met a young girl who said she was traveling with her uncle. She was trying to learn English and I happen to be a teacher. I was quite taken with the girl and wanted to help her, but I never had a chance. She got off the ferry and she was whisked into a big gray sedan that headed into town before I could talk to her." She swallowed, not sure whether to say anything more, but then decided she might as well. In for a penny, in for a pound and all that…

"The thing is, I'm wondering whether you can think of where I might look for her. Last night, I was at the night market and a man was killed. I think it was the man she said was her uncle, but she wasn't around."

The cashier looked uncomfortable as if uncertain whether to answer Phoebe's questions, or maybe she simply didn't have an answer and was upset at news of the murder.

"I'm sorry. I shouldn't have asked." Phoebe looked at her watch. Eight forty-five. God, where had the time gone? She leapt to her feet. "Shoot. Could you give me the coffee and my food in to-go containers? I've got to meet my driver and guide!"

And she was going to be late once the cashier had poured her still-hot coffee into a paper cup and had thrown the scone and the remains of the muffin into a brown paper bag. Phoebe paid and left a tip and then sprinted across the street and down the lane. A bright red motorcycle harnessed to a blue tuk-tuk-style rickshaw idled in front of the Blue Lotus, the young, male driver deep in conversation with Jorani.

Phoebe arrived puffing after her jog down the street. She set the coffee down on the rickshaw floor and rested her hands on her knees for a moment to catch her breath, then stuck out her hand to the driver. "Hi. I'm Phoebe. I think you're likely waiting for me."

Jorani introduced him as Chan. He was a grinning youngster, probably in his early twenties, with large white teeth and shoulder-length hair tied back in a ponytail with a leather cord. He wore jeans and a t-shirt blazoned with the star-spangled banner.

"Pleased to meet you, Phoebe." He tapped his shirt. "You see? America. I wear it for you."

Jorani met Phoebe's gaze, apparently recognizing Chan's error. She said nothing, seemingly awaiting Phoebe's reaction.

Phoebe turned to the proudly grinning Chan and sighed inwardly at donning her teacher hat. "That is very kind of you. America is a great country."

He beamed.

"But it is not my country."

His smile crumpled. "But she told me you were from America." He looked accusingly at Jorani.

"I am from Canada. It is a country in North America, just like America is." She launched in explaining that Canada was north of America and far larger geographically than the USA, but the glazed look in his eyes said she'd lost him, probably right when she said she wasn't from America.

"You know what? It really doesn't matter where I'm from. What matters is that I've never been to Cambodia or Angkor Wat and you know how to get there. Now, where is the guide?"

"You will pick him up on your way," Jorani said with a smile that suggested Phoebe had passed the test when she dealt with the America issue.

"Then I have my coffee and breakfast. Shall we get on the way?"

At Chan's nod, she climbed under the metal awning of the rickshaw area and settled in the seat. Chan mounted the motorcycle like he was mounting a horse, then paused to almost reverently put on a red helmet with a black-glassed front.

"Nice helmet," she said and received a beam. So maybe she'd earned back the points she'd lost when she wasn't from America…

"I borrow from friend," he said. "Someday maybe buy my own."

They set out into the city, bumping over myriad potholes and threading through traffic and out onto the main highway. There, the pavement improved as they roared past a number of posh hotels. The hotels gave way to countryside of palm trees and brown, fallow fields and the highway narrowed. Here and there, a lone man worked an ox harnessed to a wooden plow, turning great turves of the damp earth, the oxen hock-deep, the men up to their knees in mud. It looked like immensely hard labor.

Then they turned off the highway onto a long, broad stretch of what looked like newly paved, four-lane road, but left all traffic behind. She frowned, looking back at the busy narrow highway. They were driving on the best road she'd seen in Cambodia—certainly better than anything she'd seen in Phnom Penh—and yet there was no traffic. It didn't make sense.

Until a large sign announced the Angkor Wat Archeological Park was two kilometers ahead. So the paved road must be for all the tour buses that came every year, when the money could have been spent on infrastructure to help the people who lived here.

It shouldn't surprise her, but it did make her sad. From what she'd seen, there was so much poverty in the country.

Eventually they reached the gates of the park. They stopped and an older Cambodian man in a wide-brimmed, straw fedora, mirrored sunglasses, pressed black trousers, and a shirt the color of clotted cream, stepped out of the building. Chan waved him over and they talked rapidly in Khmer. She caught the word America, so apparently the other man was being warned not to make the same mistake.

"Ms. Clay," the newcomer removed his straw fedora and stuck out his hand as he peered under the rickshaw awning. His hair was slicked-back black. His voice had an educated English accent, but his eyes were invisible behind the mirrored shades. She'd always thought such glasses were the mark of someone trying to hide something. The trouble was, you never knew quite what it was.

"It is a pleasure to meet you," he said. "My name is Davuth. I am booked as your guide. If I may have your passport, I will check you in and your five-day pass will begin."

She dug out her passport and relinquished it to him. He was gone less than five minutes before returning it to her and climbing into the rickshaw beside her. He spoke to Chan and settled back beside her.

"What would you like to see today?"

"I'm not sure, " she said with a shake of her head as Chan kicked the motorcycle engine to life and they set off through the gates into the archaeological park.

"Your driver tells me you are from Canada. Toronto, perhaps?" Beyond the pavement, suddenly trees had sprung up, huge and towering white-trunked behemoths with vines and undergrowth in their shadows. Clearly, this was what the interior of Cambodia had looked like before deforestation.

Phoebe pulled herself away from the lush growth. "Canada, yes. I'm from Vancouver, on the other side of the country from Toronto."

"Aah. Vancouver. Yes." But his gaze suggested that he wasn't really clear where Vancouver was. As usual, Canada was a shadow place, barely known compared to its southern neighbor. "This is your first trip to Angkor?"

"It is." She smiled. "I've always wanted to visit."

"Angkor was made very famous by the movie *Tomb Raider*."

She shrugged. "I suppose, but I knew about Angkor long before. Oh my God, look!"

Ahead, the road traveled through an archway of ancient stone blazoned with two of the famous faces of Angkor, their almost unnerving veiled gazes peering out over the road. The slick, black stones and faces were etched with time and laced over with gray-brown and green vines and moss. She recognized one of the places from Trev's photos, though at the moment there were no monks in orange robes to juxtapose against the green.

"This is the actual boundary of the ancient city. Would you like to get out? You can climb the back of the arch."

"N-no. I just want to imprint it on my brain." She leaned forward, out of the rickshaw shade, to stare long and hard and then closed her eyes, not sure why the faces left her so uneasy. The feel of the sun on her skin cut out briefly as they passed under the arch. She sat back in her seat, but when she looked over her shoulder, the arch was lost in towering trees. "It must have been very imposing before it was abandoned."

Davuth shook his head. "Actually, the city was never abandoned. Scientists think the society gradually disintegrated and there were wars with the Thai and Burmese kingdoms, which weakened the Khmer. But there have always been people living here. They still do. They just aren't the princes and kings they used to be." He glanced behind them. "You are taken by the faces, so we will visit the Bayon first, before the tour buses arrive." He leaned forward and waved at Chan in the motorcycle's rear view mirror until he had Chan's attention. Then he shouted something at the driver in Khmer.

They passed the huge Angkor Wat temple with its wide moat and a parking lot where a fleet of huge tour buses belched diesel as they idled to release their pent-up loads of tourists. Chan turned the motorcycle taxi down a side road before coming to a stop in a parking lot dotted only with four personal vehicles at this early hour.

Long shadows fell from the trees across the parking lot. A pool of water with a small flock of white geese reflected the sky's pale blue. Stepping out of the rickshaw, the sun was an immediate weight on her head and shoulders. She ran her fingers through her hair and looked at the waiting temple. Square spires carved with gigantic faces looked out in the cardinal directions, but there weren't one or two spires with faces, there were ranks of them rising up from the temple corners and entries, tier upon tier until a single paramount spire reached higher into the sky, it's four faces like lookouts on a ship's mast overseeing the landscape.

Or like the faces of the media watching her when she left the hearing that had reviewed her actions before, during, and after the school shooting. She stopped and felt momentarily weak in the knees.

No. That was then. Over. Done and gone. Even then she'd done nothing wrong. Her principal had lied on the stand refuting the truth that she had come to him a number of times over the bullying that had led to the gun being brought to the school. It had led to the school board finding fault with her and condemnation in the court of public opinion, but it was long over. These were simply ancient faces…

She looked again.

Put the past aside and live again, her counselor had said.

The place was… indescribable. She was here. Standing by the ancient edifice. Watched by ancient, knowing eyes and perhaps found wanting—or at least insignificant. At least she felt so. Not like the person to be vilified as the cause of tragic events.

Even the air smelled different, sweet and floral. Richer than the air ever smelled in Vancouver.

Davuth stood back and allowed her to approach on her own terms. Three steps forward and the faces were doubled in the duck pond so she was caught in too many gazes, too much knowing, and she couldn't stop the shiver that ran up her back even as sweat formed on her forehead. How the place must have intimidated visitors when it was new and when it was "found" by adventurers during colonization.

Slowly, she climbed the stairs to the temple and faced a gray, stone Buddha figure garlanded with flowers. Before the Buddha, a small sand-filled urn held burning incense sticks that gave off a sweet sandalwood scent that permeated the air.

She inhaled, stilling herself, trying to simply be in the moment and forget her past.

"There are those amongst Cambodians who still believe in such things," Davuth said, disturbing her reverie as he came up behind her. By his tone, he clearly was not numbered among such people.

"The Buddha had many teachings that help us deal with our lives." Since the school shooting, she'd read a number of books on the subject and even taken a Buddhist meditation class—and recently she'd returned to those readings. Having Becca reject her had hurt immensely.

She sighed.

"I suppose there are things you should tell me about this place." Though at the moment she'd simply prefer to explore on her own. To have a chance to feel herself totally present, instead of simply floating through a landscape as she'd more or less done since the school incident. She might be a tourist, but she wanted something more from being here. She wanted a chance for the place to touch her soul. To help her heal. Johnstone Strait had done that with its beauty. For all its faults, India had done it with its kaleidoscope of color and culture. So far her impression of Cambodia was more colored by her concern for Sokha.

Maybe it was the way the heavy-lidded eyes of the statues reminded her of Sokha's veiled gaze, or maybe it was because Sokha had appeared so close in age to Alice, but she needed to know Sokha was safe so that she could get on with her trip.

Davuth led her on a circumnavigation of the temple and together they climbed the stairs up to the spires and the huge stone faces.

"The Bayon was built about 100 years after Angkor Wat, and was not 'found' until after many of the other Angkor temples due to the dense jungle surrounding it. Topological studies of the entire Angkor complex have placed the Bayon in the exact geographic center of the city of Angkor Thom."

Davuth's voice droned on as they climbed the stairs. "At first the temple was thought to be Hindu until depictions of Avalokiteshvara, the Buddha-to-be of infinite compassion, were found at the temple. Then it was correctly identified as a Buddhist monument. Over two hundred large faces on fifty-four towers top the temple."

Phoebe glazed over, overwhelmed by the fountain of information.

The top of the temple, the third level, was where most of the occupants of the cars in the parking lot seemed to be. They posed in front of the faces, lounged like they were ancient kings and queens, and talked excitedly about where they were. She found a corner and settled on her heels to watch. People drifted in and drifted out, but no one stayed very long. Davuth's overwhelming barrage of information seemed to stall.

"Would you like me to take your photo?" he asked.

"Maybe. In a bit. Right now, I'd just like to enjoy the quiet." And simply "be" here. Hopefully he could take the hint.

It appeared that he could, for he wandered over to another corner and lit a cigarette. At least the breeze wouldn't blow the smoke in her direction. She closed her eyes and lifted her face to the sun, feeling the age-smoothed stone under her hands and listening to birdsong and the distant voices in the parking lot. Simply breathe in, breathe out, and drink it all in.

She waited for the calm of the ancient faces to bless her with the same feeling, but in the distance she heard the throbbing diesel of a bus engine coming closer. Her calm thoughts skittered away like small animals. When the bus arrived, it would be madhouse here.

With that, any attempt at calm was gone. Sighing, because whatever she was seeking, she wasn't finding, she opened her eyes.

Instead of calm, the towering face closest to her glowered down like the parents of the dead children. She cringed, scrambled to her feet, and waved Davuth over. Posing in front of the faces, she handed him her little pocket camera. Davuth snapped a photo or two and she leaned over the balustrade that overlooked the parking lot.

And froze.

A dark blue Audi sedan had just pulled to a stop by the path to the Bayon entrance. There had to be a lot of dark blue sedans in the world and surely there were plenty of them in Cambodia, too. But…

Swallows darted through the air. Mists rose over the jungle from the rising sun's rays. The ducks glided over the reflecting pond and from out of the forest canopy poked the spires of other Angkor temples. But it was the sedan that held her in place. The driver climbed out. He came around to the rear passenger door and opened it.

Phoebe held her breath.

A man climbed out, dressed neatly in a light gray business suit, white shirt, and dark tie. His black hair gleamed in the early morning sun and he carried a garland of flowers. He started up the path and the confident way he moved made her sure. It was the same man that she'd seen with Sokha and her uncle. Phoebe spun around, almost colliding with Davuth.

She ducked past him and sprinted for the stairs, rushing down the precariously narrow risers and down again until she reached the main level.

"Ms. Clay? Ms. Clay? Is something the matter? Are you unwell?" Davuth clattered after her.

"I'm fine, now come on. And hurry!" What was the quickest route to the entrance? The man she'd seen looked like he was going to make an offering to the Buddha by the entrance. If that was the case, he could be done and gone before she got there if she chose the wrong path. Finally, because she wasn't sure of the route through the courtyards of the building, she leapt down the final flight of stairs to the Bayon's stone-strewn enclosure, checked her bearings, and ran in the direction she thought lay the parking lot.

At the corner of the Bayon, she paused. Yes. There was the parking lot and there was the car. She scanned the path to the temple and there was the man, retracing his path to the car, the garland nowhere in sight.

The duck pond stopped her from heading straight for him, so she ran along the front of the temple to the path, then sprinted toward the car.

She reached it just as the man was about to enter.

"Excuse me! Excuse me!"

The driver and the man both turned to her as she ran up puffing and held onto her knees to catch her breath. "Sorry. So sorry," she puffed and held up a finger asking for a minute to recover.

The man she wanted to speak to said something to the driver and started to climb in the back.

"No! Please! I—I saw you at the ferry landing yesterday."

The man paused, so surely that meant that he understood English, but he still said nothing to acknowledge her.

Davuth had caught up to her, but held back. He took one look at who she was speaking to and actually removed his hat and bowed his head.

"Phoebe, step away. You do not want to bother Mr. Yong."

She looked from Davuth to Mr. Yong and back. Davuth had a tightness around his mouth that could be anger at her, but also fear. Certainly concern. About Mr. Yong?

Considering Mr. Yong, she stepped closer to him and held out her hand. "I am so sorry to bother you. My name is Phoebe Clay. I'd like to ask you a couple of questions, if I may."

Yong still didn't acknowledge her or her outstretched hand. Instead he spat a question at Davuth. Davuth responded and she heard Canada and Vancouver in the flurry of Khmer.

"Yes, I'm Canadian. I'm sorry I'm a bother."

Yong's chill black gaze swung to her and stayed there like an icy bath.

"It's just… on the ferry I met a young girl named Sokha. She was traveling with her uncle. When we landed in Siem Reap, I saw her get into this car with you and her uncle follow on a motorcycle. Last night, in Siem Reap, her uncle was murdered in the night market. I—I just wanted to make sure the girl was safe. She must be very scared."

Yong's cold, snake gaze never wavered from her face. In fact, the damned man didn't even seem to blink.

And then, as if a window opened, suddenly he smiled and held out his hand. "It is a pleasure, Ms. Clay," he said in surprisingly perfect American-accented English. "I appreciate your concern, but Sokha is my daughter. She was traveling, but is now home and quite safe. As for her uncle's demise, it is most unfortunate. Thank you for your concern."

It was all the right things to say. All the things you might say to placate a nosy tourist, but she couldn't rid herself of the sense of Sokha's apparent fear when she was with this man. She'd even doubted that Sokha had known him, though she couldn't say why. But what more could she do?

"Thank you. Thank you very much." She tried to channel every stereotype of the vacuous tourist into her demeanor. "I've been so concerned, you see. She was such a charming girl; worrying about her kept me up last night. My visit to Cambodia will go much better now that I don't have to worry."

Yong gave a sharp incline of his head and climbed into his seat. The driver closed the Audi door, returned around the car, and climbed in. Then the sedan glided away in a cloud of exhaust, and she caught a glimpse of Yong through the tinted windows. He wasn't smiling anymore. In fact, he was on the phone.

She watched the sedan crunch out of the parking lot, then grabbed paper and pen out of her day pack to jot down the Audi's license number. Then she swung around to Davuth. "Who is he?"

Around them, the parking lot was quiet for the moment, their motorcycle taxi the only vehicle still waiting and the big buses yet to arrive. Birds called from the trees. The shadows were receding and the sun was a hammer on the back of her neck. It was time to pull out her hat. The scent of car exhaust dispersed, but the air left in its wake was no longer as sweet.

"Well?"

Davuth roused himself from whatever thoughts he'd been having. He replaced his hat on his head, but not before she caught the roll of sweat down his brow. She didn't think it was from the sun. Clearly, Mr. Yong made him nervous.

"He is a Big Man. A very Big Man. He owns many things in Siem Reap and in the country. No one questions Mr. Yong. You don't want to get in his way."

As she had.

A grudging admiration joined his fearful expression.

"So he's important."

Davuth nodded. All his self-important authoritarian crispness seemed to have vanished at the confrontation.

"A very important man. Very top man. You do not ask Mr. Yong questions. You show him respect."

She lowered her sunglasses to raise an eyebrow at him. "How do you ever know what he's doing if no one asks questions? How do you know if he's doing good or bad?"

Davuth waved away her question and started toward Chan and the motorcycle taxi.

Dammit, she'd asked him a reasonable question. She set off after him. "Are you telling me that he can do whatever he wants?"

He stopped and turned around to her. "That is exactly what I am saying. He is a very powerful man. He can help or he can destroy. He is not a good man to make angry and this morning you did. He might not have acted it, but he does not like to be asked questions. He will remember you, Phoebe Clay."

He climbed into the rickshaw seat and sat silently staring out the other side of the vehicle. She looked back at the Bayon, still beautiful and mysterious as the sun painted its faces with angled shadows. The faces looked angry. "So I take it we're done here?"

"We are," Davuth said.

5

The rest of the day had been a blur of temples. She'd visited the ruins of the iconic main temple of Angkor Wat with its vast moat and broad, interior balconies with their beautiful wall paintings and carvings. They'd climbed through the ruins of Ta Prohm, made so famous in the Tomb Raider film, and had admired the massive Tetrameles trees with their gleaming white bark and roots twining like snakes down over the stone. She'd seen children herding buffalo, men with round nets fishing chest-deep in stagnant green ponds, and flocks of blue butterflies. It had been beautiful, astounding, a little hypnotic, and mostly overwhelming.

And she felt like she'd been distracted and not fully enjoyed anything of what she'd seen.

Maybe it was because of the memories unlocked by the Bayon's stone faces, but she was pretty sure it was also because of Sokha. Where was the girl and was she safe and why had her uncle been killed? It just seemed entirely too possible that Uncle's death had somehow involved Sokha and Mr. Yong. Heck, the presence of Sokha's flower clip at the scene of Uncle's death was a good indication, and Yong's assurances simply didn't reassure her.

At all.

Chan dropped her at the Blue Lotus at six o'clock and she felt like she virtually crawled across the lobby and upstairs to her room. Who knew that riding in the back of a motorcycle taxi was so much work? But then she'd put in a few miles exploring the temple complexes, too. Climbing up precarious stairways, clambering over fallen stone walls and the long tree roots. Inhaling the scent of moist jungle and dust.

The same dust clogged her pores and stained her clothes. She felt hot and sticky with sweat and her eyes itched from the sun. Somehow the heat seemed more intense here than it had in southern India. Maybe it was the lack of ocean winds and the humidity that came off the lake and jungle.

In her room, she flicked on the ceiling fan, showered, and collapsed on her bed in her underwear, sipping a bottle of water as she contemplated what to do. Becca would say that poking her nose into anything regarding Sokha wasn't her job. It wasn't Phoebe's responsibility. She had her own demons to deal with.

But wasn't it Phoebe's responsibility to be a good citizen? A good human? Was she a good person if she let something happen to a young girl simply because it was inconvenient for her to get involved? Because she was too wrapped up in her own problems? That was the question she'd pose to Becca if she was present.

"You already know you're not going to let this go," Becca's presence whispered.

Well…

Phoebe swung her legs off the bed and pulled clean capris and a t-shirt to her. Becca certainly knew her. If she was going to do this, she might as well start now.

She headed down to the lobby and went to Jorani behind the registration desk, then found herself not quite sure where to begin.

"Jorani, I need your help. I—I'm worried about a friend. A young girl that I met on the ferry. When I met her, she was traveling with a man who she said was her uncle, but her uncle was the man killed in the market last night. I last saw her when her uncle put her into a car at the ferry with another man. The uncle followed the car when it left. I haven't seen the girl since then and I'm very worried. I don't know whether I should be and what I should do."

She looked her question at the pretty woman and wondered whether her concerns even made sense in the world of a Cambodian.

Jorani glanced at her computer screen, then licked her lips and sighed. "You may have a reason to worry. There are stories of children of poor families being sold to Thailand or to other countries. Your friend—this may be what has happened. Siem Reap—it is, unfortunately, a leaving place—a place they bring the girls together and then send them away."

For a moment Phoebe didn't know what to say. "Then I should go to the police and tell them what I know?"

Jorani thought about it a moment. "You may."

An answer that gave her no guidance whatsoever. "Surely the police would look for her?"

Jorani folded her hands on her desk, her computer screen apparently forgotten. "This is not America, Ms. Clay. Or even Canada. Such things are not uncommon."

"But surely the government wants to stop this kind of thing?"

Jorani closed her eyes as if in pain and gave the tiniest shake of her head. "It seems that the government can close its eyes to many things."

Phoebe thought a moment. "Because there are important men, Big Men, who control them."

A sad nod. "Rich men can do whatever they want. Is it not that way in Canada, as well?"

Phoebe started to say "no," then caught herself. There had been enough government scandals in Canada where no one was made to pay, to make it quite clear that Canada wasn't immune from the influence of money and influence peddling. "I suppose so, but it doesn't mean that we should just stand by and let it happen."

Jorani's sad gaze met Phoebe's. "What would you propose to do?"

Something inside Phoebe twisted at the question. This was the kind of passive response she received when she'd gone to her principal about the bullying that led to the school shooting. She should have done more then.

She'd do more now. "I don't honestly know, but something. More than nothing!" She realized the volume of her voice had increased when two other tourists entered the lobby and stopped to watch.

"I'm sorry." She softened her voice. "I need to think about this."

She left the Blue Lotus and headed down to the restaurant she'd gone to the night before, then changed her mind and headed out into the street to see what else she might find.

The evening light had turned from golden to a blue that filled shadows and darkened to secret-obscuring midnight in the crooks and crannies between the buildings. Farther down the main street there was still considerable traffic, but at her end of town there were only a few motorcycles laden with tired passengers—entire families going home, with children in school uniforms, men in trousers and wrinkled white shirts, and women in faded sarongs. The air smelled of their exhaust and of—tomato sauce?

She rounded a corner onto another street and found an open-sided restaurant called Siem Reap Pizza. The lighting was tiki lamps and there were rattan-and-glass tables, but at the rear of the eating area, a picture of the Roman colosseum was apparently supposed to convince people that the pizza was authentic. The posted menu, however, had one column of pizza toppings and another column of Chinese food options. Clearly, they were spanning the culinary variety of Marco Polo's famed journey.

She passed by and turned another corner, checking behind herself to make sure she could find her way back to her guesthouse. Across the street was the familiar curved building front that held the Trafalgar Pub.

If Trev was there, she could discuss her options with him, or maybe get clearer information about Mr. Yong. She couldn't imagine Trev being a fan of anyone involved in buying and selling children.

She hurried across the street and pushed inside, the cigarette smoke immediately burning her eyes. She sneezed, immediately drawing glances from all the patrons. From what she remembered, it looked suspiciously like the same tables were taken by the same groups of the same men. The only woman was Samphy, who washed glasses behind the counter.

She glanced at Phoebe and looked away, no smile, no nothing. So much for a place where everyone knows your name.

There was no sign of Trev, either. Phoebe crossed the worn floor to the counter. "Have you seen Trev today?"

Samphy shook her head.

"Do you expect him in?"

Another silent shake of her head. Clearly Samphy knew how to mind her own business.

Phoebe hauled herself up one of the counter stools. "Listen, I don't know how we got off on the wrong foot, but if it's because Trev brought me here last night, believe me, there is nothing going on between us. We'd just had a scare at the night market."

She cocked her head sideways at Phoebe. "You were there?" Her voice was lower than Phoebe had expected.

Phoebe nodded. "We were there, with the body, until the police arrived. Then we ran and came here."

Samphy shook her head. "It is a very bad thing. Bad that you could have brought the police here looking."

"Why would they come? We did nothing other than approach to see what all the commotion was about." She eyed Samphy. Tonight she wore loose trousers cut off below the knee and a faded Grateful Dead t-shirt that was perhaps three sizes too big. Her lustrous hair was pulled back in a bun, but stray hairs fell around her cheeks and forehead. She looked tired.

And worried.

She plunked down the glass she was wiping and turned away as if she'd had enough of Phoebe.

"Listen, do you—do you serve food here?"

Samphy turned to her. "If you want food, there are many restaurants in Siem Reap. This is a tavern."

"Could—could I have a beer, then?"

Samphy rolled her eyes but pulled Phoebe a pint and set the

sweating glass down on a coaster before Phoebe. "That will be two American dollars."

It wasn't uncommon in Cambodia to pay in U.S. dollars. Phoebe dug in her purse and pulled out a twenty but held onto the money. "I need information. Maybe you can help me."

Samphy's gaze flicked between the bill and Phoebe's face. "What kind of information."

"There is a man who lives in Siem Reap. An important man. I know that he can help or hurt people. What I want to know is where he lives and whether he has a daughter."

Samphy studied Phoebe as she wiped the already pristine counter. "Why? You are a tourist. You come, you see Angkor, you leave. Why make trouble for yourself?"

Phoebe had to smile. She shook her head. "You sound just like my sister. But the answer is that I met a young girl on the ferry yesterday. She said she was traveling with her uncle, but when they arrived at the ferry jetty, her uncle basically handed her over to a stranger. That stranger's name was Mr. Yong."

Samphy's black gaze widened. Her throat worked.

"When I asked him about the girl," Phoebe continued, "he said she is his daughter. I'm not sure I believe him."

"You spoke to Mr. Yong?" Samphy had quit wiping. Her voice had lowered to almost a reverential whisper.

Phoebe nodded. "I met him at the Bayon and asked him the question. He said she was his daughter."

"If Mr. Yong says she's his daughter, it is best to believe him." She grabbed her rag and came around the counter, going out among the tables to swipe at their surfaces.

Phoebe sipped her beer and watched the tavern keeper move around the room. She was graceful as a dancer for all her clothes were ill-fitting.

Clearly Mr. Yong was well-known and a sensitive subject to any Cambodian who knew him. Judging by Davuth's reaction, he was also someone to be feared. Judging by Jorani and Samphy's reticence, Yong and child slavery were not something to be discussed. But dammit, if a young girl was being held to be sold, Phoebe wasn't going to stand by and let it happen!

Leaving her half-full beer on the counter, she cornered Samphy while she wiped the empty table Phoebe had shared with Trev last night.

"At least tell me where he lives."

Samphy shook her head and waved Phoebe away, but Phoebe stood her ground. Samphy tried to step around her but Phoebe blocked her path. "Tell me."

"You want trouble, is that it?" Samphy hissed.

"I want to know."

"Fine. South of town, not far from the jetty, he has a large compound on a hill overlooking the lake. Everyone calls it the stilt village house because he lives above one of the fishermen's villages." She shoved past Phoebe, almost pushing her down, and went to the counter. Phoebe went to pay her before leaving, but Samphy shook her head.

"Keep your money. Just do not come back here again."

6

Daylight had fallen to dark when she stepped out of the Trafalgar Pub. The night was balmy against her skin. The scent of jasmine, mud, and car exhaust made a muddy melange of the air. The streets were quiet, but there was music down the block along with laughter and voices, but that didn't appeal to her. She headed home and stopped in at the pizza place for a platter of Chinese rice. She picked at the plate and finally forced herself to eat. It was tasty, but her heart just wasn't in it. It was a little lonely seated at her table for two.

But Sokha must be more than lonely. She must be frightened.

Contrary to all the suggestions from people that looking into Mr. Yong was a bad idea, she simply couldn't let the matter drop. And then there was the murder of Sokha's uncle. Someone should be investigating that, as well.

Yeah, yeah, yeah. It was a matter for the police. She could see Becca standing over the table, shaking her head. She could even see Becca's point that Phoebe's past interference had put her family at risk.

Well, the police might have been called, but given what Trev had said, she doubted they were doing much. And once they ran into the Mr. Yong connection—well, that would seal the deal, wouldn't it? Uncle would just be one more body in the Cambodian killing field.

She paid for her meal and left the tiki lanterns, rattan tables, and strange reek of pizza and soy sauce behind and set off home. The streetlights buzzed like an insistent mosquito. So did the thoughts of Sokha and her uncle. The turn to her narrow lane was dark. She hurried through the span of darkness and came out into the low, blue-tinged streetlights along the lane. The restaurant she ate at last night was now open, its tables empty. The lights of the Blue Lotus were on and beckoning, but she didn't feel ready for bed. At the other end of the street, the twinkle lights of the night market were on.

She headed in that direction.

The lane felt like it faded behind her as she focused on the cross street beyond. Tonight there were fewer tourist vans and motorcycle taxis than had been here last night and the crowd was thin. So word of the murder had got around amongst tourists. The kiosks were open, though. Dried frogs and snakes coiled or were hung on display. People wandered along the kiosks. Odd that there wasn't a single thing to mark where a man had lost his life.

Or maybe it wasn't odd at all. The police and the city fathers probably wouldn't like anything that would disturb the tourists and stop the flow of money into the local economy.

She stepped into the street and tried to picture it as it had been last night. The body had been… there.

It hadn't rained in the past day, but a large puddle suggested where someone had tried to hose away the bloodstain. She stopped and studied her surroundings. The same kiosks—all open. Local men smoking and talking to their companions. A few brave tourists who made it down to this more dimly lit area of the market. An old woman with the ugly red-stained lips of the betel chewer sat by her kiosk.

The same woman Phoebe had seen the night of the murder. She approached the woman and looked at what she was selling—small silken ornaments cunningly wrought in the shapes of animals, and narrow sashes woven of many colors. Phoebe admired them and the old woman stirred and stood.

"You want?" she said. Her voice was as scratchy as an old vinyl record.

"Maybe," Phoebe said, comparing a purple tortoise to a green elephant. "Do you speak English?"

The old woman nodded. Beyond the betel-stained mouth, her eyes were intelligent brown marbles held in the web of lines on her skin. Her hair was a thin clump of grey pulled back in a bun and her hands were twisted with years of hard work.

"I work in American homes through Vietnam War."

Of course. The American military had a less well-known foothold here, unlike their larger enclave in Thailand. Most likely military advisors—and spies.

Phoebe fingered the elephant trunk for luck and glanced back at the puddle in the street. It reflected the twinkle lights and ghostly shadows from down the street.

"How much?" Phoebe asked turning back to the woman and indicating the elephant.

She named her price.

"And for two? Or three?" She selected the tortoise and what looked like an egret, through its color was blue.

The woman named her inflated price and Phoebe shook her head and went to turn away.

The woman lowered her price and Phoebe turned back and offered 30% lower—a method that had done her well in India. They haggled and laughed together until a price was agreed upon, though Phoebe didn't need the ornaments. They would be nice mementos for Becca and Alice, though Phoebe wasn't quite sure how they would be received.

As signs of life from the other side of the world? Would they be relieved?

She paid, thanked the woman, and paused. They had connected through the bartering. Now Phoebe planned to use that connection.

"A man died here last night." She glanced at the puddle, then focused on the woman's eyes. Her gaze skittered away like flies off of food.

But she nodded.

"What did you see?" Phoebe asked softly.

The woman checked their surroundings. There was no one near. "Police come. They take body away."

"Before then." Phoebe caught the old woman's gnarled hand and felt ridges of scars. The woman had lived a hard life, indeed.

The woman swallowed and shook her head. "He was there. Then he was dead. I saw him fall." The voices of the market seemed to fade away until there was only this wizened woman under her orange awning.

"Who was here when it happened?"

The woman shook her head, but behind her a curtain stirred. "No one here. Just tourists. Maybe you. I see you."

"You saw me after the man was dead. I came running while the others ran away. Who ran away? Please. The—the man. He was the uncle of a young girl and now that girl has disappeared. Did you see her? What happened to her?"

The woman shook her head again. "Man there. Then knife there and man die. That what happen. Now you go." She flicked her fingers at Phoebe as if ridding herself of an annoying fly. But Phoebe was a little bigger than a fly.

"Please. I want to help the girl." Phoebe caught the woman's hand again, but this time she yanked away.

"No girl. No girl! You go." The woman fumbled with the kiosk awning, clearly intending on closing early. The awning swung down, but not before the rear curtain stirred again and a girl of about eleven stepped out. The vendor's granddaughter?

She wore a blue-flowered clip in her hair.

7

———————

From Phoebe's verandah, the next morning dawned with a red horizon and dark, heavily-laden clouds that hung over the jungle and seemed to perch on the few hills that poked out of the flat flood-land. The clothes Phoebe had washed and hung to dry overnight were still damp so she hauled on trousers and a cotton t-shirt that both seemed too heavy for the humidity-laden air. Dressed, she headed down the stairs for the lobby. It was just eight a.m. and she wasn't really hungry after events in the market last night. She'd tried to stop the woman from closing, but all she'd succeeded in doing was drawing too much attention to herself. So she'd left and returned to the Blue Lotus but felt like too many people watched where she went. All night she'd dreamed of Sokha and the hair clip she'd worn and that Phoebe had seen on the ground beside Uncle's body. It had to be the same hair clip she'd seen on the vendor's daughter. Phoebe had seen the old woman eye the clip and the body when Uncle was on the ground—probably looking for what she could take.

Darn it, she should have asked the old woman that instead of bartering for some useless ornaments that Becca could just as soon throw away as hang on her Christmas tree.

Wearily, she headed down the stairs, waved at Jorani, and headed out to the same café she'd visited the day before. A coffee would be good to wipe the morning cobwebs out of her brain.

The air was cooler this morning without the sun burning her shoulders, but there was a heavy expectancy that promised rain. She was glad she'd bought a poncho in Phnom Penh and had it in her day pack. Along the narrow street, the usual water sellers-cum-money changers were just setting up their counters and a woman arrived on a motorcycle bearing fruit and vegetables for the restaurant by the Blue Lotus. Birds called and the deep rumble of vehicles came from the street ahead. The air smelled of diesel and murky water.

The coffee shop she'd found yesterday had just opened and the same young woman was wiping the few tables clear of dust. Phoebe eyed the baked goods on display and ordered two lattes and mango-coconut scones. She took them to go and hurried back to the Blue Lotus, arriving just as Chan pulled up and took off his helmet. His dark hair was once more tied back, this time with a band woven of material much like the sashes she'd seen in the old woman's kiosk the night before. She handed him a paper cup and one of the scones.

"For you. I hope you like latte."

He tasted and his eyes lit up. "Thank you. I haven't had before." He sipped again and then tried the scone and smiled. "Good." Another big bite. "Where we go today?"

"The temples again, I think. No guide, though. You know the temples and I have my guidebook. I'd like to just be in the place instead of having someone talking my ear off the whole time. Okay? And depending on time, maybe we can take a drive in the country. If there are places you think I should go, you tell me, and if there are places along the road I'd like to stop, we'll do that, too."

He thought a moment, like one of her students deciding whether to humor her, and then nodded. "Good. We go now. Before bus line-up at gate."

He took a last draining gulp of the coffee, crammed the remains of the scone in his mouth, and slipped the helmet back on before they headed out, Phoebe's rickshaw seat hauled by the motorcycle. The route was the same as the day before, with the same overdose of car and truck exhaust and the same traffic crawl. Once they were through the archeological park gate, she had Chan pull over at the huge faced arch that marked the historic entry to the city.

"There is path over here." Smiling, he led her to the rear of the arch and pointed out a well-beaten path through the brush that led up to the canopy of trees and the top of the arch. She left Chan wiping imaginary dirt off the already pristine motorcycle and climbed the path. The jungle pressed in around her and even though she heard vehicles come into the park, it felt like she was a million miles away in another time.

At the top of the arch she was amongst the branches of lower trees, but more huge, white-trunked Tetrameles trees had grown from the archway, sending roots snaking down into the soil and stone. A single beam of sunlight turned the light a cool green-gold with butterflies flitting in the heart of the light. Through a space in the tree trunks and branches, the beam illuminated one of the great Angkor faces.

She stopped for a moment, breathless from the climb and the expression on the face. Had she ever been that peaceful? She didn't think so. Not even in her best meditation moments. Then a cloud slipped over the sun and the expression seemed to change to one of recrimination.

Closing her eyes and focusing on her breath, she tried to reclaim the calm she'd felt a moment before, but she kept seeing Sokha's face and Uncle's body. After a few minutes, she gave up. Darn it, until she knew Sokha was safe, she wouldn't enjoy her holiday.

In disgust, she retraced her path down to the foot of the gate.

"Did you like? Very many people enjoy that spot."

She nodded. "It's beautiful and I wish I could enjoy it, but... Change of plans." Hopefully he wouldn't refuse to help her. He seemed like a nice young man. "The man I talked to yesterday at the Bayon? I want to go to his home."

Chan's eternal smile disappeared. "That was Mr. Yong."

"It was."

Chan shook his head. "It not good to bother Mr. Yong. You not go to him."

"I know he's not a good man to bother. Everyone tells me so. But he says he has a little girl there and I want to make sure she's okay. If she is, no harm done other than we've driven out of our way and I've lost a day at Angkor. If she's not, then I need to help her."

He was still shaking his head. "Mr. Davuth. He tell you. Mr. Yong not like people bothering him. He very rich. Very important man."

"So? Why is everyone so afraid of him? What happens if you do bother him? Something bad?"

Chan swallowed and nodded.

"Like what?"

"A man who work for Mr. Yong stole from him. Mr. Yong fire him and he could not get a job anywhere in Siem Reap. He move away with his family. He found dead. Someone beat him."

Phoebe considered the story. Just because Yong had blacklisted the thief didn't necessarily mean Yong had killed him or had him killed, but she didn't think that would make any difference to Chan.

She grabbed his hand, deciding to try a different approach. "Have you got a family, Chan? A wife? Children?"

He shook his head "no."

"How about sisters?"

He gave a hesitant smile. "Three."

"Older? Younger?"

"Younger. Oldest fifteen. Then eleven. Then nine. The baby." His smile said his baby sister was special.

"What if someone took your baby sister and wanted to sell her?"

A deep frown settled on his face. "Not happen. I protect her."

"But what if you weren't able to? You went away and when you came back she was gone. Would you abandon her wherever she was or would you go looking?"

He met her gaze and finally shook his head. "Go looking. No one sells my sister."

"But what if she was traveling somewhere and something happened to her? You can't help her then."

"When I hear, I go to her! I help!"

Phoebe shook her head. "I know you would, Chan. If you could.

But by the time you hear anything, it might be too late. She might already be gone. Or dead." Or both. "What would you do?"

He sighed, his breath carrying the scent of latte and muffin. "I would hope she met someone who would help her like Phoebe Clay."

"Exactly." She grinned at him. "We all have responsibility to help each other. Isn't that something right out of Buddhist teachings?"

A bus trundled past them, its diesel stench overwhelming the verdant scent of jungle and erasing his answer, but he didn't look like he knew her reference. She was pretty sure she was right.

"You know where Mr. Yong's house is, right?" she asked as she climbed into the rickshaw.

Chan only nodded, pulled on his helmet, and pulled down the visor. His back was hunched as he turned the motorcycle around and straddled the seat. He looked more like a prisoner sentenced to death than a big brother rescuer.

Was she doing the right thing?

She climbed out of the rickshaw and Chan opened his visor.

"Chan, if this is placing you and your family in danger, maybe I should hire a taxi to do this."

He straightened and shook his head. "If this my sister, I would go. This right to do."

He nodded at the rickshaw and she returned to her seat, wondering whether she was going too far and jeopardizing everyone, just like Becca said she did.

The motorcycle rickshaw buzzed back the way they'd come, through the archaeological park entrance and down the road to the highway. There, Chan turned away from Siem Reap town into the countryside. The land to either side of the two-lane highway contained brown, fallow fields. Here and there, the ruins of some ancient building formed a pile of red bricks. Palm trees and low brush formed borders around the fields and ruins with what looked like shallow canals. Wooden houses on stilts sat among small farmyards with water buffalo, chickens, and gaggles of children for company. Here and there, villages grew up along the road where stalls sold displays of woven baskets and exotic fruit like pomelo and vivid pink dragon fruit. Petrol sellers had displays of pop bottles filled with pale yellow-green fuel. To one side, a massive construction site overflowed into a rice field, the torn earth taking a huge bite out of the bright green of a new planting.

Eventually, Chan stopped at a corner with a dirt side road. An old man drove three white oxen down the road to the highway where an old woman shepherded another ox while it munched on dry grass at the highway's verge. A group of four children saw Phoebe and ran for the rickshaw to stare. She smiled at them and gave them a pack of colored pencils she carried for just such occasions. She pulled out a piece of paper and drew a flower bouquet for them to color.

"Tell them they should share them, please, Chan." He translated while he haggled with a fuel seller and then filled the motorcycle's tank.

"I want to be prepared," he said.

As if he expected them to have to make a run for it or something.

"This *is* just a social call, Chan. He said Sokha is his daughter, so she should be able to speak with me. If nothing else, he'd probably like me reassured so that I leave him alone."

Chan shook his head as if he thought she was crazy, but he finished filling the tank and started the motorcycle. Phoebe waved goodbye to the children and they started down the road.

It was a bumpy ride, the rickshaw jouncing from pothole to pothole as Chan snaked the motorcycle between them. The fallow fields grew greener through the screen of palms shading the road. People waded knee deep through water, planting tender green plants so that the fields looked covered by a soft green haze. The air filled with the scent of rich mud. Another field had a man driving a team of oxen, the plough turning huge, sloppy turves. Elegant white egrets followed in the plow's wake, heads darting to scoop up small fish and frogs.

Ahead, the land was flat except for a low mound that rose up out of the rice fields, its sides covered in dense foliage, its crown obscured by what looked like a modern stone fortress.

As they neared the mound, they came to another village, but unlike the villages along the highway, this one seemed empty. There were no fruit stalls in the streets. Instead, the houses seemed shuttered within their low, stick fences. There weren't even the usual children playing, dogs lounging, chickens pecking, or women cooking in the shade under the homes.

Chan slowed, and she could see him uneasily eyeing the homes. When they'd passed through the village, suddenly the gravel road turned to pavement. Chan pulled over to the side of the road and shut the engine off.

"We close," he said, flipping up his visor and tipping his thumb at the hill. His usual smile had long vanished. "We still do this?"

She nodded and glanced back at the village. "Where do you think the people are?"

He met her gaze. "Where they told to be. Big Man own this land. Maybe Mr. Yong own this village, everything."

"Everything?"

"As far as you can see."

She craned around and looked back the way they had come. "Beyond the highway?"

Chan shrugged. "Maybe. Big Men own everything."

The warm morning air turned cold and the gentle bird cry in the trees changed from enchanting to tragic. "He owns these people?" she asked softly.

Chan shrugged just like her students had when asked something obvious.

She looked up at the hilltop compound and felt her insides tighten. This was wrong. This was positively feudal. But then, maybe she was imposing her western sensibilities on a different culture.

On the other hand, Trev had said that the tragedy of Cambodia was that the people had had their culture stripped away during the Khmer Rouge's reign of terror. From what she'd read, anyone with any education or any connection to arts or culture had been amongst the first to be killed. Doctors had been the enemy so that medical issues were dealt with by superstition and methods that weren't even folk remedies. So many more had died in the work camps that the Khmer Rouge government had celebrated as the great step back to tradition.

She couldn't imagine anyone promoting the creation of what

amounted to warlords and serfdom in a country that was trying to modernize. At least not publicly.

But then she couldn't imagine anyone with virtual warlord status taking well to anyone questioning the status quo. She was going to have to be very careful asking to see this man's "daughter."

"You walk up?" Chan's hopeful question disturbed her from her thoughts. He was looking at a steep stairway that disappeared into the hillside jungle, which must be how the villagers approached their master—when they dared.

She wanted to keep Chan out of the mix with Yong as much as possible, but to go up via the stairs could be taken to indicate she was no better than a villager. No, better to play on her western status and have Chan drive her up.

"Sorry, Chan. I need you to drive me. But you keep your visor down and maybe cover your license plate. If anyone asks, you say I insisted. I wouldn't pay you unless you did, understand?"

With considerable reluctance, he started the engine. They set off on a narrow, paved road that looped up and around the hillside. Too soon for her own comfort, the road opened out to an open area that overlooked the countryside.The road continued to a small car park and a tall, solid-steel gate set in a massive stone wall.

As if Mr. Yong planned to resist anyone who might consider attacking him or his "kingdom."

Chan pulled the motorcycle taxi up in front of the gate and turned to Phoebe. She nodded at the intercom box beside the road. She'd already spotted the security camera as it whirred its way toward them. She wouldn't be surprised if their progress had been tracked since they left the main road.

"Tell them that Ms. Phoebe Clay is making a pleasure call on Mr. Yong and his daughter, Sokha. Let's see what happens." She settled back in her seat trying to look relaxed as Chan pressed the intercom button and did as instructed.

The conversation went on longer than expected. Then suddenly there was a buzz and a whir and the black metal gate slowly swung open.

Chan swung a terrified face toward her, but Phoebe shook her head. "Don't look so scared. Pull your visor down if you must. Now let's get going."

Revving the engine, Chan closed his visor and dropped the motorcycle in gear. They jerked into motion, put-putting through the massive gate and into a veritable jungle garden of huge trees and dieffenbachia vines, elephant ear leaves, and the disturbing screech and cry of birds. When she glanced behind her, the gates had swung silently closed. She was committed to this course even if she changed her mind.

The jungle fell away and they passed into what looked like a French royal garden with hedges, topiary, pools of lily-festooned water cunningly wrought to look like natural parts of the landscape, and the opulent house beyond that looked as if it had been transported from the European countryside. It was a three-story, French chateau, built of cream-colored stone and marble, complete with stone pillars flanking the main door.

So much for Cambodian tradition.

Judging by the number of windows on each story, the chateau must stretch at least fifteen rooms across. Bigger than any building she'd seen in Cambodia including the grand palace in Phnom Penh. Perhaps Mr. Yong had a large family.

They drove past silent gardeners hunched over their labor and up to the main door, but otherwise saw no one. Chan stopped but didn't turn the engine off. He was clearly thinking of the need for a quick getaway, but had forgotten the gate.

Phoebe climbed down from the rickshaw and stretched her back. She fanned herself and turned around to admire the place, certain she was being observed.

"My, my, my. What an amazing garden, don't you think, Mr. Chan?"

His face was hidden behind his visor as she turned toward him.

"It is such a beautiful place. I imagine the house has some lovely views."

The main door opened silently, but she caught the motion from the corner of her eye. She swung around as a man she didn't know, clad in crisp white shirt, white trousers, and soft, black leather shoes stepped down the three steps to the ground to greet her. He had a narrow head and high-cheekboned face with black hair like Chan's, held back by a black leather cord. From under the edge of his shirt collar she caught a glimpse of a snake tattoo done in simple, but elegant, black.

"Ms. Clay. I am most sorry that I was not here to greet you immediately." His English was surprisingly good. "I am Vitthu, Mr. Yong's assistant. Mr. Yong is currently busy, but he invites you in for tea. He is very pleased that you made the long journey to his home. He does not get many guests."

She could just bet he didn't. She could also just bet that he wasn't pleased she was here.

"Why that is so nice of him! Such a gentleman—and after I bothered him so terribly at the temple." She fluttered her fingers through her hair, threw a warning glance at Chan to stay where he was, and followed Vitthu up the steps to the house.

It was—huge. And grand. What seemed like acres of white marble led to double, curved stairwells that ran up each side of the grand entry hall. The white marble flowed through open doors into what appeared to be a parlor and a piano room complete with a white grand piano. She wondered whether it was ever played. They passed those doors and others that gave onto more seating areas before Vitthu led her to the rear of the house and into a sunroom scattered with white rattan loveseats and chairs with cushions the purple of water hyacinths artfully arranged into seating arrangements. The expanse of windows gave views out over the countryside and the blue and white vista of Tonle Sap Lake. A single rattan table and four chairs stood in the room's center with a vase of white chrysanthemums. She didn't have to feign her reaction to the view.

"Oh my! It's beautiful." To either side, vistas of green and brown stretched away from the green jungle of the hill, the distance gradually made hazy by the moisture in the air until the land simply seemed to fade into the sky. The flat land was decorated with lush clumps of trees and fields of dewy green, fading into jungle. Here and there, red brick spires showed where ancient structures still stood. Straight ahead stretched the vastness of the Tonle Sap, the sky-reflecting water stretching to the misty horizon. At the nearest shore sat a huddle of brown structures that must be the fishing village she'd been told of. The land behind them had recently been cleared of trees—presumably to allow more farming. Farther out in the water stretched a long causeway with tiny vehicles traveling on it. The causeway led out farther, presumably to deeper water and the ferry jetty, where many boats were clotted amid the floating hyacinth.

If everything in this view belonged to Mr. Yong, did that mean he owned the ancient temples, too? And the lake? It could be, given in the distance she thought she made out the spires of Angkor.

She glanced at Vitthu, who stood attentively by the door to the room. "It is a magnificent view."

He nodded. "Please make yourself comfortable and I will bring tea. Mr. Yong should be along momentarily."

With a half bow and almost a click of his heels, Vitthu left, silently padding back down the hall. She watched him go and was tempted to try exploring the house, but that wasn't the role she was playing. Instead, she studied the landscape.

The grounds at the rear of the house were also perfectly manicured, but looked less like a showcase and more like a place people perhaps lived. A swimming pool languished in the sun, five chaise lounges empty beside it. A slide into the water and a waterfall grotto suggested perhaps there were children in this great silent house, though nothing else she'd seen supported that expectation. A broad, grass yard spread to a paved tennis court that backed onto the jungle, so the wall must run through the trees or else it didn't completely surround the house and she couldn't see that being the case given what she knew of Yong.

It was a beautiful place, but not a place for children. At least not children who were encouraged to play and grow into healthy, happy adults.

"You enjoy my view." Not a question, a cold statement as if she coveted something she shouldn't.

Phoebe swung around and smiled broadly. "Mr. Yong! How

wonderful to see you again! It truly is a most marvelous view. I can imagine you sitting here, taking your breakfast and reading your newspaper. At least that's what my dear departed Robert would have done. I suppose it would have been hard to get him out of his chair. He fancied himself a painter and he certainly would find inspiration here." So she made up a fictitious ex-husband…

She crossed to shake Yong's hand, but he showed no inclination for that kind of contact. Instead he inclined his head toward the table she'd admired. Then he turned to the door.

"Vitthu! Where is the tea I requested?"

The quick soft slap of footfall down the marble hall and the quiet clatter of china told of Vitthu's approach. He bowed deeply as he entered and set the tray he carried on the table. He quickly set it with two cups and saucers, a teapot of palest celadon green, and a tray of what looked like sugar cookies complete with white icing. Then he bowed and backed out of the room, like a servant would for royalty.

Feeling uncomfortable at the display, she seated herself at the table and Mr. Yong joined her. He swirled the teapot and then poured from a great height. She'd heard somewhere that pouring from a height aerated the tea, but not being a tea granny, she wasn't sure what that meant.

"So, Ms. Clay. What brings you here?"

To Cambodia or his home? She opted for the latter.

"Well, I was out for a drive looking for a place that sells shadow puppets. I'd been told the place is run by orphans and I thought to buy a puppet or two as gifts for back home. On the way, I thought of Sokha and wondered how she was. As I told you the other day, she was so keen to improve her English, I thought perhaps I could help her. I am a teacher, after all." She smiled broadly and sipped her tea. It was stronger than she usually drank, and with an intense smoky flavor and bitterness she that she wasn't sure she particularly liked. She set the cup down and winced at the rattle.

The last thing she wanted was for Yong to know she was nervous.

"Anyway, here we were out in the country and I asked my driver if he knew where you lived. When he did, I asked him to bring me here so that I could at least express my apologies for how I pressed you the other day, and hopefully so that I could say hello to Sokha again." Another broad smile and Mr. Yong sipped his tea.

When his lips curved it felt more like he was thinking about eating her.

8

M r. Yong's smile seemed to stifle the air. The sunroom that had been pleasant suddenly grew too hot and the view faded beyond the broad sunroom windows until there was only her and this shark-faced man. The tea tannins turned soured on her tongue and the sugar cookies were forgotten as she met Yong's dark gaze.

Though his lips curved, the man's eyes were flat and showed no emotion. She'd heard the clichés about inscrutable Asians, but this was different. She couldn't exactly say his gaze was evil—it just told her absolutely nothing about him. You could never know what a man with eyes like that was capable of. Or know what he was thinking. She, for one, didn't want to find out.

But then again, maybe she was simply caving to Chan's nervousness and western stereotypes.

Mr. Yong briefly sipped his tea, but then shook his head. "I am most sorry to say this, but my daughter, Sokha, is indisposed at the moment. She will be most sorry that she missed your visit." Yong's shark-eating smile never changed.

Was he challenging her? Testing her? Or simply dealing with an annoyance in the best way he knew how. Show just enough hospitality to get rid of the nosy tourist without exposing anything? If this man had secrets, and she was pretty sure he probably had truckloads of them, they were going to go with him to the grave.

"That is such a shame. I just love making friends in the countries I visit. I like to keep in touch after I go home, you see. I've got friends all over Asia and Europe. Some even come to visit me. It brightens my days back home. They can get a trifle lonely, you know? Now that I'm on my own."

He gave an infinitesimal nod.

"This big house of yours. It must be possible to get lost in it. I suppose you and Sokha must almost have to make appointments to see each other." She sipped her tea again, waiting for his reaction, but none was forthcoming.

"It is an adequate house. This is the best part." He nodded at the view.

"As if you are king of all you survey," she said softly and saw the tightening across his shoulders.

And his lips.

"Not quite, but I suppose one could feel that way." He took a last long sip of tea and stood. "Please accept my apologies, but I am a very busy man. Thank you for coming to see Sokha. I'm sure your remaining students miss you. Now, Vitthu will see you out."

A slight, almost gracious, nod and he left her, his virtually silent tread disappearing down the hallway. Phoebe stood, slightly stunned. Had his comment about her students meant something? She *had* told him she was a teacher… but his comment about remaining students made her think he knew her history. Had he checked on her? Her guide, Davuth, had told him where she was from, but checking on her simply because she spoke to him at the temple?

That certainly felt like an overreaction.

Or she was dealing with a *verrry* suspicious and careful man.

Considering what this could mean, she gathered her day pack and purse. Vitthu led her silently down the hallway to the broad front door. She stopped there and pulled a notebook and pen out of her daypack and quickly printed her name and an email address she kept for travel acquaintances until she trusted them well enough to give her main contact info. Then she tore the page out of the notebook and folded it.

"Please. Give this to Sokha when she is available. I would dearly like to keep in touch." As much as anything this was a test, because surely the daughter in a house like this would know how to use the internet. She hoped.

If the girl was truly Yong's daughter and not his prisoner.

Vitthu frowned, but finally nodded and accepted the note.

"Thank you. I—I truly just want to know she's okay. I'd like to be her friend."

"I—I will tell her."

She didn't dare believe him, but she thanked him again and headed down the stairs to a positively vibrating Chan.

Chan caught her arm and helped her into the rickshaw cab as if she couldn't manage herself.

"Third floor. Fifth window. Left side," he said softly.

Phoebe pretended she hadn't heard and settled back in her seat. "Goodbye!"

She waved vacuously at Vitthu as Chan started the motorcycle and they began to move. She leaned out of the side of the cab and kept waving, using the opportunity to scan for the window Chan had mentioned.

Third floor. Left side. Fifth window.

Her gaze locked on the glass opening. A curtain covered the glass, but between curtain and window a slim, feminine figure stood there, her hands pressed to the glass.

The motorcycle sped up and she craned to see, but the window was too far away, the angle too great. Then the curtain stirred and the figure disappeared as if pulled away. A male figure took her place.

Phoebe yanked back inside the cab and then leaned forward to touch Chan's back. "Faster. Let's get the heck out of here."

Chan obliged.

They whipped down the jungle corridor toward the closed fortress gate. All she could do was pray that they would be allowed to leave. And leaving was what every part of her wanted. For all the grandeur of this house, this property and the view, the place gave her the willies. No, not the place—the man who lived there. After the two brief encounters she'd had, she could truly understand the attitudes of the locals when asked about Yong.

In the words of her students, he could be one scary dude.

As they neared the gates, the huge metal closures swung open. Chan accelerated through them and they careened dangerously out into the parking area and around the corner onto the paved road down the hill. If anything, the motorcycle taxi accelerated around the descending curves so that Phoebe was forced to hold on for dear life and finally closed her eyes when it seemed they were going to drive right off the hill.

A huge bump banged her head against the cab's metal supports and the whole cab shuddered around her. She opened her eyes.

They were in the abandoned village, though this time it didn't seem so abandoned. The motorcycle taxi bounced from pothole to pothole, the pavement having ended at the bottom of the hill. Phoebe still clung to the cab uprights, but her gaze was taken by the stick-thin bedraggled people coming in from the fields. Sarongs were covered in mud. Exhausted men and women with emaciated arms and legs. A few children, just as tired and thin, with them. The bucolic scene of the rice fields she'd seen dematerialized into something far more sinister.

She glanced up at the hilltop and thought of Chan's description of the Big Man owning these people. The lord of all he surveyed, indeed. Her estimation of Yong reached a new low. The people's condition brought to mind the images she'd seen of survivors of the Khmer Rouge work camps.

They left the village behind and headed down the long straight road for the highway, Chan clearly a man on a mission to get as much distance between them and Mr. Yong as possible. At the highway he went to turn back toward Siem Reap town, but she reached over the front and tapped his back. He pulled over and pulled his helmet off. He looked distressed.

"Please! I am very sorry for the very bad ride. Please forgive me." He half bowed.

"Hold on. Hold on, there, Chan. You have exactly nothing to apologize for. You took me where I asked you to, and you got us out of there as fast as you could, and I'm happy for that. I may have bruises both top and bottom, though. And I sort of feel like all my joints have been rattled loose." She rubbed her head and her fanny and grinned.

"Very sorry, Miss Phoebe. Very sorry."

"Stop. I won't hear any more of that. You are a very good driver. Now smile like you always do," she commanded sternly. "I stopped you because I was told there's a place that makes shadow puppets somewhere outside of Siem Reap. It's run by orphans. I'd love to go there. Do you know it?"

Chan's grin bloomed anew. He nodded. "It not so far from here. We drive that way," he tipped his head back the way they'd come."Then there is a turn to Banteay Srei. The puppets are along the way."

"Then perhaps we spend our afternoon doing that. Okay?"

He nodded again. "Banteay Srei is part of the Archaeological Park. It is called the temple of women. Very fine temple. Very beautiful. You will see." He hesitated. "Along the way, there is bad smell. You hold your breath, okay?"

They set off and Phoebe nibbled on the scone she'd bought that morning, feeling guilty as she did so. She had so much compared to the people they'd passed. Soon enough they turned off the highway, but not before Phoebe felt she'd inhaled more than her share of diesel fumes. The road they turned onto was paved for the first while, but became steadily narrower. Ahead, a straight road struck off to the left. Just beyond stood a large, metal-sided building. Phoebe inhaled and almost gagged at the horrible scent. Chan hadn't been kidding. It had to be some kind of abattoir or something.

She held her breath until the building was behind them. Most of the rice fields were dry, only a few farmers out plowing, raising dusty clouds under the hot sun. Others were filled with water and newly planted rice, so they must have some way to control the water flow. Interspersed with the rice fields and the small landholdings with their swept yards, gaggles of chickens and children, were fields filled with cactus heavy with swelling pink blossoms that she realized were dragon fruit. She'd never seen them as part of a plant before. Back home, they came as livid pink amputees on grocery store shelves.

A copse of tall trees shadowed the road ahead and two large, corrugated metal-roofed buildings stood to one side. The buildings were two stories in height, the second story with rusted metal walls, the lower level mostly open-sided, what lower-level walls there were clearly pieced together with odd sheets of metal. The motorcycle taxi slowed and Chan pulled over in front of the second of the ramshackle buildings. "This is shadow puppet place. There they weave silk like in the old days." He motioned to the first building that looked almost abandoned except for two large looms that sat empty. He shrugged, clearly unimpressed that anyone would revive old arts.

Phoebe climbed out of the cab. Her legs wobbled a little and she took a deep breath to steady herself. She hadn't realized that adrenaline had been surging through her, but now it was fading and she felt the difference. She yawned and wished for a nap because, regardless of the shade, it was still darned hot. She pulled a bottle of water from her bag and drank it back. That was better, at least.

When she turned to the building Chan had indicated held the shadow puppets, she found herself facing not just a building, but a crowd of children, all with expectant faces. A man stood in front of them.

"Welcome! Welcome to the shadow puppet school!" the man said and stepped forward to shake Phoebe's hand. He might have been thirty, but still looked incredibly young. He had a mop of black hair shaved short on the sides and wore dusty trousers and a worn t-shirt as did most of the children.

There must have been about twenty boys. No girls that she could see. They seemed to range in age from perhaps six or seven all the way up to midteens, but there didn't seem to be anyone older than about sixteen.

"Thank you. Thank you for the welcome. I saw shadow puppets in town and heard they were made here. I thought perhaps I'd come here to buy. I think my niece would love them."

"Come. Come. We show you how it is done," the man said and led her inside the open-sided building. "I am Arun. I run this place for the children."

"And where are the children from?"

"Many villages. Some, their mother and father die. Others cannot afford food. The children come here. Next door we have a girl's program to learn silk weaving, but it is closed at the moment due to funding."

A sad tale, but these children looked happier and better fed than the children at the village beneath Yong's hill. She frowned and looked back the way she'd come. A break in the tree branches across the road gave an unwelcome view of a distant hill. The gleam of white stone at the top told her what she was looking at. She turned back to Arun.

"You own this land, or do you have a landlord?"

He smiled. "This was my father's land. He was very smart man and received tenure as soon as the government allowed it."

He called a couple of older boys to show her the puppet making process of tanning cowhide and then tracing designs on the leather before the leather was cut to create the shadow puppet. The other boys crowded around Arun and Phoebe. They told her that these days most of the tanning was done at a tannery down the road. She remembered the smell. Not an abattoir, then.

"Tradition says that the puppets were first made at Angkor when a great architect and artist noticed how the sun placed light and shadow through holes in old cowhides. He had the hides shaped and the puppetry was born." He pointed at a complex leather image that was about four feet high and three across. Intricate carvings showed what looked like a family walking through a forest of twining trees, birds, and flowers. "This is one style of puppet called *Sbek Thom*. These puppets are used to dance the traditional stories like the Ramayana. The second style are the *Sbek Toch*, like these."

He produced a stack of smaller puppets, all carved to look like an old man with articulated arms and legs. "These small ones are used to dance other stories. There is a third form of shadow puppet, the *Sbek Por.* They are large like the *Sbek Thom*, but they are painted as well. We do not make them here."

She eyed the gorgeous *Sbek Thom* puppet with its intricate carving. It would be spectacular at home hung against a white wall, but would take up more room than Stoney had to spare. She turned to the pile of smaller puppets, something she could take or send to Alice. She could imagine Alice's delight if she was here. She'd be oohing and aahing over the puppets. Becca would enjoy them, too, especially the large one. Maybe Phoebe should buy it and mail it to Becca. The spaces in the leather could be a reminder that she had a vacancy in her life—a family member still out in the world. Maybe make her feel the pain Phoebe felt at being abandoned.

No. Becca might have left, but she had reasons that were good to her. Sighing, Phoebe turned to the small *Sbek Toch* and rifled through the stack, but didn't see anything that would delight Alice.

"I was in the market the other day and a man there had a monkey puppet. Hanuman? Do you have any of those?"

Arun smiled. "Of course. Those are most popular with the tourists and with the children. You should know that fifty percent of each puppet's sale goes to the child who made it. Most of the smaller puppets are five dollars each." He said something and the children dispersed, only to regroup and return with the tallest and perhaps oldest among them carrying a stack of monkey puppets. He held them out to Phoebe.

"Oh my! That is so many puppets! Did you make all of these?"

He shook his head.

"Did you make any of them?"

He nodded, and sorted through the puppets until he held up one puppet. His hair, cut like Arun's, flopped into his eyes. His hands were stained brown from the leather processes.

"Did you make one?" she asked the littlest boy. When he nodded she said, "You must show me."

Soon enough the boys were each holding up their puppet of Hanuman, the monkey god. She examined each one and saw the hopeful faces of the children. If she had the money, she'd buy all of them just to see the smiles she knew would come. But she had to choose. The puppet made by the eldest student had better carving and smoother edges than many of the other children's work, but there was a playful glee in the monkey's expression in the work of a number of the younger children. Finally she settled on two and saw the disappointment in the other children's faces. She fished in her purse, found two crisp twenty dollar bills, and gave each child one.

"Please tell them that the extra fifteen dollars is to share with their friends. There were so many wonderful puppets and I am sad that I couldn't buy all of them!"

He translated and there were smiles all around. The boys crowded around the two lucky puppet makers.

She turned to Arun. "It must be very difficult to keep this place running with all these mouths to feed. May I make a donation?"

"Anything is appreciated. This is the slow season and there are not so many tourists."

She dug a fifty dollar bill out of the sweat-stained, cloth travel safe she wore on a lanyard around her neck and under her clothes.

"You said you own this land. That's unusual isn't it? I understand that most of the land around here is owned by one man."

Arun's dark gaze slipped from her face. "He has made it difficult for the traditional villages. They cannot get seed, or roads wash out and are not rebuilt. The people run out of money and then his men appear and offer help. They call it help. The people sign papers not realizing that they have signed over their lives and the lives of their children. This place—" He waved his arms at the building he presided over. "There could be fifty or a hundred more children here. Here they work, yes, but they learn to take pride in Cambodian culture. They learn to read and write and arithmetic, too. But I can only take these few. The others labor beside their parents in fields they do not own for barely enough food to live!"

He shook his head and inhaled deeply. The anger he'd displayed disappeared. "I am sorry. It is just, until this year he has ignored us, but this winter he raised the price of rice for the children. It is as if he cannot bear to see them have a future!" He closed his eyes a moment. "I am sorry again. It is no good to trouble a kind visitor with your problems."

"Arun, I don't have a lot of money, but give me your contact information. Perhaps there are people in my country who can help."

She took down his information and hated to leave, but Chan was waiting. It broke her heart the way the boys lined up to wave and yell thank you as she snapped their picture and the motorcycle taxi sped off. She palmed tears off her cheeks as they sped between the dragon fruit fields. The air here away from the lake was oddly dry and red dust rose off the road in heavy clouds. It got in her eyes and made it hard to breathe.

It made no sense given she had just been driving through drowned rice paddies and jungle.

Another turn down a narrower road, and ahead metal caught the sunlight through a screen of dusty brush. They crossed a small river and she held onto the jouncing seat and craned to see as Chan took them around a curve and suddenly they were in another parking lot that sat beside a lotus-strewn pool and a small, ornately-carved temple.

This place had neither the size of the grand Angkor Wat temple, nor the mystery of the four-faced towers that were the signature of the Bayon. Instead, every inch of the temple's orange-red stone appeared covered in artistic carvings.

Chan pulled to a stop and she climbed out into a cloud of settling dust and the hammer of sun. It was almost noon and the tourists she could see were carrying umbrellas for shade as they entered the temple. Well, she hadn't brought one. She had her baseball cap, but that would only shade her eyes from the worst of the sun. She pulled it out of her daypack and slapped it on. It didn't make much difference. The sun was still a searing red ball overhead and her shoulders and neck took the brunt of exposure.

"It's so different from the other temples," she said, standing with her hands on her hips, her gaze flitting across the quiet scene. Maybe it was just because there were few tourists here, but unlike the other temples, Banteay Srei had a sense of introversion instead of the towering faces peering outward.

She left Chan to guard his precious bike and headed across the parking lot. A sign by the arched gate entry to a causeway told her that the place had been discovered in 1914 and excavated in 1924, though the place dated back to the second half of the 10th century. It told her that the temple was made of pink sandstone, which allowed it to be carved like sandalwood, and even gave off a similar sweet scent. She leaned in to sniff the stone, but smelled nothing but dust. Still, it was a magical place—so quiet, and with the moat glimmering and reflecting the temple's colors amid the sky. She headed down the short causeway to the entry and stopped.

Close up, the carving was spectacular, with foliage and geometric patterns intertwining to cover every surface. Small figures sat between elephants rampant at the top of the final gate. She stepped through the narrow entrance, having to duck her head, and found herself in a walled inner sanctum. Unlike the Bayon and Angkor Wat temples, here the few tourists spoke in muted voices. It was—peaceful. The femininity of the place one Becca would have appreciated.

She could almost feel Becca beside her and imagine Alice rushing on ahead with her camera. Becca would tell her that it was worth the trip to visit here, to see this. She would smile and there would be no animosity between her and Phoebe.

But of course that wasn't the case. Becca had decided that Phoebe was at fault for everything that happened in India. She didn't want to see Phoebe until she would admit it.

And so, Phoebe was here alone and Becca missed seeing this place. Missed a moment together.

Phoebe's throat tightened and she swallowed. What was it about this place that she wanted to cry? That darned tears were running down her cheeks and she was so—so tired of it all. Traveling alone. It had been wonderful to have Becca and Alice to compare notes with as they traveled. Together they'd kept each others' spirits up when things got hard. She missed them both so much.

The darn tears wouldn't stop and she found a spot in a corner and let the grief flow through her. Damn it all, she wasn't a crybaby. She was strong. And Becca wasn't here because she'd chosen to go home. She'd chosen, and she had chosen Alice over Phoebe.

As it should be.

She held onto that thought and let it steady her. Well, if Becca didn't need her, she didn't need Becca, either. And Alice—well, the kid was fantastic, but she did require looking after. Besides, she was probably happier at home and exploring her newfound interest in boys.

Without her Aunty Bee to look out for her.

She palmed the tears off her face and her hand came away muddy with red dust. Great. She must look like heck. She used a tissue and water from her water bottle to try to wipe the worst of it off, but only God knew whether she'd made it better or worse.

Unfortunately, her thoughts of Becca and Alice seemed to have erased the intimate feeling of the place. Now Banteay Srei just felt old and empty. And sad.

She circumnavigated the inner sanctum because she felt she should, and left again, down the causeway to Chan. Silently, she climbed in the cab.

"Miss Phoebe? You okay?"

She shook her head. "I'm feeling a little sad at the moment. Let's head home."

Chan frowned but climbed on and started the motorcycle. He headed them out of the parking lot. The dust rose around them in clouds as they crossed over the river. On the far side of the bridge, a man in black leather and a motorcycle helmet stood beside a yellow motorcycle and watched them pass by. Phoebe glanced back and saw him swing onto his bike and follow behind.

Why anyone would choose to follow in the dust cloud her cab raised, she couldn't fathom. Most people would wait for the dust to settle. But every time she glanced over her shoulder, the yellow motorcycle was there.

When they reached the main highway and turned toward town, she glanced back once more.

The yellow motorcycle turned with them.

She sank back in her seat. Siem Reap *was* the main town in the area. It made sense that most people headed there. That had to be why the motorcycle was going the same way as them. Chan sped up and passed a truck, leaving the motorcycle behind and she sighed in relief.

When Chan finally turned onto the main street through town, she was glad that she was almost home.

Until she glanced back and the yellow bike was once more behind them.

9

"Chan." At a stoplight she leaned forward and managed to catch his attention. He glanced at her over his shoulder.

"There's someone following us. A yellow motorcycle has been behind us since the temple."

He flipped up his visor and nodded, his expression grim. "I see him. That's why I pass truck. I lose him." A huge grin, and he flipped his visor down. "Hold tight," he called.

She did as told and braced herself as the light changed. He raced off the mark, dodging through traffic more swiftly than she'd thought possible or ever wanted to go.

They roared down the street, barely making a tight, left-hand corner at the next light and accelerated down the road, whipping past bicycles so close Phoebe swore she could have wiped people's noses. At the next corner the light changed, but he roared through the intersection anyway, barely missing an orange-robed monk who stepped off the curb.

They were going to have such bad karma if Chan wasn't careful. She glanced back. The yellow motorcycle was a good way behind, probably slowed by the heavier traffic on the main road. But Chan was taking them onto less trafficked streets and the yellow motorcycle was catching up. Clearly the motorcycle taxi was no match in power or speed.

Chan must have seen, for he took a corner so sharply that Phoebe screamed. The motorcycle taxi cab went up on two wheels and the metal roof squealed as it scraped along a building wall. Then the cab crashed down to level and her head smacked into the metal crossbar on the ceiling. She bit her tongue. They were in a narrow lane sided by tall brick walls. Broken glass gleamed at the tops in the late afternoon sun.

Tasting blood, the motorcycle taxi's engine roaring in her already ringing ears, she closed her eyes and wished for the whole thing to be over. And then suddenly Chan stood on the motorcycle taxi brakes. She held on tight as the vehicle swung hard right through a gate. Chan was off before the vehicle stopped rolling and shoving shut a solid gate. Then he ran back and shut the motorbike off, shushing her queries with a finger to his lips.

"My house. It safe. But must be very quiet. He can still hear us."

They were in a small, still, concrete-block walled courtyard that held a traditional stilted home of wood. Chickens scratched at the warm, dusty soil, but along one wall a garden of flowers grew in a profusion of bougainvillea, jasmine, and calla lilies. A line of laundry waved in the sun and filled the air with the scent of flowers and laundry detergent.

From beyond the solid walls came the roar of a motorcycle engine, so their pursuer had tracked them this far. Phoebe held her breath as the vehicle roared past to the other end of the street, but her relief was short-lived. The motorcycle turned back and ran along the laneway again. It sounded like it even slowed as it came even with their gate.

Then the engine revved and the motorcycle departed with a squeal. Phoebe sagged against the side of the cab.

"I wonder who that was," she said.

Chan looked at her through the tops of his eyes.

"Okay. I'll bet we know who he works for."

Chan nodded. "Tomorrow we just go to temples, okay?"

"Deal." She smiled. She just hoped that their pursuer hadn't pinpointed where they were. She hadn't realized how risky the visit to

Yong would be. She didn't want to do anything more that could bring something bad down on Chan or his family.

They spent the next hour having tea, seated on small benches under the house. Chan made the tea because his mother was at the market where she sold tomatoes and other vegetables that they grew in a small garden on the other side of the house. The youngest of Chan's three sisters, nine-year-old Chantou, a spritely girl with long black hair tied back with a pink bow, arrived home from school and was thrilled to have the opportunity to practice her English with a native speaker. The three of them chatted, with Phoebe offering words when Chan's little sister got stuck and the afternoon filled with the girl's delighted laughter. When they were done with their tea, Chan spoke to his sister in Khmer and the child turned serious.

She left the courtyard and was gone a few minutes before returning through the gate pushing another motorcycle. She shook her head.

"Yellow motorcycle man has left," Chan said. "Chantou says there is no sign of him, so I can take you home."

"On that?" she nodded at the motorcycle. It was black, but the paint had worn in places and there was rust on the spokes.

"My friend loan us his bike. It safer and faster to get you home."

With trepidation, Phoebe gathered her daypack and climbed on the rear of the motorcycle after Chan started the engine. Chantou ran to open the gate and Phoebe waved to her as she and Chan roared out of the gate and down the street.

Wind blew in her already tangled hair and an insect splatted against her cheek. The shadows were getting long in the streets and people were clearly heading home after a day of work. Women carried baskets of fruit and vegetables. Men drove motorcycles home with two or three children crowded behind them. They looked so casual about the whole thing, while she clung to Chan's waist and wished that she never had to ride a motorcycle again.

She wasn't built for this. Was too old for this.

Becca would be nodding her agreement.

Chan wove a circuitous route through areas that were mostly homes. The air was rich with evening cool and the scent of rice water and curry, though Cambodians seemed to have less spicy cuisine than Thais.

The motorcycle slowed as they wove down a street crowded with small wooden kiosks that she was surprised to recognize as the night market street. Phoebe looked for the woman she'd spoken to last night, but her kiosk was shuttered and looked deserted, while the others were being opened for the night. Strange.

Chan turned down Phoebe's street and the closed kiosk was lost from view. He slowed and came to a stop before the Blue Lotus and turned to her. "Home, Miss Phoebe. Safe and sound."

She climbed down from the motorcycle cab and went to him. "I owe you a lot today, Chan. Thank you for all you have done to keep me safe." She handed him a twenty-dollar bill tip for the day.

"But, Miss Phoebe. No! We have more days to go. You will tip me at the end."

She clasped his shoulder and met his gaze. "I will tip you whenever I want to, Chan. Today you gave me great service at great risk to yourself. If I'd realized what kind of man Yong is, I wouldn't have asked you to do it." Though she couldn't be sure, she hoped that was the case. She *did* have a history of dragging other people into her investigations. "Use the money toward getting your own helmet. I know you want one." She patted his shoulder and climbed the stairs to the lobby to head for her room.

"Ms. Clay. I have messages for you," Jorani said from her perch by the registry desk. She stood and gracefully came down the few stairs to meet Phoebe, surprisingly handing her three pink slips of paper.

Who would call her? Who knew she was here?

Thanking Jorani, Phoebe headed for her room, but the pink slips of paper had sent a chill up her spine. Something at home? She'd emailed her plans to Becca; could something have happened that she needed Phoebe? Or maybe Becca had come to her senses and was apologizing finally.

Like that was going to happen. And even if it was an apology, Becca would go off the deep end if she knew what Phoebe was doing, because there was no question now that Phoebe was in it for the long haul. Until Sokha's safety and the death of Uncle had been resolved.

In her room she sank down on the extra bed next to Stoney and checked the messages. It was surprising how tired she was given she'd hardly walked anywhere today. It must be the heat and the emotional toll of fear, guilt, and grief. It had been an emotional rollercoaster of a day, what with the meeting with Mr. Yong and then the time with the shadow puppet orphans and then the fear that came from being pursued.

The first of the messages was from Davuth, her guide the previous day. All it said was to call him and left a number. Odd. She had no remaining business with him as she'd arranged direct payment through Jorani. She set the message aside, intending to call him once she'd showered.

The second message was from Trev and so was the third. The third one said "urgent." Again, she set the message aside for after her shower.

She rinsed out her dusty clothes and stood in the warm shower, watching red dust run off her body and down the drain. When she was clean, she gradually turned the water cool until she felt revived from the day and ready to return calls.

Dressed in blue capris and a red pin-striped blouse, she toweled off her hair and picked up her phone.

Pacing the room, she dialed Davuth first because she was sure it would be a shorter conversation. He picked up on the first ring.

"Davuth? This is Phoebe Clay returning your call."

He was silent a moment and then cleared his throat. "Ms. Clay, I fear that I may have done you a disservice by not fully explaining…" His voice sounded strained as if he was unhappy to speak to her.

"I don't understand. You were an excellent guide yesterday. You told me more than I could ever remember, I'm sure. Thank you so much, again."

"No."

She could almost hear him shaking his head.

"Yesterday… yesterday at the Bayon. You spoke to a man. A very important and powerful man."

She looked at the phone. "Mr. Yong. Yes. And you told me in no uncertain terms just how inappropriate that was."

"I did. But I understand that today you had your driver take you to Mr. Yong's personal residence. Miss Phoebe, this is most unacceptable. You cannot do such things to such men!"

What the heck was he talking about? Then a place deep inside her went cold. "Are you threatening me, Davuth?"

"No! No! I would not do such a thing. But this afternoon I received a visit from a very angry man. I was told that you make powerful people very unhappy and I was to ensure it did not happen again. They —they asked me where you stay and I—I told them."

Phoebe's legs went weak. She sank down on her bed. That was why the yellow motorcycle hadn't been waiting. They'd found out another way where she would be going.

"I was not thinking. I was scared. I am so sorry."

She hung up on him and realized her hands were shaking. Davuth hadn't said as much, but it was pretty clear that Mr. Yong was a dangerous man and he wasn't above intimidating people who irritated him.

Like Phoebe Clay. And if he couldn't get to Phoebe directly, he'd get at the people she knew. He must have already figured out that Phoebe cared about other people's welfare. Heck, she'd told him as much!

She considered Trev's messages and wasn't sure she could handle whatever he was going to tell her. Besides, she was hungry after only having a scone all day. She abandoned the messages on her bed and left her room to find dinner.

With a nod in Jorani's direction, she left the lobby and checked both ways down the street. Not that there was traffic. At this time of evening it was mostly dead, but that didn't stop her from checking. She'd been abducted in broad daylight once before.

The lane was dark except for the pools of blue streetlight and the glimmer of moth wings. Insects hummed rhythmically in the trees as if crooning children to sleep. Shadowy figures passed her on the other side of the street and she found herself slowing to keep an eye on each one.

She had to admit, she was worried—both for Sokha and herself. And Chan, for that matter, and Davuth and Trev. Heck, she should be worried for Jorani and the Blue Lotus, too. If Yong had reached out to Davuth to put the fear of God into him, then he was apt to do it with anyone who associated with her. Her sense of vulnerability led to her returning to the little restaurant on her street. She once more ordered the baked pumpkin, preferring its authentic custard texture and nutty, curry flavour over the mediocre Chinese food or pizza farther down the street. She settled herself at a back table facing the street and close to a rear exit.

Paranoia much?

Nothing was going to happen. Davuth had just delivered his warning. Surely Mr. Yong would wait to see whether she stopped her enquiries.

The more serious question was whether she would.

This was the first time in her adventures that she'd felt personally threatened just for asking questions. Well, no. That wasn't quite true. There'd come a point in each of her "investigations" where things had degenerated and she had been scared.

But this case was different. In the others she'd been prepared to put herself at risk because her family were in danger. In this one, there was no family connection, just a girl and a dead man she didn't know except to recognize.

Was she prepared to place herself at risk for them?

"Yes." She spoke out loud and smiled at the waitress. She probably thought Phoebe was another weird tourist.

Yes. She'd said it and she meant it, because all the things she'd said to Chan were true. People had a responsibility for each other. To help each other.

But at what cost?

Becca's voice sounded like she stood right at Phoebe's shoulder. She glanced around.

Of course no one was there.

She looked back to the front of the restaurant as two heavy-set local men entered and settled themselves at a table. Both wore dark trousers and floral shirts that seemed glued on over their bulging arms. One had a round head with a crew cut while the other had long straggly hair that touched his shoulders. She smiled at them and then gulped back some water and tried to ignore them.

They waved away the waitress when she approached them. Their flat gazes never wavered from Phoebe.

Okay. She got the message.

Maybe Becca was right and she should go to the police. But Trev had told her that was a bad idea that could easily backfire into her becoming a suspect. She really didn't fancy the idea of spending the rest of her days in a Cambodian prison.

She shifted uncomfortably in her seat. She was darned if she was going to let them scare her, but still... Maybe...maybe she should contact the Canadian Embassy and let them know that if anything happened to her they should look at Mr. Yong as a suspect. She pulled out her phone and looked for a number. There was one for an office in Phnom Penh. Tomorrow she would do that.

Satisfied, she settled back in her chair and tried to relax—or at least appear so. In fact her gut was twisted so tight she felt ill. The scent of her curried pumpkin almost undid her.

She barely managed to force down five or six mouthfuls before paying and leaving. She kept her back straight and walked right past the men as if they didn't matter, but when she got out on the street, she was tempted to break and run. Instead she held a steady pace back to the Blue Lotus and climbed the stairs to the lobby. She dared a look back and the two men were there, standing in the light from the restaurant.

Watching her.

10

Back in her room, Phoebe set the locks on the door and slumped on her bed in the dark. Her hands shook and her guts felt unsteady. Those men had been goons sent to intimidate her and they'd done a very good job. She was afraid to turn on the lights for fear of telling them which room was hers. Instead she turned on the fan, pulled the curtains closed over the window, and sat there feeling queasy from the curried pumpkin. She inhaled and exhaled slowly, trying to slow her racing heart.

Maybe she should just pack up and leave. That's what Becca would advise. Heck, Becca would be changing her travel reservations right now. But Phoebe wasn't Becca. She had her own ideas of what was right and what was wrong and clearly a very different perspective about personal responsibility. But then Becca was looking out for Alice, too. Responsibility like that could change the risks you took in the world.

But there was only so much Phoebe could do. She was just one person. And Becca would tell her to let the police do their jobs. The only problem was that the police didn't even know about Sokha and even if they did, Trev's reaction to their approach didn't exactly leave her with a sense of confidence. If she trusted his advice. But why shouldn't she? The guy had exactly nothing to do with anything that had happened. He'd helped her when she had blood on her hands and had even counseled Phoebe to stay out of it, just as Becca would.

Not the police, then, but the embassy, and she wasn't going to wait until tomorrow.

She grabbed her phone and made the call to Phnom Penh. Of course no one answered, but she left a message that outlined who she was, her passport number, and that she'd been looking into a missing girl. If she disappeared, they might ask Mr. Yong about it. When she hung up, adrenaline was pinging in her veins. Making the call had brought home the danger she'd placed herself in.

Well, she was safe for the moment and she might as well use the fact that she was awake to her advantage.

She changed to her pajamas in the bathroom and, in the weak light through the bathroom door, settled on the bed with a paper and pencil. It might help to outline the pros and cons of leaving or staying.

Starting out, she channeled Becca and wrote down all the dangers of staying in Siem Reap. It was, unfortunately, a fairly lengthy and convincing list. Then she started in on reasons to stay.

First and foremost was the missing girl. Even from their brief meeting on the ferry, Sokha had been a charming young woman. Phoebe dearly wanted confirmation that the girl was safe before she left the area.

Then there was the fact that she had yet to see Angkor fully. She still hadn't had the experience she was seeking—but then maybe she never would. Maybe she was fooling herself thinking that she could find something in those ancient ruined temples. She wasn't even sure what it was she was looking for.

Peace? Tranquility? Forgiveness?

Why here?

It didn't make any sense to expect to "find herself" here, if that's what she was doing.

So what else held her here?

Her thoughts kept returning to Sokha. A young girl who had briefly talked with her and whose uncle had been murdered. A girl who might have been abducted.

She thought for a moment.

There was not wanting to prove Becca right by running home at the first sign of things getting difficult.

There was that, though Phoebe wasn't sure it was valid.

But really, given the threat made to her person and potentially to those she knew, maybe it made more sense to leave.

And leave a girl trapped in what might be her abductor's home, not to mention a man murdered.

Just what did she know about the case anyway?

A girl escorted to Siem Reap by her uncle. A girl who had looked afraid to get into Mr. Yong's car. The uncle found dead in the market, Sokha's hair clip next to him as if she'd been there when her uncle was killed.

If he was her uncle.

Hadn't the girl referred to Phoebe as Aunty? In some countries, wasn't that a term of respect for an elder?

She didn't even know whether Sokha was really Mr. Yong's daughter. If she was, had she run away and been dragged back to him? Could Phoebe quit worrying because it was a family matter?

Her gaze kept circling back to the sentence about the girl possibly abducted and a man murdered. There were very basic things she didn't know about this whole case, like the identify and relationship between the people involved.

At least in the school shooting, she'd known the players. She hadn't in Johnstone Strait, and look at the trouble it caused. And not knowing the true identities of the people involved in the last murder in Kochi had almost resulted in Becca and Alice's murder. She needed to know whether Sokha really was Yong's daughter and the identity of the murdered man before she could decide whether to cut short her Cambodian vacation.

That made sense.

And it was something she could find out without Mr. Yong knowing.

Hopefully.

There had to be some sort of birth registry, and at the ferry she remembered Sokha and her uncle having to show some kind of ID. That meant there was some kind of government registry. And surely the police had to have identified the murdered man by now. She could ask.

That meant she knew what she was doing tomorrow, and if Chan didn't like it, she'd hire another driver. Actually, maybe she should do that anyway, because she didn't want to put him and his lovely family at risk.

She'd talk to Jorani about it in the morning.

She stood to turn the bathroom light off and noticed the pink messages Jorani had given her. She hadn't called back Trev, but not calling him was likely doing him a favor if her discussion with Davuth had been any indication of what had happened today after she left Yong's house. She was frankly surprised that Jorani hadn't asked her to leave.

She left the messages where they were, turned the bathroom lights off, and shifted the curtain the barest amount to peer outside.

The sky overhead was verging on black, with the paler shadows of clouds passing over the stars. Below her window, the streetlight pooled along the lane. The restaurant lights had turned off and nothing moved, but down the street toward the main part of town, a brown car she hadn't seen before was parked. As she watched, the glow of a cigarette illuminated the cab. Two figures.

Watching.

She let the curtain fall and climbed into bed.

S leep had been almost impossible to find through the night. Every sound beyond her room doorway brought her upright in bed until finally she did fall asleep and was woken by someone knocking on her door.

Insistently.

She sat up and groaned. There was too much light in the room even though the curtains were closed.

The knocking continued and she sighed. Stood shakily for a moment before looking for a weapon—the best she could come up with was her day pack loaded with a couple of bottles of water to give it heft if swung. She heading for the door, her heart pounding in her chest.

"All right. All right! Who is it and what do you want?"

The knocking stopped. "Phoebe? Are you okay?" Trev's voice.

"Of course I'm okay." But she unlocked the door bolts and pulled the door open wearing only her sleeping t-shirt and shorts.

Light filled the landing outside her door and backlit Trev, this time in his brimmed hat, so she couldn't see his face.

"Well, I'm definitely not." He shoved past her into her room, so she left the door open and turned to him, her arms crossed over her far-too-exposed braless chest.

"Well, let me invite you in," she said, resenting his presumption. "Why don't you make yourself at home?"

"Bloody hell, Phoebe. I've been worried sick about you. Are you sure you're fine?"

"Fine. Good. Well. Okay. Whatever you want to call it except I could use a bit more shut-eye—something you have well and truly disturbed."

That seemed to slow him down a moment. He looked at his hands. "So no one threatened you yesterday?"

"Followed, yes. Watched, yes. Sent messages of warning through other people, yes. But overtly threatened, no." She settled on the end of Stoney's bed and pressed her hands between her knees. "Trev, what's happened? What's got you so worried?"

He seemed to hesitate, but then he took off his hat. The left side of his face was swollen with purple and green bruising.

"My God! What happened? Are you okay?" The threats suddenly became much more real. She felt sick to her stomach.

"Better than some of my villagers. One or two have broken fingers and arms." He hauled out the chair from the desk and eased himself down. Besides the bruises, he looked awful. His hands were bruised and the knuckles scabbed. He hadn't shaved, so pale stubble shone on his cheeks, and the twinkle had gone out of his eyes.

"You *are* hurt!"

He shook his head. "My pride, mostly." He shifted on the chair and winced. "I may have cracked a rib."

He exhaled. "I'm glad to see you in one piece. Yesterday I was visiting one of our villages east of here. There's been some worries that the people are being pressured to give up their land but that's one of the first things we do with our villagers is support them to secure land tenure. Our villagers own their land, but that doesn't stop the land grabs by some of the bigger owners. So I went out to reassure them. That was one of the reasons I went down to Phnom Penh—to petition the government to be more diligent about protecting village land claims. Again." He shook his head.

"But that is another story, my dear. Yesterday I arrived and the village head man and I were discussing the situation when a truck rolled up with six men armed with clubs. They climbed out, ignored the villagers, and came after me telling me to keep my nose and yours out of other people's business. Of course the villagers defended me and a terrible brawl ensued. I think the villagers gave as good as they got, and the truck and men left, but I was worried about you. The men specifically mentioned your name and then you didn't answer your phone or respond to my messages. I was frantic thinking something had happened to you!"

Phoebe plucked the pink messages from off the bed beside her. "I'm so sorry. I should have returned your call, but I was exhausted and, frankly, scared." She told him about Davuth's call and the men at the restaurant. "They haven't done anything to me so far, but it seems they're trying to get to me through anyone that I know."

"What the bloody hell have you been doing? And who is 'they'?"

"I told you I was concerned for Sokha, the girl from the ferry. She disappeared into that man's car and hasn't been seen again." Other than a brief glimpse of a figure at a window that could have been any young female. "It was her flower barrette that was beside her uncle's body.

And then there's his murder and the fact that Mr. Yong claims that Sokha's his daughter, but when I went to his house, he couldn't or wouldn't produce her to set me at ease."

Trev sat with his mouth slightly agape, his brows raised in horror, made more horrible by the awful colors and swelling of his face. "Mr. Yong? You spoke to Mr. Yong and went to his house?"

When she nodded, he closed his eyes.

"God save the Queen," he murmured. He opened his eyes. "No wonder this happened. Phoebe, do you have any idea who you're dealing with?"

She blew out a breath and seriously wished for her toothbrush and a shower before getting into this further. The sunlight on the landing outside her door had intensified and reflected unwelcome heat into her room. She stood and closed the door. "According to Davuth, my Angkor guide, he's a very Big Man who doesn't like people to bother him. From what I've seen, Davuth's assessment was right."

She turned back to him to see him shaking his head. "Phoebe, you've no idea. A Big Man? Bloody hell, Yong is as big as they get. Up to now *Cambodia Prosperous* has been trying to fly under his radar by focusing on villages in areas not close to his properties. Unfortunately, the village yesterday has had him acquire lands in the surrounding area. More villages than we knew had given over their land due to his tactics. After yesterday, I'd say we were firmly on his radar and that can mean nothing good. The man is almost a god to those who work for him and he holds much influence with the government. In fact, I think he finances the campaigns of most of the politicians in Siem Reap so that no matter who wins an election, they'll do what he wants or at least look the other way."

"So he grabs the land and he doesn't do it in a nice way. That still doesn't mean we should ignore that a young girl has disappeared."

Wearily, he scrubbed at his face. Then he looked at her. "There's more about Yong you need to know. There have been people who claim that Yong is actually the son of a man named Ye Thol who was the right had man of Im Chaem." He held up his hand to stop her question. "Im Chaem was one of the leading Khmer Rouge charged with genocide and crimes against humanity. Ye Thol used to bring his son to see the prisoners tortured. It is said the boy even helped. Both disappeared and were presumed killed in the overthrow of the Khmer Rouge, but some say they recognized Yong's father and Yong from another time and place. Of course he disputes it."

"You're saying that I had tea with a man who participated in untold deaths and torture?" Her stomach clenched and the room seemed to sway a little. "A man who had participated in that kind of thing as child could easily grow into a monster." And the Khmer Rouge hadn't been shy about killing foreigners, either.

It was hard to breathe and the room was too hot. She stood and turned on the fan above Stoney's bed but it didn't help. What was she going to do? Stoney was just waiting for her to pack up and go home.

Becca was, too. And Alice.

But going home was giving up. Going home was leaving a murder unsolved and a young woman in danger. She'd left Rick Hames to fend for himself before and look what that led to. Three students dead and her career and life in ruins.

But even if Sokha was Yong's daughter, she didn't deserve to be imprisoned by a monster.

She looked back at Trev. His gaze clearly reading her resolve. She saw the same thing in him.

"You've been working to outmaneuver Yong," she said. "You've known all along who he was and you've been working to undermine, or at least curb, his fiefdom."

He inclined his head. "Something like that."

She thought a moment. The room smelled stale—like her hand-washed clothes and dirty sandals.

"How long have you known about Yong?"

He shrugged. "About as long as I've been in country."

"In country. Isn't that a term used by military or diplomats?" She met his gaze and held there. He was the first to look away.

"Which are you?" she asked softly.

"I spent most of my childhood in Cambodia. My father was a diplomat during the war. When the Khmer Rouge took over, we barely escaped and most of our Cambodian household staff and family friends were slaughtered. My dad's business associates, too. Back home, I ended up becoming involved in the security services and conducting investigations. So when the Khmer Rouge tribunals began, I volunteered to be an investigator. I thought perhaps I could locate friends and help them. Turns out there was no one left."

His gaze had turned bleak, his expression stricken—swiftly swept away to the smooth countenance of the professional.

"So how did you end up here?"

"After I was back, I was determined to help the people.At first I was looking for friends, but then I realized that everyone was suffering and the people on the land most of all. I could see a land grab free-for-all in the making what with the country just opening up. I set things up with *Cambodia Prosperous* and then stepped away to act as an investigator for the tribunal. But I could see how things were going. Yes, there were some convictions, but someone was getting to the Cambodian judges. The case of Im Chaem was the final straw. Samphy's family were killed by the Khmer Rouge and Im Chaem was in charge of the camp they were in. She barely survived herself, but only after numerous rapes and beatings. She would have given evidence, but at the last minute the case was dismissed. I'd worked that case and the evidence was solid. When the appeal ended in deadlock and nothing was done, I quit and came back here. Imagine my shock when I happened to see Ye Thol and his now-grown son stepping out of a fancy car in Siem Reap one day. Samphy approached him and he laughed and said she was delusional. Not too long after that, her eight-year-old son was hit by a car. It devastated Samphy. She was sure Ye Thol arranged it and blamed herself. Then she blamed me for the tribunal dismissing the case against Im Chaem. Our friendship has been strained ever since even though Ye Thol has since passed away. I've been using *Cambodia Prosperous*, to stand against Yong as much as I can."

Phoebe could imagine. She could also imagine the toll that case dismissal and Samphy's son's death must have had on everyone. No wonder the poor woman hadn't wanted to answer Phoebe's questions.

She felt like hell for asking them.

"There's nothing you can do, Phoebe. You need to get out of here while you still can in one piece. I'd suggest you book a flight back to Phnom Penh."

She was so deep in thought that she only half heard him. She shook herself and scrubbed her hands across her scalp. "What? Leave? Leave Sokha in danger?"

"Bloody hell, Phoebe. You don't even know if she *is* in danger. If she is his daughter, she could be perfectly safe."

"I agree," she said. "But then why wouldn't he let me talk to her? Why did I see a young woman in one the windows of the house and see her pulled away and a man look out?"

"What? You saw that?"

"I did. My driver saw her in the window and pointed her out. But we were in a hurry to get the heck away from that house. It didn't feel safe—at all. Even if she *is* his daughter, I don't think she's safe in that home." She shook her head and stood. "I'm staying—at least for now."

She could imagine Becca almost howling at the moon at Phoebe's decision to put herself in danger.

"Phoebe, no. Please, think about this. Yong is a very dangerous man."

She faced him, hands on her hips. "Are you suggesting that I haven't given this a great deal of thought? I was up half the night thinking about it. About Sokha and about the people I put in danger by staying. But from what you've told me, those people deserve to be safe from people like Yong. Heck, maybe that's why they're helping me. They *know* what Yong is and what he's doing. They're just too afraid to do anything themselves."

"I suppose I'm not doing anything, either." Trev's voice was soft, but his expression had hardened. Fatigue seemed to have pressed down his shoulders and the corners of his mouth. He stood to face her.

"I didn't realize you had a death wish, Phoebe. But then perhaps I should have, given your history. A psychologist would likely have a field day with you. Survivor's guilt, perhaps?"

It felt like he'd slapped her and she staggered back.

She squared her shoulders to face Trevor, wishing she wasn't doing so with her breasts only covered by a thin t-shirt, with her hair in a knot and her mouth tasting like a nest of mice had made their home there overnight. "I survived. So did you. You're not that different from me in that regard. Now what do we do about Sokha and what do we know about the man who was killed?"

11

____

Phoebe held her breath waiting for Trev to respond. The fan whirred overhead, swirling the tepid air over her skin. Beyond the drapes and the louvered windows, the sound of motorcycle engines increased in frequency and volume. She wondered whether the men she'd seen last night were still watching the Blue Lotus, or if she dared open her curtains. But then maybe she shouldn't. She could already feel the heat of the sun radiating from the small balcony into the room.

Trev stood in the center of her bedroom, a shocked look on his battered face. His tired gaze tightened in momentary annoyance, then loosened to frustration and finally acceptance.

"You are a bloody piece of work, Phoebe Clay. Who says I'm going to help you if you stay? Who says I'm going to help you find a girl who might be perfectly safe and happy, or investigate the death of a man I barely met, let alone, saw?"

She shrugged. "Maybe the fact that you're here? The fact that you care about people just like I care?"

He looked as if he didn't quite know what to say.

"You know, I'd love to talk more about this, but I really need a shower. And to brush my teeth. If you don't mind waiting downstairs, I'll meet you in fifteen and take you for a coffee to discuss it."

A single nod from him and she ushered him out of the room and closed the door. What she really wanted was to go back to bed and pull up the covers, but the notes she'd made the night before gave her a roadmap of what she had to do. Having Trev's help would only make the job easier.

She showered with Trev's words swirling in her head. She was, for all intents and purposes, dealing with a vestige of the Khmer Rouge. And she was doing it out of survivor's guilt, just like Trev was working here trying to save the people's land for them.

What was it her counselor had said? What Becca had said? That Phoebe didn't think she deserved to live? That she was trying to rescue everyone else instead of rescuing herself?

Maybe rescuing everyone else was the process she needed to rescue herself. To prove to herself that there was a reason that she lived. To rid herself of survivor's guilt.

Dressed in last night's blue capris and red pinstriped shirt, she headed down the stairs.

After asking Jorani to have Chan wait for her return, Phoebe followed Trev to a new place for breakfast. It was on a corner in the Blue Lotus area—the area Trev referred to as the budget traveler end of town and only a block away from Trafalgar Pub and around the corner from the coffee shop she'd frequented for her lattes in the morning. How she'd missed it, she didn't know. The building was two stories, whitewashed, and looked like there were apartments on the upper floor beyond large, shaded balconies. The restaurant was at street level and had lovely white tablecloth-covered tables on an open-air terrace by the street. Potted palms provided a lush barrier from any traffic. Through the open glass doors, more white tables were inside and a dark wooden bar filled the far wall. One of Trev's photos graced an inside wall, this one of a tree growing out of an Angkor wall with a lone, orange-clad monk seated on one of the twisted roots.

Trev ushered her to a table in a corner. There was only one other occupied table, this one by a couple of western women of about Phoebe's age. They were hunched over a guidebook.

Phoebe and Trev settled across from each other, both vying for the seat with the best view of the street.They ended up compromising by shifting the table around so that both of them could see the street. Phoebe's back still felt vulnerable without a wall behind her.

The waitress, who had watched the whole thing, approached with menus. Phoebe scanned it and ordered a latte and granola, fruit, and yogurt. Trev opted for tea and bacon and eggs.

When the waitress had left, they eyed each other. Finally Trev sat back with his arms crossed.

"Well? What is it you wanted my help with?"

She pursed her lips. "You could look a little happier about it."

"I'd be happy if I was taking you to the airport, but that's not going to happen, is it?"

She shook her head and thanked the waitress who brought Trev his tea and Phoebe's latte. Phoebe sipped. Good. Strong and hot.

"I've decided I'm here until I know Sokha is safe. I figure there's two places to start. The first is finding out about the girl: birth records, school records, medical records if we can get them. The second thing is to find out about the man who was killed. All we know is that Sokha called him Uncle and didn't seem that happy around him. Why was he killed? Was Sokha there when he died? The fact her hair barrette was at the scene suggests she was. And if she was, what happened to her?"

Trev hadn't moved, his tea before him still untouched. The morning sunlight had found its way into the street and it placed a gleam across their cutlery but didn't reach into the hat-brim shadow to illuminate Trev's eyes. If anything, they seemed more shadowed.

"You, Phoebe Clay, are a woman of many questions."

She grinned. "My sister tells me I missed my calling. Should have gone into police or science instead of teaching."

His mouth twitched and he unfolded his arms and tried his tea. Apparently satisfied, he sat back again.

"I think I can help you. At least I think I know how we can get some of the information. If she is Yong's daughter, then she likely would have been born in a hospital here. She also is likely to have gone to one of the private schools, like the American School in Phnom Penh. Or the Sisters of Our Holy Father Mission School here in Siem Reap. Both have excellent academic programs and are used by Cambodia's elite to ensure that their children can obtain higher education. *Cambodia Prosperous* offers scholarships to both schools for the top students in our village schools. As a result, many of our teachers are now from the villages they teach in. A few have gone into teaching at the scholarship schools."

She could see where he was going. "So we ask them whether Sokha attended either school and who her father is. If she is a student there, perhaps they're familiar with the man called Uncle."

"Those thoughts had crossed my mind. I'll see what I can do. But Phoebe, if we don't learn anything, I think you should seriously reconsider and climb on that plane."

"I'll think about it."

Their breakfasts came and Phoebe was thrilled to see the fresh dragon fruit, pineapple, and mango that came with her granola and plain yogurt. Trev's bacon and eggs looked less appetizing, with runny sunny-side-up eggs and bacon that looked like a cross between back bacon and shoe-leather, but Trev seemed not to mind and tucked right in. They ate in silence, the texture and crunch of the granola and the natural acidity of the fruit a wonderful reprieve from the baked goods of the past few days. It was real food.

Of course Trev hadn't mentioned their other access to information —the local police. It almost seemed like he was avoiding any direct approach and trying to keep a low profile. She glanced up at Trev and caught him studying her, a study that was quickly diverted back to his food. Were there things she should know about Trev? She barely knew him and yet her tendency was to trust him. He had seemed very open with her about who and what he was. Was she wrong to trust him? That was the thing. In a foreign country, everyone was a stranger.

And the stranger across from her was avoiding the police. She was sure of it. Surely, the police would have identified the dead man by now. Heck, it might have even been in the local newspapers. She could ask Jorani if there was any mention of the murder. She could even follow up with the newspaper. Surely any reporter would speak English.

She finished her granola and looked at Trev brightly. "So what should I do while you ask around? Lock myself in my room?" As if she would.

The light had shifted again and she could make out his rolling eyes.

"I could. Lock myself in my room, I mean. If I wanted."

He leaned his elbows on the table and leaned across to her. "Phoebe Clay." His voice was soft enough, she had to lean toward him. "If there is one thing we have to avoid, it is you with time on your hands. I recognize a woman with a penchant for getting into trouble." He smiled. "Is there an alternative? You do have a driver arranged."

"I read in a brochure that there are tours of the stilted villages along the lake."

"Fantastic idea." He checked his watch and waved for the waitress. "Go on that tour. If we get you back to Blue Lotus right now, you just might be able to make it to the jetty on time."

Phoebe waved off Trev's offer to pay for breakfast and paid for their meal herself. It was the least she could do. They walked back to the Blue Lotus, the market traffic gradually building around them with motorcycles bringing women with baskets of vegetables and fruit and even a huge pig tied across the motorcycle's back seat. Monks in saffron robes strolled with their begging bowls down the street. Merchants swept out their store entrances. It was vibrant place, filled with life, unlike the times she'd been here either earlier in the morning or after dark. Aside from dodging traffic, she felt perfectly safe.

At the Blue Lotus, Chan was waiting and appeared deep in a conversation with Jorani. The two Cambodians stopped talking to watch them approach.

"I'll check in with you tonight, hope you enjoy your tour of the lake." Trev nodded and slung his leg over his motorcycle, gunned the engine, and left.

Phoebe watched him leave, a little unsettled that he'd just assumed that she'd really go on the lake tour. She turned to Chan and Jorani.

"Chan. Good morning. How are you and your family?" Please don't have let the bruisers she'd seen come after him.

He grinned. "I am well, Miss Phoebe. A-okay. My sister sends her hello. She very much enjoyed speaking English with you."

"As I did with her." She turned to Jorani. "Hopefully there have not been any problems for you, either. Has anyone warned you to stop renting me a room? There were two large men around here last night. They seemed to be watching me."

Jorani gave a furtive head shake as if someone might be watching. "Everything is good. There are no problems." Her gaze scanned the building across the street, so Phoebe's skin itched between her shoulder blades. Someone was there. Someone was keeping an eye on her movements.

Or she was being paranoid.

Phoebe turned back to Chan. "I thought today might be good for a change. Maybe take the lake tour to the stilted villages. Do you think we can make it to the jetty on time?"

When he nodded, she ran up to her room for a bottle of water and then climbed into the cab of the motorcycle taxi. Doves cooed from the telephone lines and children in white shirts and navy trousers and skirts dawdled down the lane just like children around the world. The young girls held hands with their friends and she thought of Sokha, so alone. Chan flipped down his helmet visor and started his motorcycle. They bumped down the potholed lane to the street.

At the lane end, Phoebe reached forward and tapped Chan's shoulder. "Change of plans, Chan. I need you to take me to the police station."

He flipped his visor up. "Police, Miss Phoebe?"

How should she answer? She'd been chased and more or less threatened. At least people close to her had been. There was absolutely nothing right about that. "There was a man murdered in the night market the first night I was here. I want to find out about him."

The way his lips tightened and his eyes narrowed, he clearly didn't think this was a good idea.

"What is it? Tell me, Chan."

He held up a finger to wait and he zipped the taxi around the corner and down the street to a parking spot.

"I read about dead man in newspaper. Not good." He shook his head. "Police not good people, Miss Phoebe. You go to them. They look at you."

She wasn't quite sure what he meant, but was clear on his concern. Frankly, after her experiences in other places, she wasn't too sure the police were her friends. Especially not in an undeveloped country when she was asking questions. She had no confidence the police in an undeveloped country would do their job, or even that they were trained to do it.

She thought a moment. "What about the newspaper? I could speak to the reporter who wrote the article."

Chan looked doubtful, but the tightness diminished from around his eyes. "I take you to newspaper, but then we go on tour, okay? I take you back to Angkor, okay?"

If that was what it took to get to speak to someone about the murder, then it was okay by her. She hadn't had enough chance to explore the jungle ruins so far.

When she nodded, Chan positively beamed. He gave her the thumbs up sign, gunned the engine, and headed into the street. Men in western trousers and white shirts and women in sarongs hurried down the streets as Chan wove through traffic of bicycles, motorcycle taxis, cars, and large, brightly painted trucks that belched exhaust fumes. Chan drove through Siem Reap's downtown area and then turned down progressively narrower streets until he came to a narrow street lined with houses. Most were surrounded by tall, broken glass-topped concrete block walls relieved only by high, solid metal gates. But Chan stopped in front of a small, stilted, yellow-painted wooden house surrounded by a garden awash with color. A low, intricately constructed brick fence created a lattice around the yard and allowed flowers to flow through the spaces and beautify the otherwise ugly street. Beside the wrought-iron gate, a sign spelled out something in Khmer. Beneath the Khmer lettering, *Siem Reap Register* was spelled out in English.

Chan turned off his motorcycle and dismounted. Phoebe climbed out of the cab and Chan opened the gate for her. They both went through. At the house, Chan climbed the ladder to the open door and knocked on the doorframe while Phoebe waited in the garden.

It was a truly lovely garden, with overflowing bougainvillaea around the fence and climbing the outside of the neighbor's walls. Jasmine grew up over a trellis and lilies and other flowers that she didn't know grew in profusion. Through the open area under the house, she could see a small plot in the rear that looked like it held tomato plants and pumpkins.

A shuffling sound came from inside the house and a wizened, bald man appeared in the door. He was hunched as Quasimodo, though without the hump. He wore the ubiquitous white shirt and black trousers, though his shirt had the sleeves rolled up over ropy forearms and the rolled cuffs were frayed and stained gray in places. His eyes were wide spaced over a small nose that provided a precarious perch for a pair of thick pince-nez glasses.

His magnified watery gaze flipped from Chan to Phoebe and back again. He said something in Khmer and Chan responded in kind. Then he turned and motioned to Phoebe.

"This Miss Phoebe Clay. She from Canada. This gentleman name Mr. Leng, my uncle. He newspaperman."

The old man half-bowed. "It is a pleasure to meet you, Miss Clay. Come in. Come in."

He stood back from the door and Phoebe and Chan climbed the ladder stairs. The house was dimly lit from the door and from light leaking in beside the high rafters. She stood in a large common room that held a desk and chair and filing cabinets. Stacked papers and books filled shelves on the walls so the room smelled of newsprint and ink. Filling one wall stood a larger machine that she didn't recognize.

Leng shook her hand and smiled up at her. Close up, he didn't appear as wizened as she'd thought. His stoop seemed something more physical than the product of age and his face, while lined, didn't have the deep grooves of the truly ancient.

He said something in Khmer. Chan hurried into a back room and returned with two more chairs that he set before the desk. Leng hobbled around the desk to sink into the chair. There was something about the way he walked that made her think his legs were crooked. Open, in front of him, was a laptop computer that he shifted to one side so that he could see the screen, but she couldn't.

"What brings a Canadian tourist to my door?" Leng said in surprisingly perfect English with a slight French accent.

"Thank you for seeing me. Chan said you were a newspaperman."

He glanced at Chan, seated quietly beside her. "My nephew is correct, though that still does not give me an answer."

She had to smile. She'd avoided reporters and media like the plague after the school shooting—especially after the school board suggested that it had been Phoebe who may have incited the shooting. They'd chosen to believe her principal, who denied Phoebe's assertions that she'd brought her concerns to her principal numerous times. He'd lied to protect himself and Phoebe had taken the heat—including from the media. And now here she was, asking for help from a newspaperman.

"There was a man murdered in the night market three days ago. I'm trying to find out who he was and why he was killed."

Leng steepled his hands. He had long fingers, most of which had horribly swollen knuckles and deformed ends. She looked away, suddenly understanding. Leng had been tortured. His infirmities were the legacy of the Khmer Rouge regime. She felt horror. She felt ill. She felt pity.

He must have read it all on her face. Leng nodded. "It is all history. Now I ensure that history is not forgotten. Before the Khmer Rouge, I was a runner for a young reporter. I am one of the few who walked through the doors of S-21 and managed to stumble back out again."

S-21. She'd read about it in her guidebook and had intended to visit when in Phnom Penh, but simply could not face the grim reality such a museum would make her face. She'd had enough of killing in her lifetime already and S-21 was one of the worst. Formerly a secondary school, it had become Security Prison 21 and now was Tuol Sleng Genocide Museum. From 1976-1979, approximately twenty thousand people, including children, were tortured and killed there and it was only one of between 150 and 196 such places around the country.

To meet a man who had survived so much darkness trivialized her own experiences. She swallowed.

"You are a very brave man."

He shrugged and winced. "Excuse me. My scars trouble me more as I get older."

She nodded. "That's the thing about age. Our scars seem to gradually take over our lives."

He placed his twisted hands on his desktop and met her gaze. Outside the front door came the voices of people walking down the street. The morning breeze brought in the scent of the jasmine.

"If I may enquire, why is a Canadian tourist asking about a dead Cambodian?"

Here it came. All the questions. She either told him everything or let her question stand as it was. Either way, she was pretty sure this man would be checking up on her after she left. Once he found out who she was, she doubted whether he'd help her again. It was now or never.

She decided on everything and described meeting Sokha on the ferry and everything that happened until the murder in the night market. "So I'm concerned for the girl. I've read enough to know that Cambodian women and children are trafficked for the international sex trade. She seemed a lovely young woman and so I'm concerned for her safety. And was more concerned when the man she claimed was her uncle turned up murdered. I was there and I saw a barrette beside him that was identical to one Sokha wore in her hair on the ferry."

She left out the matter of Mr. Yong and the motorcycle that had pursued her and Chan, as well as the men who had been watching.

Leng fussed with some papers on his desk. Then he looked at her and nodded. "There is not a lot to tell. The police have not released the man's identity, nor anything about the murder. But then that is their usual modus operandi. They do not like there to be murders in a town dependent upon tourism. To have a murder occur so publicly in a tourist market—well, I believe they would like to assume the position of the three monkeys."

He demonstrated covering his eyes, his ears, his mouth.

Phoebe slumped back in her chair. She'd hoped she could get information here. Anything at all that might help her understand what was happening around Sokha.

"Thank you for seeing me. I appreciate your time." She went to stand, but Leng waved her back to her chair.

"Please. I told you the police know nothing or aren't saying, but that does not mean that I do not have information. I am, after all, a reporter, Ms.Clay. Ever since the end of the Khmer Rouge, I have dedicated myself to sharing the truth. I have been known to stick my nose in places people would prefer I not go. I believe that is something you know something about."

She froze in her chair.

"I'm sorry?" she managed. It was more like a squeak than a question.

"I said that you know about asking questions some people would rather not be posed. I believe that led to the solution of a murder in your home country."

Oh, God, no. The man had researched her. How? She swung around to Chan. She hadn't seen him make any call.

"Last night my nephew called about the fact that you were followed. And the fact that you visited the home of one of our town's more notorious residents. He told me about you and I decided I needed to know more of such a strong-willed woman."

He'd investigated her just as the reporters back home had investigated her, and he knew that she'd left out important information. Usually, she would simply walk away, but she needed his information.

"Then you know that I don't tend to turn a blind eye to things that disturb me. I'm sorry I didn't tell you everything."

Leng gave a single nod and sank back in his chair, his hands steepled once more. "You do not let things go, yes."

"So what do you know about the murdered man?" Damn it all, she didn't have time for silly games. Just give her the information.

His bald head gleamed in the soft light from the doorway. Chan stepped down the ladder-stairs and lit up a smoke in the front yard.

"It seems someone relieved the dead man of his wallet and identification before the police arrived. That wallet and its contents found its way into my possession." He opened a desk drawer and pulled out a well-worn cloth wallet and pulled out a piece of identification. Uncle's face looked out at her, still wearing the frown she remembered. "His name was Chum Nath. To date his death has not been confirmed, but the contents of his wallet indicate that he was a senior functionary at the Cambodian Land Registry. He was a keen advocate of addressing land inequities and in reducing foreign ownership. They are issues plaguing Cambodia, particularly here in Siem Reap, in Phnom Penh, and in the areas along the coast."

She studied the face in the identification. "What else was in his wallet?"

Leng shrugged one shoulder. "Identification from the Land Administration. An image of him with his family. Receipts for the Phnom Penh-Siem Reap ferry. A few American dollars and some riel." He named the Cambodian currency.

"Anything that would indicate why he came to Siem Reap?"

"I thought he escorted a young woman."

"Sokha might be as old as fifteen or sixteen, I think. Your Mr. Yong claims she is his daughter. Do you know whether that's true?"

His brows knitted together and his lower lips jutted out. "I seem to recall that there was a marriage and children. The wife died of fever, but I've no idea whether the children were boys or girls. I could check for you, if you like."

She nodded, glancing out the door at Chan. He still stood in the garden, but had moved to the gate and was peering up and down the street. There was no one else in the street that she could see, but the rumble of traffic came in the distance.

"I would appreciate that. The girl's hair barrette was seen near the dead man's body. Did the source of the wallet see anything? See what happened to her?"

Leng shifted in his chair and finally stood to limp around the room.

"The girl was there? I've heard none of that." His gaze turned distant and he stopped next to the massive machine that she was pretty sure was for printing his newspaper. His gaze came alive again and he came to her to perch on the side of his desk, but she could see that he was in pain. "It is true what I read about you. You see things and you don't give up. I will look into this girl's disappearance."

"Thank you." She stood, wanting to give Leng a chance to rest. Dealing with constant pain was a tiring process. "May I come to visit you again? It will likely be with more questions, so think carefully before saying yes."

He smiled, revealing betel-stained teeth. "Come any time. Next time I will be a better host and offer tea. But from what my nephew has said, you must be very careful in your enquiries. The Khmer Rouge did many things, but most of all, they destroyed the heart of my people. Many have lost their faith, and people without a faith can lose their souls very easily. This is especially so when money is involved."

And Mr. Yong clearly had enough wealth that he could probably buy every soul he wanted.

She shook her head. "Where money is concerned, it's not just Cambodians who lose their souls. Thank you again for your time."

Back in the motorcycle cab, she waved to Leng where he stood in his doorway. He looked wizened and ancient, but when she did the math, he likely wasn't much older than her. But then, life experiences did that. They reshaped the body and the mind, just as hers had been reshaped the day Rick Hames brought a gun to school.

She leaned forward in the cab. "He's an amazing man."

Chan nodded. "Respected in Siem Reap. He a Big Man, too. Just not so big here." He touched his wallet pocket and gunned his engine before they sped away.

They unspooled through the tight residential streets until they were on the main city streets. Chan pulled over. "Where to, Miss Phoebe? You miss the regular boat tour."

She thought a moment. "Is it possible to arrange a private tour?"

"It can be done. If boatman there."

"Then let's head for the water." She glanced up at the sun. At least she'd thought to stuff her hat in her day pack. On a private tour, no one was going to get in the way of her thinking about what she knew. Besides, a breeze off the water would be a good thing.

12

It was a long, bumpy ride to the jetty. She hadn't noticed it before in the shuttle van, but in the motorcycle taxi, the lack of suspension meant every pothole jarred up her back. It was worth it, though, for the flecks of cloud in the blue sky reflected endlessly in the expansive sheet of the flooded fields around Tonle Sap Lake. Here and there a copse of trees or a stilted house jutted up out of the water, and boats floated across the flooded rice fields.

She thought about what Leng had told her. The dead man, Chum Nath, could easily have been killed by one of Yong's men. If Yong was grabbing land, that would give him a reason to want dead a man who was a proponent of land tenure. What she didn't understand was Sokha traveling with such a man. Why would a man like Yong allow it?

Unless he hadn't.

But even if he hadn't, why was the girl there? She hadn't been Chum Nath's prisoner, because she'd spoken to Phoebe and Trev. She needed to know if Sokha really was Yong's daughter.

She sat back in frustration, just as another deep pothole jolted her up to the ceiling. She banged her head and bit her tongue. Tasting blood and nursing her sore tongue, she held on tightly as the motorcycle taxi ran past empty restaurants hung with what looked like hammocks and through the small town built along the sides of the elevated road and then out onto the barren stone jetty.

A few men lounged beside the front of an old wooden boat that had been pulled up on the jetty side. The narrow boat was about twenty feet long with an open sided canopied area in the middle.The men leapt up when Chan's motorcycle came to a stop and Phoebe stepped down. Out on the lake, the floating village of boats was busy with small boats traveling from craft to craft selling produce. Children splashed in the water. Still other children rowed an unwieldy-looking round coracle across the blue water. Beyond the village, the mats of water hyacinth placed a green and purple haze into the distance.

"Tour boat! Tour boat!" the men called. The place smelled of sun-heated water with the faint scent of burning propane—probably from the floating village.

"You let me talk to them," Chan said, and left her by the taxi.

She stood there with the sun beating down and the slight breeze off the water ruffling her hair. The breeze lifted dust off the jetty that got in her eyes.

In a few minutes Chan returned from discussions. He told her the price for a two-hour tour and that it would take her to one of the stilted villages and back with time for exploration in the village.

She thought a minute. Fifty American dollars wasn't a lot of money, but she had to be careful with her dollars. Her pension in Canadian funds wasn't huge and was feeling less sufficient as she doled it out to finance her travel. Still... she was only going to be in Cambodia once.

"All right."

The boatmen must have seen her nod, for they shoved the boat halfway into the water.

Chan went to gather her things from the cab, but she stopped him. "How about you come with me?"

He looked at her with wide eyes. "Really?"

Clearly he'd not had such an invitation before.

"Yes, really. You speak English and those fellows probably don't.

You can tell me what we're seeing. Besides, waiting here at the jetty can't be much fun…"

He raised his chin back the way they'd come. "There are restaurants."

Of course there were and he would probably prefer to go there.

"Then you choose." She smiled and claimed her things from him and started for the water.

The sound of footfall behind her told her Chan was coming. He carried his borrowed helmet with him.

They loaded onto the boat and chose cushioned seats under the canopy. It was lovely with the breeze and without the sun beating down. The boat was pushed off with a single man to manage the long-tailed propeller that gave them their direction. Then they were off, passing the floating village and circling around the jetty and then southeastward heading toward the distant shore.

The engine was loud so it was hard to talk. Phoebe simply sat back to enjoy the view. Chan put his feet up and pulled on a peaked baseball cap emblazoned with a silhouette of Angkor Wat temple. The boatman smiled and nodded to her. They picked up speed.

It seemed like forever that they skimmed over the cloud-dappled water, but finally she could see what she thought were trees along the shore. When they neared the trees, she realized she was wrong, for the lake lapped at the tree trunks just below the branches. Liquid shadows danced under the spreading foliage and on the plumage of white egrets perched on the branches. Butterflies fluttered in the treetops. The boatman cut the engine and the silence descended. The slap and hum of water against the trees. The thunk of some bit of flotsam hitting the hull. The twitter of smaller birds in the trees.

Phoebe inhaled the musty scent of water and felt—full. As if she could feed herself on this experience and be whole.

From under the trees came six smaller canoe-type boats, each guided by a woman in a Chinese coolie hat. The boats rafted up with Phoebe's boat, the women calling to her.

"They want you to take a tour of the flooded forest," Chan said.

The trees were tempting, but the small boats less so. She shook her head, but the women persisted, calling with too-pink mouths, reaching for her with thin arms and begging hands, and any desire to be in this place disappeared. Too many people had reached for her, had needed her, and it never turned out well.

She shook her head vehemently and squeezed her eyes shut. "Let's go, please."

The boat didn't move.

"Let's go!" she cried and Chan roused the boatman from discussion with one of the women.

The boat's engine roared to life and the women released their canoes from the gunnels. Phoebe's heart raced as her boat pulled away and she hauled a bottle of water from her daypack. She was too hot and felt almost faint. She cracked the bottle open and drank deeply. It helped.

Some.

She glanced over her shoulder at the small fleet of boats now receding into the trees. Why the heck had that happened? In the past she'd have at least given the women something. It felt like she was vibrating so fast a piece of her was coming loose. Her stomach flip-flopped and she sipped the water and closed her eyes against the up and down movement of the deck.

The breeze helped, stripping away some of the sticky sweat that had suddenly coalesced on her skin. Finally, she opened her eyes and spotted what had to be a village along the shore. It was built of silvered, ten-foot-tall, water-stained wood stilts evidence of the water's height at times in the past, but today there was still some exposed earth beneath the houses. The walls and roofs of the houses were of rough, age-darkened wood. Doors gaped open, and here and there it appeared as if boards or entire walls had been removed. Nothing moved except an egret that fluttered up at their approach.

"It looks abandoned," Phoebe said.

Chan nodded. "Government come. They say this place no good. The people move to larger village where we go."

Phoebe looked back at the village. It looked perfectly serviceable from here. Beyond the houses, a copse of trees looked like it held a spreading mango tree and two or three tall, thin papaya. So even if the area flooded, the fruit trees survived.

They left the abandoned village behind and continued along shore. More trees stood waist deep in water. Every tiny hillock held a small shed or stilted house. Boats glided past them, some clearly fishermen with their decks piled with nets, while others carried things like firewood, or fruit and vegetables, or even packages of the salted peas and peanuts found in the markets. All of the boats had eyes painted near the bow.

Beyond a flooded copse of trees, a silver-and-white spire jutted into the sky. The boat chugged on around the trees to another stilted village. This one had long fingers of lake water reaching under some of the houses. A central "street" was bare earth, but lay covered in tarps and nets. The boatman edged their craft into shore and used a plank for Phoebe and Chan to step down to dry land.

Without the boat's movement, the air was sultry and Phoebe immediately began to sweat. She hauled on her peaked Canuck's Hockey cap and almost wished she had an umbrella to keep the strong light off her shoulders and neck. Beyond the line of stilted houses closest to the water, men worked in the sunlight, folding nets or spreading the pale green netting to dry. Here and there, orange tarps had been spread in the sun. What appeared to be rice had been spread on them. Ten feet up, above long ladders, she spotted movement in the shadows of the house interiors, but no one peeked out at her. It was as if the place was half deserted.

"Where is everyone?" she asked Chan.

Chan shrugged. "Many work elsewhere on farms."

"But they still live here?"

He shrugged again. "Many generations live in each village. It is where their families have always been."

"And the people from the other village? You said they moved here."

He nodded. "At first they come here, but there no place. They move again. Some to Siem Reap, some away." He shrugged. "Many people come to Siem Reap."

She thought of the shanty-like villages she'd seen along the river in town.

"So they were told to move here, but there was no place for them."

He looked at her as if she was being obtuse or something. It might be a simple thing to understand, but she couldn't fathom the thinking behind it. It reminded her too much of the kind of thinking that had been her school's policy that complaints of harassment had to be brought by someone with direct knowledge of the harassment—in other words, either the victim or someone who witnessed it. Of course people who were victims were the least likely to risk coming forward.

So victims continued to be victimized.

And here in Cambodia, somebody successfully made a land grab and the people were displaced. Her gaze was caught by a rise of land in the distance. Layers of lush green lifted up the hillside, and at the top lay something white. Windows flashed in the sun.

She pulled her gaze away feeling suddenly very exposed. This was the village that Mr. Yong looked out over. Her gaze traveled back down to the village and villagers. The men looked fit and healthy. A father had three young boys helping him repair a boat, all looked healthy and well fed.

She skirted the edge of the drying fishing nets and followed the central road toward the temple. It sat on a slight rise of land, the ornate building surrounded by white, wood balconies where saffron-colored robes had been spread to dry. Not a temple.

A monastery.

A saffron-clad monk of perhaps fifteen came around a corner, grinned at Phoebe, removed a saffron robe from the railing, and disappeared around the corner again. She heard a burst of laughter. Then three young monks came around the corner, one clearly still adjusting his robes over his shoulder.

"How are you?" the first monk she had seen carefully articulated his question.

Phoebe stopped. "I'm very well, thank you. How are you?"

The young monk's gaze widened as if he had never had anyone ask him anything before. He turned to his friends and there was much muttering in Khmer. Beside Phoebe, Chan swallowed a smile.

"Don't help him. Let him try himself," Phoebe said to Chan.

He nodded.

The muttering complete, the young monk faced Phoebe and swallowed. "I am fine, thank you very much."

Phoebe touched her chest. "My name is Phoebe. What is your name?"

More whispers amongst the monks and then, "My name is Bou Mey."

She didn't hold out her hand because she'd heard that monks should not be touched, so she inclined her head. "I am very pleased to meet you, Bou Mey."

He looked thrilled that he had gotten this far in an English conversation. His friend elbowed him out of the way.

"I am Pheakdei. I am pleased to meet you, Phoebe Clay." He spoke much more easily. Clearly he'd practiced with tourists more.

"You live here?" she asked, though it was fairly obvious.

"Yes." Pheakdei placed his hands on the shoulder of his two friends. "We live here."

Phoebe thought a moment. "Are your family from the village?"

The confusion in his eyes said she'd gone beyond his comprehension. "Mother, father, there?" She pointed at the stilted village.

He shook his head and pointed inland toward Mr. Yong's hill. "Mother, father there."

She frowned. From what she'd seen and heard, Mr. Yong seemed to work his people to collapse. She couldn't imagine him letting the labor of three strapping young men slip through his fingers. She turned to Chan. "Who built this monastery? Who supports it? Surely it isn't only this village?" Judging by the silver on the stupa, this monastery wasn't exactly impoverished.

Chan shook his head, but he spoke to the three monks. All three pointed inland.

Toward Yong's hill.

13

———————

It didn't make sense. It just didn't make sense.

The boat ride back to the jetty seemed to go on forever, even though the boatman was taking a direct route back instead of following the shoreline. The drone of the engine vibrated up through the cushioned seat to settle in her shoulders against the hard seat back. The breeze fluttered her bangs against her forehead. Shimmering blue water seemed to stretch forever and reflect her thoughts back at her in never-ending circles.

It didn't make sense that a man like Yong would not only donate the land, but finance the monastery's construction and support it afterward. Yes, she'd seen him bring an offering to the Bayon temple, but she couldn't see the man she'd been told so much about condoning the youth from "his" villages entering that lifestyle. Not if it meant losing viable members of the workforce.

At least not if what she knew about him was true. She pulled out her phone and Googled Yong, Cambodian businessman, because she didn't know his first name. She searched through the listings but nothing seemed to reflect the man she'd met. Sighing, she shoved the phone away in her pack.

But what did she really know? All her information was secondhand except for her discussion at the temple and then at his home. In both instances he'd been, if not friendly, at least decent, though he hadn't exactly been forthcoming with information. Or welcoming. He hadn't been threatening either time, really, though she'd taken him as threatening—mainly due to Davuth's and Chan's reactions. Maybe she'd had her perceptions colored by their worries. Maybe things weren't as they seemed.

Maybe. If that was the case, it raised a lot more questions. And she still couldn't believe that Sokha was Yong's daughter. Well, hopefully Trev would confirm it one way or another this evening.

She squirmed in her seat, unable to get comfortable. The thing was, the most damning information about Yong had come from Trev and it simply didn't fit with what the young monks had told her. It was likely nothing, but she would ask him about it when they spoke.

She finally found a marginally more comfortable position in the hard chair and wished the trip was over. Even the breeze was no relief from the muggy heat off the water. The distances of the lake were lost in haze that combined sky and water and just left her tired.

She shouldn't have come on this trip today. It hadn't distracted her and, in fact, had led to more confusion that made her worry. She felt completely blind to the truth. The information she had simply wasn't adding up.

The boat passed two large fishing vessels, hauling in nets, before reaching the end of the jetty and turning into the more sheltered water by the floating village. When the boatman cut the engine and the boat coasted into shore, she was already standing as waiting men hauled the vessel up the gravel and placed a plank from the gunnels to the shore.

Phoebe paid the boatman and gave him a generous tip, then hurried over the plank to shore. Chan had beat her up to the motorcycle taxi and turned it around as she trudged up from the water.

Chan grinned at her and pulled the borrowed helmet on. The motorcycle purred under him. "Where to, Miss Phoebe?" His eagerness suggested the boat trip hadn't drained him the way she was feeling.

"The Blue Lotus, please. I think I need to get out of the sun for a while." And a nap would be good, too, though she wasn't going to admit that to anyone. She was not *that* old.

She climbed in the cab, every part of her aching, and Chan revved the engine. Before he could release the clutch, she leaned forward and tapped him on the back.

"Yes?" He turned to her.

"Chan, when we went to Mr. Yong's house, you were very worried."

He nodded, his gaze going guarded.

"Why were you so worried? Those monks said he built their monastery and supports it."

"Mr. Yong very, very important. He not like to be bothered. I not want him angry at Miss Phoebe."

That put his hesitance in a somewhat different light. So where had she learned to be concerned for her own safety? She'd been afraid before she ever learned Yong's history from Trev. She thought a moment.

"What would he do if he was angry?"

Chan seemed to pale a little. "A Big Man like that. You not want to know. Big Man can make life very bad."

"Have you seen him get mad before? Or heard about it? You told me about a man who was forced to move away. Have there been other things like that with Mr. Yong?"

Chan thought a moment, but then shook his head. "Not Mr. Yong. No. Other Big Men. They make things bad for enemies."

"But I'm not Mr. Yong's enemy. I just want to make sure a girl is safe."

He seemed to digest that a moment and then met her gaze. "It look bad if foreigners think a father not keep daughter safe. Very bad. He lose respect of people if they hear." He nodded in emphasis and then grinned. "Blue Lotus. We go now."

He flipped his visor down, revved the engine, and released the clutch. The motorcycle taxi bounced over the gravel and Phoebe sat back, holding on for dear life as they whizzed through the small village that had seemed to go somnolent in the afternoon sun.

Forty minutes later they wound through the shanty town that had grown up among the spreading trees along the river. She scanned the dwellings built of cast-off metal, wood, and cardboard and wondered whether any of the people she saw squatting around small cook fires had once lived in the abandoned stilted village. Then they left the tree-shaded river and wound through the tourist end of town, past a market and open shops. She really should explore the area more. Unfortunately, the murder in the night market had stymied those efforts.

She needed to go back to the night market, too, and ask more questions. Why would Sokha have been there with a government official?

She scrubbed at her face trying to erase her fatigue. It didn't help, but thankfully Chan pulled up in front of the Blue Lotus.

"We go temples tomorrow?" he asked as she climbed stiffly from the cab.

"I think so. I think I need to just enjoy the ruins. I'll see you tomorrow morning. Go enjoy the afternoon with your lovely family."

He grinned and nodded and she paid him for the past few days and then watched him leave, the rickshaw bouncing through the potholes in the lane. When he was gone, she made her slow way up into and across the Blue Lotus lobby toward the stairs.

"Miss Phoebe?" Jorani called. "There is another message."

She hurried around her desk, as usual crisply neat in her skirt and white blouse. She handed the pink slip to Phoebe, actually half-bowed, and retreated to her desk.

Clutching the message, Phoebe climbed the stairs to her room. When she let herself in, she flipped on the fans. She'd left the louvered windows closed, so the room was dim, though slatted light filtered in. With the fans whirling, she stood in the cooling breeze as she scanned the message. Mr. Leng, Chan's uncle, was inviting her to tea at her earliest convenience, but had left no phone number for her to call. Apparently he expected her to be with Chan, who presumably did have his number.

Letting her day pack slip off her shoulder to the floor, she doffed her sandals and clothes and headed for the shower. After fifteen minutes in cool water, she toweled off, pulled on clean underwear and bra, and lay on her bed and then checked her watch. Almost three thirty.

She could call Chan back, but she hated to take him away from his family and friends. She could phone Leng and arrange a taxi to go to see him immediately, but that would likely put her at his home at his dinner time. And there wasn't anything exactly urgent about the message, just the invitation. No, better to go tomorrow when Chan was here and not let more people know her comings and goings.

She lay back on the bed and closed her eyes letting the cooled air pummel her damp skin.

Why did everything this time leave her tired?

In India she'd been a driven woman and had the energy to pursue her investigation. Here, though still driven, she just felt tired. Was it because, in India, it had been her sister who had been threatened, just as in Johnstone Strait it had been her niece? Was she that kind of person? Was that one of the reasons Rick Hames and the others had died? She hadn't cared enough?

She covered her eyes with her forearm, but it didn't help the sick feeling in her stomach. It made too much sense. She'd spent the afternoon touring the lake, while something horrible could have befallen Sokha. She would *never* have considered doing anything like that when it was Alice or Becca who were threatened.

She'd been lying to herself and everyone else when she said she cared. Well…she cared. She apparently just didn't care enough.

She rolled over on her side and curled up in a ball.

Phoebe Clay wasn't the person she'd thought herself to be. She wasn't the face she showed the world, because she had a double standard.

Unable to get comfortable on the suddenly too-lumpy bed, she rolled over to her other side. It didn't help.

Who was she kidding? It wasn't the bed that had lumps, it was her insides. Lumps and bumps and ugliness.

She groaned and sat up.

This sort of thinking was getting her nowhere. She needed to be up. She needed to be doing—something. Anything! Maybe she should go visit Leng.

Not quite sure what she was doing, she pulled on clean clothes and rinsed out those she'd worn that morning, hanging them on her balcony to dry.

She folded Leng's message into her pocket and headed out the door with her day pack. Maybe… maybe she'd explore some of the town that she'd seen on her way home. She'd do that and have dinner and then go to the night market on her way home. Hopefully, the kiosk vendors would be there by then.

Day pack in hand, she headed out the door. In the lobby, Jorani smiled and waved. Phoebe waved back.

Ask her to call a taxi? The trouble was, Phoebe wasn't even sure where Leng lived. No, better to just stretch her legs after spending all morning on the boat. She'd meet with Leng first thing tomorrow.

She headed down the lane past the restaurant to the main street. Traffic was light and she easily ducked across the pavement, then headed in the direction she'd seen the people going this morning. The market was likely pretty much over, but this would at least give her an idea of what it was like. She could always come back another day if she thought she might like it. The buildings along the street shrank to small, one-story shops. She passed shop fronts offering tours of Angkor and other Cambodian tourist spots, including the lake tour she'd done this morning. Another sold souvenirs the sign said were all ethically and sustainably sourced. She ducked inside for a look around and found wallets woven in Cambodian tribal patterns, more of the cute silk ornaments along with silken scarves, small carvings, and shadow puppets. She puttered around, spotting locally made hand creams and insect repellents and even scented candles, but she left the store empty-handed after thanking the young shopkeeper. Thoughts of Sokha stopped her from enjoying the shopping experience.

She continued down the road and came to a low, metal-roofed building with wooden sides. Motorcycles and bicycles were parked along the curb, and along the sides of the building women had spread cloths where they sold colorful dragon fruit, oranges, and papayas.

The entry to the building didn't look or smell particularly inviting. It was dark inside with only a few bare lightbulbs gleaming among the shadowed rafters. The smell was a melange of fruit both fresh and rotting, fresh meat, and fish.

Holding her breath, she stepping through the doorway and had to wait a moment for her eyes to adjust. Four long rows of vendor tables ran the length of the building with two rows of tables back-to-back. Closest to her was an aisle that ran between two rows of produce vendors. Unfortunately most of the produce looked picked over and many of the vendor tables were empty, their business clearly finished for the day.

She stepped aside to allow others to enter and leave and walked around to the other aisle. This explained the smell. Silver fish laid out in display. Something—she suspected it was a pig—had been butchered and fly-speckled pieces of meat sat on tables with bored vendors flicking away flies with straw whisks and sluicing the meat and fish with water. Other vendors had packages of dried shrimp and fish that reeked of salt and the distant sea. She picked up a package of the dried shrimp. She'd had some in Thailand in her pad thai noodles and they were salty and crunchy.

"You like?" The female vendor said. She was a woman of about Phoebe's age, dressed in a sarong and a blouse that likely hadn't been white in a very long time, thought it was still very clean. She had her hair coiled behind her head and eyes that looked like they liked to smile. "Very good." She rubbed her stomach.

Phoebe smiled and nodded. "I know. I have eaten them."

"You try?" The woman grabbed a few from an open pack. "Very good. You try." She grabbed Phoebe's hand and, nodding, placed a few dried shrimp in her palm.

Well, dysentery, here she came. Phoebe popped the shrimp in her mouth and chewed. Very salty, but with a hint of nutty sweetness from the shrimp meat. She nodded. "Very good. Where are these from?"

"Sihanoukville," the woman said, naming a town on the Gulf of

Thailand coast. "We bring." She pointed at another woman who sold dried fish and then tapped her chest proudly.

So this woman was a merchant.

"Are you married?" Phoebe asked.

The woman shook her head and laughed. It sort of made sense given the land tenure issues. Women would be even less likely to have land to grow food on, so they had to make a living another way.

"You married?" The woman asked.

Phoebe shook her head. "No one would have me."

It took a moment for the woman to translate, but then she threw her head back and laughed. She called to her friend, who burst out laughing, too, and the laughter traveled down the row of vendors. The woman grabbed Phoebe's hand. "Sister!" she said.

Phoebe caught the woman's fingers in her own. "Sisters." She pointed her finger at the woman's chest. "From Sihanoukville?"

The woman shook her head. "Siem Reap." She said it proudly and pointed at her friend. "Siem Reap." Then she spoke in Khmer for a moment before catching herself. Phoebe caught only one word.

Yong.

She felt like backing up and leaving, but she couldn't be sure. Besides, what harm would it do to pursue given she probably misheard anyway?

"Mr. Yong?" she asked.

The woman vendor nodded, her smile broadening.

Phoebe thought a moment, and then pointed in the direction she thought lay Yong's home. Then she pantomimed driving up the winding road to the top of Yong's hill. "Yong?" she asked.

The woman nodded again and she caught Phoebe's hand. "He give money." The woman indicated the stall, the dried fish. "Number one. Mr. Yong number one!" She released Phoebe and gave her a thumbs up, the gesture echoed by the woman's partner.

Phoebe wasn't sure what to say. Their information flew in the face of most of what she knew about Yong. She looked at the two women. "Mr. Yong bad?"

A vehement shake of two heads.

"Good. He very good. Big Man."

In thanks for their conversation, Phoebe bought a bag of dried shrimp from each woman and said her goodbyes. The shrimp she'd likely give to Jorani or Chan because there was no way she was putting something that smelly in with her clothes, but she had no idea what to do with the information. It didn't make sense. Had the women misunderstood her? Could they mean someone else?

But they'd actually used the phrase Big Man to describe him and that was the same as Davuth. Chan, too, had called him that. If Yong had helped the women start their business and financed the monastery by the lake, he wasn't the person she'd thought he was, or the person she'd been told he was.

Was he? Could a person who had benefited from the Khmer Rouge have a good side? Yong was only the son of a Khmer Rouge officer who had been taken to observe the tortures… He'd been a child… Or was that story simply not true?

But Trev had told her that story… Why would he lie?

She didn't know what to think or how it might factor into Sokha's disappearance—if she truly had disappeared—and the murder of the government man.

Darn it all, if anything, the case was getting more confusing. Her plan to ease her questions through a walk wasn't paying off.

In the lengthening shadows of the sweltering afternoon, she left the market with her thoughts whirring. She traipsed around the block in the direction of the Blue Lotus, but took a parallel street to reach the road with the night market. It was late enough in the day that the sun had fallen behind the tops of the spreading trees along the river. The air felt cooler and she inhaled deeply, enjoying the scents of flowers and evening cooking instead of the reek of the fish market.

The night market street was quiet. Bathed in deep shadows, few of the vendors were about, the kiosks mostly closed up tight. She walked past the place where the man had died, but the old woman she'd spoken to previously was nowhere in sight. There was no one else around either, which seemed odd, given the number of open shops that lined the street.

She carried on to the small square that had held the shadow puppet booth and Trev's display as well as the greater part of the market's vendors. The small kiosks were all closed, their fold-down shutters apparently locked up tight. Not much chance of getting information here.

With a sigh, she turned around to head back to the guesthouse, but stopped at the sight of two men examining the ground near where the government man, Chum Nath, had fallen. One of the men wore the ubiquitous dark trousers and white shirt, but had a dark tie added to his sartorial splendor—not something she'd seen in Cambodia before. It suggested that he had status and was trying to retain it. The other man wore a dark blue police uniform that must be sweltering in the heat.

She wasn't sure what to do. She could take the long way home by wandering back to the main street—she figured she could find it. Trev *had* warned her against speaking to the police and she already had a less than stellar opinion of police outside of Canada, even though she'd been pleasantly surprised by her dealings with the Indian police.

But there was the chance she could gain information from them. More so, when she thought about information she could trade them. Like Sokha likely having been present and the old woman having seen more than she would let on. Most of all they could probably clear up her confusion about Mr. Yong.

Girding herself for what she was about to do, she headed down the road toward the turn to the Blue Lotus.

She arrived even with the two men as the man in the tie straightened from examining the ground. Phoebe stopped.

The two men glanced in her direction and ignored her as they talked. They glanced at her again when she stayed where she was. She stood with her hands folded in front of her, clearly not a threat, but clearly not planning on going anywhere.

Finally the man in the tie stopped talking.He was close to Phoebe's five-foot-six in height, and his age looked similar as well, but in a developing country, fifty-five could look much older or younger depending upon the life the person had lived. He had wide-set eyes under heavy epicanthic folds that might appear sleepy, but his gaze caught her sharply. "May I help you?" he asked in surprisingly unaccented English.

"Thank you," Phoebe said. "But I think I may be able to help you."

The man's already sharp gaze seemed to narrow on her. She felt his inspection. "How?"

"I think I may have information for you. I was here the night the man was killed."

His chin came up a little and he glanced at the uniformed officer who shook his head. "You were not here when my men arrived."

Phoebe swallowed, now doubting her decision to speak to these men. "I was advised to run. Everyone else did so I did, too."

"Did you see who killed him?"

Phoebe shook her head.

He crossed his arms over his chest. "So what information do you have that might help my investigation?"

Well, she might as well do this.

She held out her hand. "My name is Phoebe Clay. I'm visiting Cambodia as a tourist, but I have been involved in several police investigations in the past."

Her hand hung there, but the man simply waited.

She took back her hand and continued. "The night the man was killed was my first night in Siem Reap. I walked to the night market square and was speaking with a man I met on the ferry from Phnom Penh when someone screamed and there was a commotion. People started running away, but, well, I ran down here to see what had happened. The man was on the ground and already dead. The weapon wasn't there, but beside him lay a blue flower hair barrette. Do you know what I mean?"

His gaze flickered when she mentioned the barrette, but his arms were still crossed.

"When I came back the next day, a girl working at that kiosk was wearing the barrette, but I don't think it was hers. I think it belonged to the girl I saw the dead man with on the ferry."

There. If that didn't pique his interest, nothing would.

"What did you see on the ferry?"

"I saw the dead man and the girl waiting for the ferry. They were just in front of me. At first I thought it was father and daughter, but the girl didn't seem happy. They boarded and went into the cabin, while I chose to sit on the bow. We left Phnom Penh and later the girl joined me and a man I had met." Given Trev's misgivings about the police, she'd leave him out of things if she could.

"The girl was perhaps fifteen, but could have been younger or older, and wore a blue floral barrette in her hair. She told me her name was Sokha. She said she was traveling with her uncle back to Siem Reap. That was all I understood of the conversation. The rest was in Khmer. Then her uncle called her back inside the cabin. When we landed on the jetty, the girl drove off in the back of a blue Audi sedan while Uncle followed on a motorcycle. I thought at the time it was very odd and I worried about the girl because she didn't seem happy to see the owner of the automobile." She glanced down at the muddy spot where Chum Nath had lain. "Who was he, do you know?"

The detective shrugged. "A government bureaucrat on holiday from Phnom Penh."

If they knew he was a government bureaucrat, then the police likely knew more about him.

"We believe his death was a simple case of robbery gone wrong. His wallet was missing. This girl you say you saw on the ferry. Can you provide a description? She may be the killer."

Great. She'd made Sokha a suspect. So not what she'd intended when she'd opened this conversation. The trouble was, aside from her concern about Sokha, she really had no right to be involved in this investigation and this fellow who hadn't even introduced himself clearly didn't think she mattered.

"She was a pretty little thing. Slight build. Dark hair pulled back in a bun. She wore a sarong and white blouse." As did pretty much any woman or girl who wasn't working on a farm.It wasn't much to go on, unless you knew what she knew. "I'm worried that she's disappeared."

The detective in the tie nodded at the police officer to take down the information. Then he turned his attention back to Phoebe. "Thank you for your time. May we have your name again and where to find you?"

She told him and then hesitated. "There is one more thing. There— there might be a connection to a wealthy man who lives in Siem Reap. A Mr. Yong. Do you know who I mean?"

Both men looked at each other, then back at her, but their gazes had shuttered. "Thank you for the information. Now let us conduct our investigation," the man in the tie said. He turned away and both men bent their heads together conversing in Khmer. She caught what sounded like Yong's name, but both officers pointedly ignored her.

So Yong was clearly important and the police didn't want to know of his potential involvement. Frustrated, she sighed and walked to the Blue Lotus's laneway. She looked back when she turned the corner. In the market square, vendors had begun to filter in. Kiosks were opening. But the man in the tie and the uniformed police officer were both looking at her.

She nodded once and hurried toward home feeling a little shiver run down her spine. She might feel relief that she'd told them about Sokha, but maybe Trev had been right and she shouldn't have talked to them.

14

———

The late afternoon placed shadows like ragged fangs across the lobby floor of the Blue Lotus. There was another message waiting for her, this one was from Trev. It said he'd pick her up at six and they could go for dinner and he could tell Phoebe what he'd learned. When she checked her watch, it was almost five thirty and she thought about canceling, but she really needed the information Trev had said he'd gather.

If she could trust him.

No… she trusted him as much as she trusted anyone in this country of strangers because she couldn't see where he'd have anything to gain from what had happened. Whatever inconsistencies existed in his information had to be the result of a misunderstanding.

She hurried up to her room to throw water at her face, brush her teeth, and change her shirt into a saffron-colored tunic that didn't smell like the fish and meat market. Her capris she left unchanged. She washed out her sweaty top and hung it on her balcony, taking in her clothes that were dry, then sat there, sipping water and watching the sun fall toward the horizon. As with every tropical sunset she'd seen, the sun fell rapidly and was gone, this one disappearing beyond the ragged horizon of trees sending up streamers of light into the sky that quickly faded.

The dusk air felt cooler on her skin as the laneway streetlights flickered on and the scent of rice water reached her from the houses in their walled courtyards. The tiki lamplight from the restaurant spilled into the street and shadowed figures walked the gravel lane in both directions. Down the street a small, battered sedan sat at the side of the lane. The flare of a cigarette said someone was inside.

Frowning, Phoebe set her water bottle down. The car might be different, but it was in the same position as the car the two threatening men had sat watch in. Damn and double damn. If it was them, she'd clearly shown them which room was hers.

She eased to her feet and retreated into her room, feeling like a prisoner. Darn it, she was half a mind to go down to that car and confront whoever it was.

But Becca would have a bird if Phoebe did that and it wouldn't be the smartest move she ever made. Instead she opened the louvred windows and turned on the fan to move the room's stale air.

It helped. A little.

She looked around the room and missed the neat pile of belongings that signified Becca and the wild explosion of clothes that went with Alice. If anything, Stoney-the-pack looked lonely. Or she was feeling lonely. It was hard to admit, but she missed them. The chiding, the laughter, the feeling of family on an adventure together.

The caring. She missed having someone to care for and about. Her throat tightened a little.

Darn it, she was not going to cry. Traveling alone was what she'd planned all along. The family trip to India had been an aberration, even if it was a nice one that would likely never be repeated.

The sound of a motorcycle engine in the street brought her out of her thoughts. The engine cut out close by and she checked her watch. Six p.m. on the dot. She could do a lot worse than having a friend who was punctual. A male friend, no less.

Smiling at the surprised expression Becca would have at such news, she quickly grabbed her daypack, did a last check of her hair—

not much she could do about the wind-blown look she sported—and headed out the door.

Downstairs, Trev was chatting with a young woman who had taken over from Jorani for the evening. He left their conversation and greeted her, then looked her up and down.

"That's a great color on you."

Surprised at the compliment, because surely to goodness this wasn't a real date, she looked him up and down in return. "And khaki becomes you."

He looked down at the trousers and cotton shirt that could have been the same ones he wore on the ferry except these looked a trifle brighter. "Good thing, I guess. I live in these things. So how was your tour?" Then he shook his head. "Hold on. Let's get to the restaurant and then you can tell me everything."

He caught her arm proprietarily to lead her to his motorcycle and she almost pulled away. She wasn't his. She was able-bodied and with her own mind. When had she ever indicated that she was interested in him in *that* way?

She stopped herself. What the heck was she going off on Trev for? He'd done nothing but be a friend and help her. If he was interested, it was flattering, actually. What was it Becca said? Phoebe kept pushing people away?

It wasn't true, but this sudden aversion to Trev might suggest Becca was right. If that was the case, what else was Becca right about?

She climbed on the back of the bike, feeling ridiculously intimate with her hands on Trev's waist and the insides of her thighs skimming his backside.

He started the engine and they headed out to wherever Trev was taking her.

He could take her out into the countryside and kill her and no one would be the wiser. Becca and Alice would be devastated at her disappearance. Well… maybe Alice would be. Becca would probably just think Phoebe got what was coming to her after running into danger for so long.

But all those happy thoughts were moot given Trev pulled into the circular driveway of one of the swanky tourist hotels and stopped by the front steps.

"What are we doing here?" she asked when he turned off the engine. The air was full of the scent of jasmine, and insects whined in the lush foliage and palms that made up the hotel's gardens.

Trev glanced at her over his shoulder. "They have a first-class kitchen here. I thought you might enjoy a nice dinner."

She looked up at the hotel—they stood in front of what must be the administration and dining wing because the room block was a curved tower behind. The administration building advanced back on what was likely a man-made hill in glass-fronted steps. Through the main doors spilled golden light, soft classical music, and the tinkling of a fountain. It was lovely and inviting and a far cry from anything her budget would allow. She wondered if they were going dutch or Trev was paying for their meal. She wasn't looking forward to the menu prices.

"Does it meet your standards?" he asked when she looked back at him.

"Exceeded them by far. Maybe a little too much. I'm used to eating in places in town."

"Aah. It's one night. Splash out a little." He climbed off and offered her his hand as she dismounted. She managed on her own.

In truth, the whole evening was beginning to overwhelm her a little. She wanted Trev to help her in her investigation, not for a date, though his attention might be flattering. But she walked up the stairs and inside beside him. The fountains she'd heard bubbled in the middle of a grand foyer with potted palms and ferns creating a man-made glade around it. Overhead was an open oval of roof that allowed in the perfumed night air, but in daytime would illuminate the plants and fountain with sun. Frosted lamps and wall sconces gave a buttery color to the gleaming wood walls and floor and the main registration desk that faced them under large rotating fans.

Trev caught her elbow again and steered her to the left past more potted plants and through the entrance of what was, by the white tablecloths and low lighting, clearly a dining room. A maître d' greeted them in English and Trev responded in Khmer. Phoebe was sure he slipped the maître d' some cash, but she didn't see how. Regardless, suddenly the man gave a forced smile and led them to a table secluded behind more potted palms.

They settled into wicker chairs with thick jungle-patterned cushions. A single tea light burned in a large glass snifter with an orchid floating beside it in water. The light from the candle placed flickering shadows on Trev's face.

He smiled. "Nice place, yes?"

She glanced around, feeling a trifle off-balance because this was seeming more and more like a date. "It is, indeed. What's the occasion?" She kept her tone light.

"As I said, I thought you might enjoy an evening of normal food."

Normal food? So far she hadn't found any truly local cuisine, unless the pumpkin counted. Everything else had been western. If anything, she *wanted* Cambodian food just so she knew what it tasted like. She couldn't simply assume it was like Thai food—which she loved.

"Well, thank you for being so considerate." She smiled at Trev as a Cambodian waiter hurried up to the table and produced two menus. He explained that the special of the day was a lake fish cooked in saffron butter and a medley of fresh vegetables. It sounded lovely until the price of thirty-five dollars was quoted.

Way above her pay grade!

She flipped open the menu and scanned the prices, feeling herself blanch a little.

"What would you like to drink?" Trev asked. "Shall we share a bottle of white wine?"

Feeling way out of her league, she nodded. Trev said something to the waiter in Khmer and he hustled away, returning with a bottle of French Sauvignon Blanc. He poured Trev a taste and when Trev nodded his approval, the waiter poured them both generous portions.

"So how was your tour? You did make it out onto the lake, I hope?"

Trev sat back in his chair sipping his wine, the menu apparently forgotten.

"I did. It was a bit of a madhouse getting there, but Chan took care of everything. It was a gorgeous day to be out there. The water was like glass. I saw a few fishing vessels and the flooded forest and then we went to a stilted village. That was interesting. There was actually a Buddhist monastery there." She settled in her chair and tasted the wine. It reminded her of pears and sunshine. She closed her eyes and sighed. "Very nice."

"I'm glad you like it. It sounds like it's been a full day for you."

"It was, but you were the one doing all the work. I just got to go on a tour." Why wasn't she telling him about meeting with Leng? About the wallet and the identity of the man?

"So what did you find out?" She set her wine down and pulled her attention from the glorious sounding food and the off-putting prices in the menu.

"Perhaps we should order first. They can prepare the food while we discuss things. Do you know what you want?"

What she wanted and what she could afford were two different things, but she had her credit card and plastic could solve anything. "The lake fish special sounded good…" And was the most reasonably priced item on the menu.

"Fish for you, then. I'm going to have the chicken almondine." She had actually eyed the chicken, but the price of near fifty dollars U.S. had steered her clear. He waved the waiter over and placed their orders, though Phoebe would have preferred to order herself.

What was wrong with her? He was just being polite as he'd always been. Besides, he probably didn't get a chance to meet single western women his age very often.

Who was she kidding? The tours were full of them. He just wouldn't have found them traveling on their own very much.

The waiter took their order and left and Trev refreshed their wine, though Phoebe protested that she wasn't much of a drinker. The problem was, even though she sipped her wine, it was going down faster that she wanted and the last thing she needed was to get tipsy during the meal. She had no plans to do anything with this man that she might regret in the morning and she wanted to stay sharp to hear what he had to say.

She wished she hadn't neglected to ask the waiter for water. She cautiously sipped her wine, then set it down and clasped her hands in her lap. "So what did you learn?"

Trev shook his head. His blond-gray hair curled nicely over his ears and the lines around his eyes enhanced his smile—things she shouldn't be noticing. In the dim light, the bruises and swelling on his face were almost invisible.

"Unfortunately, I haven't much to tell you. Sokha, it turns out, truly is Yong's daughter, so I seriously doubt she's in any danger. Turns out Yong has two daughters, Sokha and Neary. Sokha is the older of the two and apparently quite brilliant. She is also supposedly the apple of her father's eye. She has been attending school here in Siem Reap, but recently had an interview for the American School in Phnom Penh. That's probably when we met her. She was coming home."

Phoebe considered his information. It was a relief to know that the girl had a positive home life, even if Yong seemed too dangerous to Phoebe's western sensibilities. She had made it home to her father. The question was what had happened afterward. There was the matter of the blue floral hair barrette abandoned by a dead man's hand.

She said as much to Trev.

"I don't know, Phoebe. I'm sure Sokha isn't the only girl with a blue flower barrette in Siem Reap."

Around them came the light clink and scrape and soft conversation of the other diners eating their meals, but the ambience and the scent of rich food couldn't dispel Phoebe's ill ease. She shook her head.

"Think about it. Whether the dead man was from Siem Reap or not, he clearly knows the Yongs well enough to escort Yong's favored daughter, so it could have been Sokha with him in the market. What chance is there of him knowing another girl with a blue floral barrette in Siem Reap if he does live here, and if he doesn't live here, the chance would be even less. I think there is a good chance that Sokha was there when he was killed and that she knows who killed him."

Trev sipped his wine and looked at her as if he was weighing her words. Finally, he nodded. "Makes sense. But if she was a witness, clearly her father doesn't want her getting involved. No wonder he wouldn't let you see her. He's probably got her secreted away somewhere to avoid the police. Maybe he's even sent her out of the country if she was somehow involved. I doubt he'd ever chance allowing you to see her."

Which made sense, too.

The waiter brought their meals and they tucked in. Trev asked about her tour and she regaled him with descriptions of the scenery, of the birds in the drowned forest and of the villagers at the stilted village. She even mentioned the monastery, how lovely it was, and Yong's apparent patronage.

"It's a karma thing," Trev said around a mouthful of chicken.

"Karma like reincarnation?" The lake fish was very tasty, cooked tender in a pandan leaf and bathed in a lovely saffron sauce. It came with a medley of carrot, bok choy, and baby corn, with white rice alongside to soak up the sauce.

Trev replenished her wine, but when had she drunk what she already had?

"Karma, like building up credit to offset the bad things you've done so that you come back to the good next time, instead falling back down the levels of reincarnation. You see it all the time—Big Men who do terrible things. They think they get off scot-free if they build or support a temple. Or monastery." He shrugged. "I guess it's sort of like a Catholic going to confession and saying five Hail Marys to gain forgiveness for past misdeeds. Heck, a lot of Europe's cathedrals were built by wealthy men to prove they were good men after the wars."

His gaze twinkled in the candlelight. He really was an attractive man, but something about what he'd said didn't sit right. The monastery, sure. But the women in the market? It might be the right thing to do, but it didn't fit with the man Trev had described. She just didn't want to challenge him on it—it simply wasn't something you did on a "date."

"You're probably right, of course." She took another bite of her fish. "So I've really gotten sidetracked from my visit to Angkor. Can you recommend which of the temples I should spend time in tomorrow? I'd love to find a time when the Bayon's less busy, so I definitely want to go back there, but where else would you suggest?"

Apparently not wanting to bolt his chicken, Trev sat back in his chair. "For my money, Preah Khan, Ta Prohm, and Ta Som are the best. You can practically hear the Tetrameles trees growing though the ruins. You might also want to climb Phnom Bakheng. A temple sits on a hilltop and has spectacular views of Angkor Wat and the lake at West Mebon. The best time to go is sunrise or sunset, but go early to get your spot. There are crowds."

She made a mental note of his suggestions. The candlelight gleamed on their wine glasses turning the liquid amber. A light breeze from the overhead fans stirred in the nearby palm leaves and in Trev's hair. Phoebe shivered.

"It must have been hard to see the damage done to the country," she observed.

He nodded.

"What is it that makes you stay? What do you love the most about the country? Or the least, for that matter?" Maybe it would help her understand Trev better. Maybe she would understand why she was both attracted to the man and had reservations.

"I stay because of the work, of course. I've been working here for so long building the company, I'm not certain I could do anything else. As for what I love, I suppose it's the people. Those I've gotten to know are very trusting—which is surprising given all their country has been through. As for what I hate, well, the graft and bureaucracy, of course, but also the lack of women. Or should I say western women." He smiled and nodded as if she was the example of what he'd been missing.

The odd thing was she didn't believe him. Not one bit. A lot of western men came to countries like Cambodia just to meet women who weren't inculcated with women's rights and equality. They came to meet women who were less demanding. Women who would accept a man's authority. Besides, the tour buses were full of western women, although it was likely more difficult to meet one of them. Feeling uncomfortable, she changed the subject.

The two of them talked about the great culture that had been the Khmer until their meal was almost done. Trev cleaned his plate and she picked at the last of her delicious fish before finally placed her knife and fork on the plate. "That's a lot of food, but I don't know if I could eat that rich all the time. Do you eat this well every night?"

Trev burst out laughing. "Hardly! A lot of rice and a vegetable and a little fish or chicken. That's the meals around here. Most people just eat rice. It's the staple."

She glanced around the dining room. It really was a lovely place, but so far from what she'd seen of Cambodia, it was like another world. There was soft music playing that she hadn't even noticed before, but most of the people were finishing their meals and leaving. Probably had plans to head to the temples again tomorrow and that made for an early morning.

Like she should be planning for.

"Dessert?" Trev asked as if he wanted to lengthen the evening.

"Thank you, no. I don't think so." It had been a lot of food, but more than anything, she was feeling a little woozy from all the wine. "It's been lovely, Trev and the food was great, but I think I should be getting home if I'm going to visit the temples early tomorrow."

He waved the waiter over and refused Phoebe's offer to go dutch for the meal.

"You are my guest tonight. I wanted to show you the other side of Siem Reap. With a little western money, you can live very well."

Interesting, given she'd found a lot of things expensive in her short time here. But maybe she didn't know where to shop, given she was just a tourist.

They went outside, but Trev steered her away from the motorcycle to a path through a lush garden of night-blooming jasmine, ferns, and bougainvillea, all illuminated by strategically placed spotlights. She inhaled the heavenly scents of earth and flowers and allowed Trev to steer her along the path. They came out at a lily pad strewn pond with blue colored lotus spread wide for the night around a central Buddha statue draped with gold fabric. The pond was illuminated from below, placing an illusion of a halo around the Buddha figure, and the air was rich with a sweet, heady perfume that reminded Phoebe of the tropical jungles of her imagination—from the lotus blooms she surmised. Huge orange and gold koi floated languidly in the crystal water.

"It's beautiful," she said, dipping her fingers in the cool water.

"I thought you might like it," Trev said, coming up behind her. "It's one of my favorite spots in Siem Reap."

She could understand why. If she lived here, it would be one of hers, too.

Trev caught her shoulders and gently turned her around. "Phoebe, I'm so glad we met. Living here has been quite lonely for me some time."

He dipped his head and kissed her before she could respond.

She went to step back, but the pond was in the way. Instead she had to push him back to step out of his grasp.

"No. I'm sorry, Trev, but no. I don't think of you that—this—way. I —I've enjoyed getting to know you, but this is all too fast. Perhaps if we had time to know each other better, but we don't. I'll be leaving in a few days, remember?" But then, maybe that was what he was counting on. Maybe it was what he thought she was looking for. "I hope I haven't led you on."

His tongue lightly touched his lips as if he tasted her still. But then he sighed and nodded. "I understand. I'd best get you home. Please forgive me if I've caused you discomfort."

His formality was disconcerting, but he held her hand to lead her away from the pond back to the hotel. They claimed his motorcycle and left the hotel. The night air was balmy and humid. Huge cumulonimbus clouds overwhelmed the southern stars as if the weather was changing. The monsoon rains she'd endured in Phnom Penh were headed this way.

Trev stopped and turned the motorcycle off at the Blue Lotus and they dismounted.

"I am sorry, Trev. You're an attractive man, but I'm just not looking for that kind of thing at the moment. I've too many other issues to deal with, without adding one more."

He quirked a brow at her. "So I'm only an issue. That's hard for a man to hear." But he caught her hands and looked her in the eye. "Phoebe, nothing more might come of it, but I'm glad that we've met. And I'm relieved that I could find out enough about Sokha that you can spend your last few days in Siem Reap as a tourist. I would hate for anything to happen to such a lovely woman." He smiled down at her and kissed her on the cheek. "I know you have tomorrow planned with your driver, but if you would like another local guide, I would be honored to serve."

She didn't know what to say. Well, she did, but she couldn't very well have Trev tagging along when the first thing she wanted to do tomorrow was visit Chan's uncle Leng. She nodded.

"Thank you. Thank you for everything. You've been a wonderful friend in a foreign country. I hope we can stay in touch."

He looked sad when he released her hands and climbed on his motorcycle. With a bare salute, he started the engine and zoomed away.

Phoebe watched his taillight disappear around the corner onto night market street and almost wondered whether she'd done the right thing. But she had. She *wasn't* looking for a relationship or a one-night stand or booty call or whatever they called it nowadays. She was alone.

Well and truly alone since Becca and Alice returned to Canada.

For a moment her throat tightened and grief threatened to overwhelm her. Then she shook herself.

She was alone in Cambodia and she had another mystery to solve and, darn it, she would, if for no other reason than to prove that she could.

Regardless of what anyone else might think.

Determined not to regret her choice, she crossed the Blue Lotus lobby and took the stairs to her room two at a time. Oddly, she had trouble sleeping when she went to bed. She lay in her sleeping t-shirt with the fan gently paddling the air and her thoughts whirring.

Apparently regret had followed her home.

15

———————

She woke exhausted after a meagre sleep and lay staring at the ceiling fan whirring overhead. It didn't help. She felt hot and sweaty and her legs were sore, as if she'd run for miles. According to her dreams, she had. All night long she'd had a recurring dream of running down the corridors of her school. Unlike previous dreams, this time she'd been running for herself and trying to escape huge faces that she recognized as the effigies of Angkor. She'd been alone, too.

Alone and feeling the walls pressing in and in and in and she couldn't get out and those huge eyes were watching and weighing her. She could never help anyone because she couldn't even help herself. She'd woken frequently through the night, panting and confused with the realization that there might be a reason she was alone. She couldn't be trusted with anyone else. That was what the eyes were saying.

And oh, God, maybe it was true! Didn't they say that your dreams could set you free?

The room reeked of her sweat and damp bedsheets, so she got up feeling unsteady on her feet. When she checked her watch, it was six a.m., still plenty of time to get ready for Chan. She bundled the sheets up and set them outside her room door, hoping that would be a hint to the housekeeper that she wanted clean ones on her bed. Then she had a warm shower and dressed in navy capris and a white cotton blouse. Hopefully cool enough in the humid heat.

Even at half past six it was already hot and humid enough for her capris to stick to her skin almost immediately when she stepped out of her room. She went downstairs, told Jorani about the sheets—better to make sure housekeeping understood what she wanted—and headed out down the street toward town.

The traffic was unusually busy, but then she realized it was people taking their wares to market. Chickens hung upside down by their feet from poles strapped across motorcycle panniers. A pig lay across the passenger seat of another. Women carried baskets of fresh produce on their heads and others rode motorcycles with their children behind them and empty baskets, ready to purchase provisions for home. A pair of monks strode down the road toward the center of town, their saffron robes vibrant in the early morning sun. The air still carried the cool sweetness of night jasmine…

And that took her back to her last conversation with Trev. She felt bad that things had ended the way they had, but she'd only been honest. But he'd kissed her and that left her confused. It had been so long since anyone showed an attraction to her that she really hadn't known how to react. Maybe she could have let him down easier, but what was done was done. She just had to hope that he didn't hate her.

She tried the coffee shop she'd been to her first couple of mornings, but it was still locked up tight. Stymied, she decided to look around because surely there had to be some place open at this hour. Heck, it was almost seven, and *everyone* left for the temples around eight. There had to be some arrangement to feed the tourists.

Sure enough, the café she had gone to with Trev the other morning was just setting up. Tablecloths were going on the patio tables and silverware and glasses soon followed. Phoebe seated herself at a table in the corner and dug out a piece of paper while she waited for the waitress to take her order. On the paper she listed what she knew and the questions she still needed answered.

Chum Nath had been a government man from the Lands bureau who had accompanied Sokha from Phnom Penh to Siem Reap. He had apparently handed Sokha over to her father and then had followed them into town. Later that night, he'd been murdered and she suspected Sokha had been with him.

Sokha's barrette had been by the body, but her father had said she was safely at home.

Her father was the son of a Khmer Rouge officer, a "land baron" and a Big Man in the area. He reportedly treated everyone like serfs, and yet—she tapped her pen on the edge of the table and realized the waitress was standing over her.

"I'd like a large latte and a bowl of granola, yogurt, and fruit." She hoped to replicate the wonderful breakfast she'd had with Trev.

The thought made the meal a little less appetizing, but the waitress had departed and she didn't feel like anything different, so she turned back to her list. Where was she?

The village monks and the women in the market. What they'd said didn't quite jive with the other information.

But Mr. Yong was still the most logical suspect in Cham Nath's death. Had Cham Nath come to Siem Reap to stop Yong's land grab? That could be a reason for Yong to kill him.

More taps of her pen.

But why would Sokha be with him on the ferry? And why would she be in the market if she'd just arrived home? If she was Yong's favored daughter, why wouldn't she be spending time with him? What could bring her into the market that evening with a man she barely knew?

Unless she knew him from Phnom Penh.

Hadn't Trev told her that she was going to attend the American School there? Maybe Cham Nath was more than a bureaucrat. Maybe he was a friend of Yong's? Maybe he helped Yong bilk the land out of the villagers…

But if that was the case, then why kill him?

Darn it, she couldn't see anything to explain this muddle. Or maybe it was her brain that was muddled this morning. Lack of sleep and a kiss.

That could do it.

"I am too old for this," she muttered as the waitress arrived with Phoebe's meal.

Regardless of the reservations she'd had about the food, the granola was exactly what she needed, the latte even more so. With a good dose of caffeine flowing through her veins she almost felt like her brain was working again. She tucked the list in her day pack and finished her meal, then paid and headed back to the guesthouse. It was a quarter to eight when she got there, but Chan was already waiting.

Phoebe made a quick dash to her room to use the washroom and grab her hat, daypack, and water and then they were off with a wave to Jorani, but at the end of the street she used Chan's rearview mirror to wave him over.

"I want to go to the temples today like I said, but first I need to see Leng. He left a message for me yesterday and I have some questions." Actually, her head was full of them.

Chan nodded and they began the winding route that would eventually find the newspaperman's house again. She realized that last night there was no way she could have given a taxi instructions.While he drove, Chan called ahead.

As it was last time, the street of high, concrete walls was quiet, but the flowers of the old man's garden's blushed profusely in the early morning sunlight as Chan pulled up at the gate. He held the small garden gate for Phoebe as Leng appeared in his doorway and gestured them up to his home.

"It is a fine morning," the old newspaperman said, catching Phoebe's hand as she finished climbing the small ladder into his house.

"It is, indeed. We are off to the temples, but we came to see you first." Phoebe smiled and squeezed his fingers gently.

He motioned her toward his desk and busied himself with a tea service on a tray balanced on a pile of books.

"Your garden is a marvel. Why didn't you put up a wall like everyone else?"

Leng paused and the teacup rattled in his misshaped hand. "Perhaps it is because there have been enough walls in Cambodia. I breathe better with the light and the leaves and flowers." He sighed. "And I like to see who comes and goes past my house."

And who approaches, she could surmise. Chan had once more taken up station by the garden gate as if worried they were followed. At least this morning the car she'd seen parked in the lane last night was gone.

Leng limped across the room carrying the tea cups, the fine porcelain rattling, until she reached up to take the cups from him and place them on the desk. He slipped around the desk to his chair and settled, a furrow between his brows painting a pained expression on his face.

His gaze met hers. "My neighbors must forgive a nosy old man. Old habits are hard to break. I think they built the walls to avoid my and other's constant gazes." A brief smile touched his thin lips. "It was not always so. Once we were a community, but many of the homes burned during the bad years, and those who rebuilt also built walls. Whether to keep people out or to keep them in, I cannot say."

"So much changed with the Khmer Rouge," Phoebe said softly. She picked up her teacup and sipped. The tea had a slightly musty odor but was rich with tannins and slightly sweet.

"It did. No one who did not live with it can fathom the changes to my people, both outside and in."

That echoed something Trev had told her and she nodded.

"And how was your day yesterday? Did you go to the temples?" Leng used two hands to pick up his tea cup as if to steady it. Carrying the two cups at the same time must have been a huge exertion.

"Actually, I took a tour on the lake to see the stilted villages. It was very beautiful, but also raised questions for me. You see, while I was at the village, I met three young monks from the monastery built there. They told me that the monastery was built and supported by Mr. Yong. That seemed to fly in the face of everything I've been told about him. Is it true?"

Leng set his tea cup down with a rattle. He steepled his fingers and considered her over them. "Yes. As far as I know, it is true. Mr. Yong is known for his Buddhist faith. He has sponsored many temple restorations as well."

"I see." It made the women's stories more believable, too. "So he's trying to rebalance his karma?"

"Pardon me?" Leng pushed his chair back from the desk, the wheels squealing too loudly in the quiet house.

His confusion was so clear Phoebe reconsidered what she would say.

"Mr. Yong. The man who lives on a hilltop southeast of town. The man who told me Sokha was his daughter."

"Yes. And I can indeed confirm that Yong has a daughter named Sokha, but I do not understand your reference to rebalancing karma by building temples. Yes, Mr. Yong builds good karma through his works, but rebalancing? I was not aware that he had negative karma to rebalance."

"But that can't be possible. My guide seemed truly afraid for me when I spoke to Yong. Even Chan was very concerned when I wanted to speak to Yong and was terribly afraid when we went to his home."

"My nephew has the proper respect for Big Men and knows the potential repercussions if you anger one. In Yong's case, he may have over reacted. Yong is not a typical Big Man."

"But I've also been told that Yong—that he is the son of a senior Khmer Rouge officer named Ye Thol and actually participated in or observed the tortures when he was a child."

As she spoke, Leng had gripped the edge of his desk. His hands were white, his swollen knuckles vivid red. "Who told you this?"

Tell him? Did she really want to drag Trev into this?

"A man I met on the way to Siem Reap. A westerner."

"Well your westerner is wrong. I'm sorry, Ms. Clay. Perhaps gathering information for you has been a bad idea." He pushed up to his feet and shuffled to the door as if expecting her to follow.

She had to find a way to undo this, to convince him to help. Without Leng, there was no one else to help her ensure Sokha was safe and to find Cham Nath's killer. "The same man told me that Sokha was safe at home and that I could quit worrying. At least tell me whether I am wrong to listen to him."

The light from the doorway lit half of the newspaperman's face, leaving the rest in darkness. It was a lot like how Phoebe felt, except more than fifty percent of what she needed to know was lost in darkness.

"Please," she said.

Leng's face remained still, as if he had not changed his mind, but then he shuffled back to the desk and sank down in his chair. He motioned her to follow so she returned to her chair.

"This westerner lies. Since you and I last spoke, I have extended my reach as far as it can go regarding the girl, this Sokha. She is well known, if you know the right people to ask. A brilliant student, but with health issues that have stunted her growth, so that at eighteen she still looks a child. She is her father's daughter—strong-willed, but giving to all around her. She has strong friendships and was accepted into Oxford University with the intention of studying economics and environmental studies with a focus on land management."

His gaze suggested he thought he'd told her enough, but not everything.

"So there was a connection of interests between Sokha and Cham Nath."

"It would appear so." Leng nodded, but something had changed between them. He did not know whether to trust her.

"That could explain why she was with him in the night market."

He arched a brow at her.

"Perhaps they had become friends. She could have been showing him around."

Now Leng looked at her over the tops of his pince-nez glasses. "That does not make sense to me. If he was a friend, why would he not stay at her father's home?"

It was a good question and one she had no answer for. But at least Leng was talking with her—talking the interpretations through. Perhaps her questions had eased any concerns he might have about her connections to such beliefs about Yong.

"So why wouldn't he stay at her father's home?" Phoebe asked. "He doesn't want to appear to be a friend?"

Leng thought and nodded. "That could make sense if he wanted to appear unbiased."

"If that's the case, why would Sokha be with him in the night market? And on the ferry, for that matter?"

"Perhaps there was something that they must do together?"

"The trouble is, we've no idea what. All that we know is that whatever it was ended in Cham Nath's death and Sokha's apparent disappearance. But then, I've been told she's safe at home. You haven't confirmed that for me yet."

She met Leng's gaze and picked up her tea cup. Sipped. She could wait as long as he could. The Angkor temples weren't going anywhere. After years of waiting out surly students, she was pretty sure she could out-wait a reporter.

From the street came the sound of a bicycle bell and greetings passed between the cyclist and Chan. She sipped her tea.

Finally, Leng nodded. "You are very determined, Ms. Clay. So I will tell you what I have found. I contacted those who I thought would know the girl and from there went further to contact those she is truly close with. None of them know where she is. None of them have spoken to her since the day of the night market, though all of them have tried and a few of them had engagements planned with her— planned while she was in Phnom Penh. Unless her father has her locked in his home, which apparently is unlikely, it seems the young woman, Sokha, has truly disappeared."

16

——————

The shadowed room and the sultry Cambodian heat suddenly vanished. Phoebe sat in a frigid School Board hearing room, under unforgiving fluorescent lights, listening as her principal lied about her interactions with him. How she had never come to him to warn him of the harassment occurring to Rick Hames' little sister. Assuring the School Board that any such information would have drawn swift and decisive action on his part. The room reeked of coffee and tea and her own sweat—inside her blue wool fitted jacket. Though her flesh had gone cold at his testimony, her white blouse was drenched and it was hard to catch her breath.

Her chest ached just as it had back then. Betrayal was never an easy thing to accept, but this time she had to.

"Ms. Clay? Are you unwell?"

She shook herself and clutched at her porcelain tea cup. It shook as she brought it to her mouth and sipped. From outside Leng's small house, Chan and the cyclist's voices rose and fell, but she didn't understand a single word. Much as she had been hard pressed to hear the Board when they'd made their findings in the "Rick Hames Matter." With it, they had erased the truth from the record.

And now someone else was trying to do the same.

Trev.

She thought of his quirky smile, the twinkle in his eye, and the casual way he caught her elbow. She thought of the soft kiss in the hotel garden.

Then she thought of his assurances.

"I—I'm fine. I think." She met Leng's gaze. "The man I told you about from the ferry? I've just realized he's an even bigger liar. He told me Sokha was at home and fine. That I didn't need to worry and could finish my tour and go home with no concerns."

She took another sip of tea to steady herself and savored the tannins as they gradually bloomed on her tongue. Bitterness followed, but that was right somehow. It went with her anger.

The facts she knew began to assume a different pattern. But it was all conjecture at this point. She needed information.

"What do you know about a western man named Trevor Morgan and a society named *Cambodia Prosperous*?"

Leng frowned and removed his pince-nez glasses. "Why do you ask?" The light from the door caught on his disfigured knuckles.

"Because he's the man who told me Sokha was safe. He's also the man who told me that Mr. Yong was the son of a Khmer Rouge war criminal—and other things."

She felt like she held her breath as she waited for his response. The reporter replaced his glasses and slowly pushed to his feet to shuffle across the room to a stack of books. These he shifted aside to reveal a small locked cabinet that opened with a key he kept on a chain around his neck. Unlocked, a drawer slid open revealing what looked like about a dozen thick files. He pulled one out, slid the drawer shut, and relocked it before returning to the desk.

He sat down and opened the file with his twisted hands resting on the documents as if to protect them. "You've spoken a name well-known in this country. He lives in Siem Reap now, but his tentacles stretch to many areas. Ruby and sapphire mines in the far west, resorts along the southern coast, farmland and lake frontage here in Siem Reap."

"I thought he ran a nonprofit? I thought *Cambodia Prosperous* was dedicated to helping villagers complete projects that make the village more viable. Like building bridges or schools, or helping individual families get bicycles so they can take produce to market?"

Leng slumped back in his chair and steepled his fingers. "It sounds very good, does it not? I, and so very many others were taken in by these promises of opportunities for those who need them most. Cambodia is a very poor country and the farmers are the poorest of the poor. Easy pickings, one could say, if the right bait was offered."

Phoebe finished the dregs of her tea. "What are you saying?"

"What is the English saying? If something is too good to be true, it probably is?"

She got up and went to the teapot, swirled it, and brought it back to the desk to refill their cups. Leng nodded his thanks as she sank into her chair again.

"*Cambodia Prosperous* offered just such promises. With the District headmen's approval, they selected a village and then went in with an agreement to assist the village to build a school and a bridge, as well as operate the school after it was built. Such a wonderful promise required the villagers to have tenure of their land, so *Cambodia Prosperous* guided illiterate villagers through the bureaucracy before they began."

Phoebe nodded. "That's all good, right?"

Nodding, Leng picked up his cup and sipped. "So far, yes. But *Cambodia Prosperous* then required the villagers to sign an agreement. The agreement was in Khmer, but of course the villagers couldn't read it. The agreement effectively sold their newly tenured land to a company called *Cambodian Prosperity Lands*. The company is Cambodian and even has Cambodian board members as are required under the Cambodian Lands legislation. Foreigners are not allowed to own Cambodian land. Only a Khmer individual or company may. The trouble is, as far as I can tell, *Cambodian Prosperity Lands* has only one purpose and that is to facilitate the acquisition of lands, leaving more of our people landless and working as peasants for the company.

"My research so far has been unable to confirm why, but I suspect that there may be foreign interests partnering with the company to finance large resorts. There has been something like that happening in the south around Sihanoukville. The villages along the coastal beaches have been bought out and been forced to move so that resorts catering to foreigners can be built. I suspect something similar is planned for Siem Reap given the ongoing interest in Angkor. There has been much activity here."

He turned the file toward her and lifted his hands to expose a map covered in red blotches. "The red is owned by *Cambodian Prosperity Lands*."

Phoebe leaned forward to scan the map and felt weak at the expanse of the poxy marks and the potential scope of the *Cambodia Prosperous* plan. She could imagine a landscape of rice fields filled in, vast resorts with shimmering swimming pools and golf courses and Siem Reap expanded ten-fold by the burgeoning shanty towns of the displaced landless.

"But I heard that Mr. Yong was the one purchasing land. That he was the one displacing villages."

Leng shook his head, his thin hair shifting on his head. "He has purchased land, yes. When *Cambodian Prosperity Lands* bought the lands adjacent to Yong's residence, he knew that he had to do something." His finger tapped the map where a small island of white was surrounded by red. "He had to fight back for his people. So he learned from *Cambodia Prosperous'* methods and began to sign agreements of co-ownership with villages and in exchange funded monasteries and other things the villages needed."

"You're saying that the fields and village at the base of Yong's hill are not his." And all those starving villagers.

Leng nodded.

"But he has that…that castle…"

Leng met her gaze. "I did not say he wasn't a rich man. His family were wealthy before the Khmer Rouge. They escaped to Thailand and grew their business and wealth there through the jewelry trade. When the Khmer Rouge were deposed, he returned to Siem Reap. Excess is not a crime, Ms. Clay. The man is house proud."

And the stilted village—he was a patron there. "When I was on the lake tour, we passed a stilted village that looked in almost perfect condition, but was abandoned. It looked like someone had been scavenging building materials there."

His nod confirmed her suspicions. "That is a very sad case. The people of that village only know Tonle Sap Lake. They can read it as a westerner would read one of your books. But *Cambodian Prosperity Lands* forced them out." He shook his head, his lips pressed into a line, angry furrows spreading out from his eyes. "Now the village is empty and the people live in the shanty towns around the city. An entire village wiped out and for what? The lake floods annually. I hear tell of plans to use fill to build a hilltop hotel and causeway so that foreigners will have a lake view when they visit Angkor."

He set his cup down with a rattle and stood to limp around the room. "I know this, and yet I can do nothing about it. The Board of *Cambodia Prosperity Lands* is filled with influential Cambodian men. Big Men. Bigger men than Mr. Yong, but still he battles on, trying to protect the little man."

"Where does Trevor Morgan fit into all of this? You said he's well known…" Phoebe bit her lip, not sure she wanted to know the answer. The light from the open front door drew her. Out into the sunshine. Out to the temples where she could simply be a tourist without a care in the world. She didn't have to know about Trev's involvement in robbing the Cambodian people of their most basic right to their land. She could simply pretend he was a nice man she'd befriended.

"He is called their Senior Advisor to the Board, though his work is that of a CEO. The man named CEO is more like a figurehead, but all of it allows *Cambodia Prosperity Lands* to operate within my country's current land rules."

"But his business card only said he was the Manager of *Cambodia Prosperous.*" She felt a total fool as she shook her head.

"And so he is the smiling face of the men who would rob my people of their heritage. I have been researching this quietly for years, but have been unable to make anyone listen in this country. I fear the government has been bribed to look the other way, or worse, senior government men stand to profit directly."

Shoulders slumping and hands suddenly gone still, if anything Leng looked more tired and forlorn—as if he had disappointed himself.

"Would Yong have tried to negotiate with them?" In some ways it made sense. If Yong was as big a deal as Davuth and others had made out, he had earned the respect to have a face-to-face with his adversaries.

Leng once more removed his pince-nez, this time to clean them with a hanky. "Who can say? He does have local authority and respect. If they didn't meet with him, it would be a total sign of disrespect. On the other hand, do the men behind *Cambodian Prosperity Lands* even care? I don't know." He resettled his glasses on his nose, but they sat crooked making his face look misaligned.

Thinking, Phoebe drummed her fingers on her knees. "What if Yong couldn't go himself for some reason. He'd want to send someone he trusted as his envoy, right?"

Leng nodded and steepled his hands.

"So he sends Sokha in his place." Phoebe plunged on. "They needed a neutral place to meet and decided that the seven-hour trip on the ferry would provide a good place to begin the process. They'd have Sokha for Yong, Cham Nath as mediator/arbiter and…and Trevor Morgan on behalf of *Cambodian Prosperity Lands*. The only problem was that I got in the way." Or Trevor Morgan made it look that way. He had started the conversation. He had moved up beside Phoebe to talk.

And Sokha had been taken in by the situation and so had feigned ignorance of English so she could converse with Trev…Trevor Morgan. Phoebe couldn't let herself think of the Trev who had kissed her.

"I don't understand why, but he sabotaged the meeting on the ferry." She met Leng's gaze. From outside, the voices had faded and the clump of Chan's footfall on the ladder drew her attention to the time. She'd been talking to the newspaper man for over an hour.

"But why?" Leng echoed the question she was asking herself.

"Clearly, because it didn't suit his purposes. The ferry is very public, but it's also very controlled. Here's a wild thought: What if they wanted to have a hold over Yong? Maybe even get him on board to hand over the lands he's been acquiring? What better way to do that than abducting his favorite daughter? But that's hard to do on a public ferry. So Trevor Morgan sabotages the ferry meeting, but they agree to meet in another public place that same day—the tourist night market. A place less controlled, where *Cambodia Prosperous'* men could do what they wanted. They wanted Sokha. I'll bet Cham Nath was only collateral damage. He probably tried to stop the abduction."

It made sense. Cham Nath and Sokha would be coming to meet Trevor Morgan, but again Phoebe got in the way. Trevor had called her over to get her out of the way so she couldn't possibly see events unfold, but then the confusion unfolded and she did what most people would never do—she ran toward the scene in time to see it before they could remove any signs of Sokha. Trevor's quick thinking to get her away had allowed them to do what was needed and Trevor had likely been keeping an eye on her ever since.

She felt sick to her stomach. She needed to move. To walk. She pushed to her feet and paced the room between the stacks of books and Leng's desk. Finally, she stopped to lean down to him.

"Tell me. Trevor Morgan came to me yesterday looking like he'd been beaten. He said Yong's men were responsible. Could that be true?"

Leng met her gaze. "I think not. I have heard one of his villages attempted to take their rights back. They actually caught Trevor Morgan alone and beat him—until he managed to escape and call for help. He sent his men back to the village. A woman was killed."

She felt sick her stomach at the news, but also determined. "So it's been Trevor Morgan all along. He might not have killed Cham Nath outright, but he arranged for it to be done. He's also most likely the one who has Sokha if she's still alive. The question is where he'd keep her."

Leng shook his head, clearly mystified.

If he didn't know, she doubted anyone did.

"Would Yong know?" she asked.

"If he did, he dares not act for fear of reprisal on his daughter."

"So they have him right where they want him. He has to do what they want or risk Sokha's life."

"That is my assessment as well." Leng nodded.

Phoebe returned to her pacing. "We can't let them do this. I saw some of those villagers. They look like Auschwitz victims. It's like you said, their land is their heritage. The Cambodian people have already suffered so much. They don't deserve to be disinherited from their country by an international group and their local cronies."

"What are you thinking?" Chan asked from the doorway.

For a moment Phoebe wasn't sure whether he meant it as a critique of her comments, but then she saw the gleam in his eyes. Chan had been listening and, even though the discussion had been in English, had understood far more than she expected.

She turned back to Leng. "We do what Yong can't. We find and rescue Sokha."

In the back of her mind, she could picture Becca shaking her head.

Leaving Leng to identify locations Trevor Morgan might have hidden the girl, Phoebe and Chan headed to Angkor. Trev could have men at the temples reporting on whether or not she turned up. Heck, there was every possibility that he'd even had her followed to Leng's. But the reporter had said he'd be careful and Chan had called a friend to keep an eye on Leng's home. There wasn't much more she could do, other than act like nothing was wrong.

The prospect of the ancient temples was a poor distraction from the whir of information in her head. She sorted through what she already knew or suspected and how she might use it.

The traffic was heavier than she'd experienced given the later departure today, and the diesel fumes had her coughing in the open cab. Chan seemed to know she was suffering, or maybe he was, too. He wove between the trucks until he turned off on the empty four-lane road to the gates to Angkor. It wasn't quite so empty at this time of the day. A long line of full buses idled at the gates awaiting passport approval, with groups of western tourists clustered outside their respective vehicles. There was even one bus with a cruise ship logo, so they must fly people to Angkor from one of their ports of call. She couldn't imagine trying to see the huge complex of temples in only a day.

Given Phoebe already had her pass, Chan scooted past the buses and soon they were passing beneath the ancient arched gate with its many-sided faces. Chan slowed, flipped his visor up, and looked back at her. "Where we go?"

"The Bayon?" she suggested.

Chan checked his watch. "Bayon very bad this time of day. Many, many people."

"Then take me to what you think I should see."

He gave her a thumbs-up, pulled his visor down, and sped on. They drove past Angkor Wat temple where flocks of buses and minivans disgorged a parade of tourists up and over the causeway moat and into the huge inner temple. The temple's iconic spires stood out darkly against a sky filled with towering cumulonimbus clouds lumbering up from the south. Monsoon clouds she'd already learned to recognize.

Past the huge temple complex, they entered jungle where the Tetrameles trees snaked huge, knotted root runners across the jungle floor. Thick brush grew up amidst the trees and mist still hung along a small river. It would be beautiful if she wasn't so distracted.

They came into the gravel Preah Khan parking lot and were almost alone. Another motorcycle taxi sat idle, its driver dozing on the passenger bench. There were no other tourists in sight. Perfect. She could explore and hopefully settle her thoughts. If she was really lucky, she might accomplish what she'd hoped to do on the first day of her visit—simply be *here* and enjoy the wonder of it. Feel it seep in and hopefully change her. With a clear head, she might even come up with how to find Sokha.

Phoebe hauled her day pack onto her shoulder and stepped down from the cab. "It's okay for you to wait here, Chan. I'll be fine. I really need time alone."

He hesitated, but finally nodded. "Be careful. Stay on paths, please. There are still rumors of bombs left behind by the Khmer Rouge."

She nodded. Davuth had said the same things to her on her first day and she'd read about the possibility of old Khmer war ordinance still being discovered across the country, including at the archeological site. The last thing she planned to do was step on a landmine.

She had enough of those in her head.

Once away from the parking lot, she became aware of the quiet. Birds sang in trees. A flock of small blue butterflies danced around a flowering bush so she could understand where the movie Tomb Raider got its inspiration. The butterflies, however, didn't lead her through the ruins and neither did a small child. Instead there was only quiet, the massive, tumbled ruins, and huge trees that grew up around, through, and over the stone blocks and spread green shadows over the earth below.

She found a corner filled with a beam of light and leaned against the sun-warmed stone. Across the courtyard, a single tree with smooth white bark raised twisted branches from the top of the wall, its equally smooth roots cascading down, as if reflecting its form in the stone.

Raising her face to the sun, she let the warmth fill her face and eyes, while her lower body remained in cooler shadows. She breathed in and out as her counselor had shown her, savoring the damp earth and green growth-scented air. Slow her heartbeat. Slow her thoughts. Concentrate on the feel of the breath only. If she could just settle her thoughts…

But Sokha's face kept getting in the way. Every time Phoebe thought she was relaxing into the moment, the girl appeared. Sokha wouldn't be calm—or maybe she would be. One thing Phoebe had noticed was how the people of Asia seemed to be able to overlook their current circumstances. Equanimity the Buddhists called it. The ability to experience calm composure no matter the negative circumstances they found themselves in.

But Sokha was in a lot of trouble and she would know it. She would know her father would give up just about anything to have her released. She would also know the cost to the Cambodian people and that she wouldn't like. Just from the very brief interaction Phoebe had

had with the girl, and from the trust her father put in her, this was a very unusual young woman. One who deserved to be helped.

Sighing, Phoebe opened her eyes. She was getting nowhere fast trying to meditate. Better to concentrate on what she knew and what she could do.

She could go to Yong and offer her help, but she could imagine the man would tell her to mind her own business. He wouldn't want someone he viewed as simply an old busybody getting involved. It could result in Sokha being hurt or worse. Maybe he was right.

She really had no reason to pursue this, no skin in the game, so to speak. So why *was* she so determined to find Sokha and help her?

She could almost hear Becca and her counselor speaking to her, telling her she was doing this out of guilt. But it wasn't true. She wasn't doing this because she hadn't been able to help Rick Hames and his little sister. She wasn't doing it to prove that she *could* help.

Was she?

Surely she'd proved that to herself when she rescued Alice. She really had nothing to prove at all. She simply wanted to do what was right, and helping Sokha and the Cambodian people was right.

Darn Becca and the counselor for getting into her head. She was doing just fine. So she ran to help when others ran away. That's what firemen did. It's what police officers did. It's what heroes did. She might not be looking to be a hero, but there were lots of people who simply did what was right when confronted with a situation. She simply happened to be one of those people.

So if she was going to try to help, what could she do?

Let the police know what she suspected? She wasn't sure about that given even Leng seemed hesitant to work with them. And given the graft in the country, wasn't it likely that they were working for *Cambodia Prosperity Lands*? If she told them what she knew, she could place herself in the very danger she was trying to avoid.

So that meant she had to do something directly herself to find where Sokha was held. Darn it all, if she'd only known, she could have led Trev on and used her feminine wiles to get him to tell her.

The laugh burst out of her, sending two doves fluttering up into the tree branches. The sound seemed to echo around the courtyard.

Feminine wiles. Like she'd had any of them at any time of her life, let alone now in her fifties. Nope, any feminine wiles she'd had, had long ago worn off leaving behind the wrinkles of a fledgling crone.

But Trev *had* been interested—or he'd acted like he was. To control her? Maybe she could use that and turn the tables on him. Give him a call? Arrange to see him again? Apologize for how she'd acted and say she regretted what she'd done? She could say that part of it was that she just didn't know him that well. Maybe ask to see the work he did? Even offer to teach a few classes of English? These days it was the lingua franca in the developing world. Speaking English well opened up a world of possibilities in employment and education.

She'd say she wanted to give back to the country and the people who had been so kind to her. That sounded like something she'd say. Actually, it sounded exactly like something she'd say.

Smiling to herself, she pulled a bottle of water from her pack and drank deep. Around her, mist rose off the stone and her sweat dripped into her clothes.

Through the stillness, she heard the growl of diesel buses along the jungle road and climbed to her feet. Time to go. Time to let Leng and Chan know her meagre plan and then put it into action. She ran her fingers over the rough stone and turned back for the parking lot, picking her way back through debris-laden hallways, past galleries with ancient Buddha figures that someone had draped in saffron and surrounded with lit candles. The butterflies were gone from the path to the parking lot, and the birds seemed to slumber in the late morning heat. It would be good to sit down and it was getting near lunch. Her stomach was actually growling. A huge bus was just turning in to the parking lot, its diesels shattering the quiet. Otherwise the lot was empty.

The motorcycle taxi and Chan were gone.

17

———

Feeling somewhat dumbfounded, Phoebe stood on the gravel parking lot in the glaring sun. Chan must have gone on a quick errand. Maybe for food or a washroom. He wouldn't leave her in the lurch. She pulled out her phone. Had he texted her a message? But she hadn't given him her number, had she?

Stoopid, stoopid, stoopid.

The huge tour bus stopped, and its doors hissed open. A parade of lily-white passengers in Tilly hats, Angkor t-shirts, Bermuda shorts, and cameras began to disgorge, their chatter destroying the quiet. They were followed by a slim Cambodian woman in trim navy skirt and pale blue blouse who opened a red umbrella.She shepherded her flock to the side of the parking lot and pointed out a statue sculpted into the wall.

"This is one of seventy-two garuda statues carved into the outer walls of Preah Khan temple. Its arms are up, holding the tails of three-headed naga serpents. The garuda is the guardian of the heavens and the naga of the earth, therefore they are thought to represent the earth and sky of the temple. Each of the statues is five meters high."

The woman droned on and Phoebe wondered whether she dared interrupt her and ask for help. Clearly she spoke English. But Chan and the motorcycle taxi would be back soon enough. He was a responsible young man. He wouldn't just leave.

At least she didn't think he would.

She found a shady spot at the edge of the parking area, and settled on a fallen stone to wait. And wait. She knew Chan would have her number and she would have his if Alice was here. Alice was the one who was tech savvy and had taken care of things like that on the trip to India. Here, Phoebe had simply forgotten. It hadn't seemed necessary because Jorani always called Chan.

A second tour bus arrived and then a third, each following the same process as the first, except the tourists were German on one bus and Chinese on the other. Two minivans arrived and smaller groups of tourists followed a similar process. Did any of them realize they were simply widgets on the Angkor tourist conveyor belt? The good thing was it brought much-needed money to the Cambodian economy. The sad thing was so little made it down to the people who needed it the most.

After thirty minutes the first tour bus departed, but two more took its place. The sun had shifted enough that Phoebe's spot was no longer in the shade and, frankly, she was darn tired of waiting. Chan had never done anything like this before. Had something happened to him or his family? That was the only reason she could think of for him leaving.

Tamping down on a curl of fear, she stood, took a sip of water from her rapidly depleting supply, brushed off her capris, and crossed the parking lot. The road east-and-west was quiet. A single minivan zoomed past.

She set out walking back toward Angkor Wat temple. She'd noticed a series of restaurant stalls there on her first morning. Though her hope was diminishing, there was a chance Chan was there. He could have gone for a meal and lost track of time…

At least the road was paved so the dust was at a minimum, but it was narrow so the huge tour buses forced her off the road into the edge of the jungle. It was the cumulonimbus clouds overhead that had her most concerned. They seemed to have snagged on something and were gathering to the north and backing up toward her. From the pristine white they had been when they floated overhead, they had turned into a shoal of bruised purple and gray that promised rain.

The road had curved back toward Angkor Wat temple when she felt the first raindrop. It splatted on her forehead and was soon followed by a few more. Large, fat drops left splatter marks amongst the dust at the side of the pavement. A sudden wind gust tore at the trees and her hair. The jungle opened up to a field with a couple of minor shrines leaning amongst the tall grass. She could take the time to pull out her poncho or take a chance on beating the worst of the rain and cut across the field.

She decided to try to beat the rain and cut across the field, hurrying at first, and then running as the rain turned from a sprinkle to a steady downpour. Regretting her decision, she hauled her daypack off and held it over her head. Bursts of wind whipped the tall grass around her legs. She angled toward the road and was forced to climb an ancient, rough, stone wall. She half fell onto the pavement and picked herself up. Heavy raindrops bounced on the hot pavement and the air smelled of steam and wet earth. She jogged down the road, her day pack still raised—not that it did much good.

She was soaked when she reached the parking lot—empty—and the line of small restaurants and souvenir vendors. She ducked under the tarp awning of the first restaurant and relished the end of the rain pounding on her head. Now it thundered on the tarps and ran in heavy streams off the edge. She found a table and collapsed, scanning the parking lot in vain, hoping Chan or another taxi driver might have pulled their vehicles under the trees. There was no one. A woman brought her the restaurant menu.

"Taxi?" Phoebe asked.

The woman shook her head. "All gone. Much rain. No tourists."

Phoebe sighed and ordered fried rice and a cup of tea. Then she dug through her pack for her phone.

Of course there were no calls from Chan, but she dug deeper in her daypack for her wallet in search of the Blue Lotus business card she'd taken when she checked in. What she came up with instead was Trevor Morgan's business card.

She considered it as they brought her the cup of tea. She sipped, thankful for the warmth for the wind was chill and cut through her wet clothes. She shivered and held the cup with both hands to warm her fingers.

She could keep looking for the guesthouse business card, or she could take this as a sign. She'd already made the decision that she was going to reconnect with the man in order to try to learn where Sokha was. Her situation provided the perfect excuse. Call him and ask him to take her back to her guesthouse. Then invite him out to dinner in thank you. If romance "bloomed," it would give her an excuse to visit him. If not, she could ask to see the villages he worked with and maybe volunteer to teach English. She had an open ticket home. She could stay in Cambodia as long as she wanted or leave any time. Surely she could figure out where Sokha was. She didn't have to rescue the girl herself. She could get the information to Yong and let him rescue his daughter himself.

So calling Trev to ask for a ride back to Blue Lotus wouldn't be taking much of a risk, which would make Becca happy.

Before she could change her mind, she opened her phone app and punched in his number. The dial tone purred in her ear.

"Hello." Trev's crisp tone.

"Trev?" She didn't have to fake the tremble in her voice.

"Phoebe? Is that you?"

"It's me." Her teeth actually chattered. "I'm in a bit of a pickle. I was out at Preah Khan and my motorcycle taxi disappeared on me. There're no other taxis because of the rain. I'm stuck and I wondered whether you could come and get me and take me home? I'm sorry to ask... I've probably caught you in the middle of something."

"No. No. Don't be sorry. Are you still at Preah Khan? I can be right there."

"No. I'm at a restaurant by Angkor Wat."

"Stay there." He hung up.

Whether it was the right thing to do, it was done. She contemplated the phone a moment. She should tell someone, but she had no one to tell. She didn't have Chan or Leng's numbers. Call Becca? Call Jorani and tell her Trevor Morgan was bringing her back to the guesthouse? Jorani wouldn't care, but if someone asked, she could tell them…Still, she should tell someone. She opened her email and sent a quick note to Becca saying that she was having fun and had made a friend named Trevor Morgan who was the manager of a nonprofit called *Cambodia Prosperous.*

Becca could keep or delete the message, but if something happened to Phoebe, there would at least be a name for them to look at. Shivering at the thought, she considered the phone. She should have gotten Leng's phone number. And Chan's, but she hadn't.

Stoopid, stoopid, stoopid.

Please let her be doing the right thing.

She still held the phone. Phone Jorani or not? What did it matter if the woman thought she was weird? She dug through her daypack for the card, but just as she found it, Trev and his motorcycle zoomed into the parking lot. She shoved the card in the daypack's front pocket and stood, her tea and her order of rice forgotten. He wore a helmet, rain jacket and pants, but stripped the helmet off as soon as he came to a stop.

When he spotted her, he crossed to her in long strides.

"Oh my God, you're soaked." He said, catching her arms and looking down at her. "And you're shivering!" He pulled her into his chest and she forced herself to relax into his arms. Warm. Strong. Unfortunately, she liked the soap and water smell of him.

But these were the arms of someone who tricked people into signing away their land, and then worked them like slaves. She stiffened.

Trev held her away and studied her face. "Are you okay?"

She shook her head. "I just feel really stupid for getting caught in the rain. I have a poncho for goodness sake, but I thought I could get here before the clouds let loose. Guess I was wrong." She looked down at her soaked clothing and shook her head. Another gust of wind hit her and she shivered.

"We need to get you out of the wind and into some dry clothes, but first we need to get away from here. How about you pull out that poncho?" Trev said, all business and in control.

Obediently, she returned to her table and dug for her poncho. Against her objections, Trev paid for her meal. Regardless of what he'd done, he was apparently still a gentleman.

She pulled the poncho out of its plastic envelope and managed to open the thin plastic material in the gusting wind. Pulling it on, the poncho stuck uncomfortably to her damp clothes and skin, but she shimmied it down and pulled the hood up over her sodden hair.

Trev shook his head. "That's not the most useful poncho, but I suppose it will have to do."

It was the cheapest she'd seen in Phnom Penh, meant for a single emergency use she had hoped she could avoid. Well this was an emergency, wasn't it?

She felt like an imposter and a fool letting Trev take her arm to guide her through the rain to his bike. At least the downpour was lessening. He assisted her on, though she didn't need his help, but then maybe this was the way to learn things. Act like a helpless tourist and no one thought you were a threat. When he climbed on, she gripped his waist tighter than she had previously. He started the engine and they left the parking lot toward the Archeological Park main gate.

Rain still bounced off the pavement and spray rose off the road from the hissing tires. The wind plastered the plastic poncho to Phoebe's skin and she huddled closer to Trev for warmth. Who knew that you could get so cold in a tropical country? She felt chilled through. They zoomed through the ancient Angkor gate and past the passport checkpoint. The line of buses hadn't decreased, though the tourists were only visible as rain-blurred faces in misty windows.

Trev increased speed down the four-lane highway until they reached the main road. He turned into traffic, but not toward town.

"Where are we going?" She yelled above the road noise.

"My place. It's closer. We need to get you warmed up."

His voice floated back to her through his helmet.

A flutter of concern clenched her stomach, but she tamped it down.

She'd planned to somehow get herself invited back to his place and here it was happening. A little sooner than she'd planned, but all good. She huddled in closer and breathed in Trev's man-scent. Under different circumstances she really could be attracted to this man. Too bad he was a criminal.

To her left, not too far ahead, through the rain she could make out a single hill that had to be Yong's place. Around it, fields of newly planted rice created a green haze over the landscape. But Yong's place was a heck of a lot farther away than the Blue Lotus Guesthouse. Just where was Trev taking her?

She sat up a little straighter and Trev seemed to slow the motorcycle in answer. They turned off the highway onto a road she thought she recognized. Wasn't this the way to the women's temple called Banteay Srei and the puppet carving school?

The road was potholed pavement—the kind that could bounce a motorcycle taxi passenger around. She was pretty sure that this was the way Chan had gone, but then Trev turned down a narrower side road. This one wasn't paved, and mud flew up around them as he slewed around puddles that must mark potholes. Mud splattered Phoebe's legs and dotted her poncho. Brush closed in on both sides of the road, but where it thinned, the earth fell away to a deep ditch between the road and the fields. She spotted pairs of young boys fishing with a round net in the ditch. Beyond them were more fields, some fallow and some being ploughed. A few held stooped figures patiently replanting delicate rice plants into the knee-deep mud.

Then they were past and traveling up a slight slope past yellow and red stone ruins amongst a copse of palms and what might be spreading mango trees. A cluster of traditional stilted houses sat in an arc around another ruin, this one with a large Buddha figure draped in rain-sodden saffron-colored cloth. Beyond the Buddha figure and an open central square sat a low, ranch-style building elevated about three feet from the ground by cinder blocks. The building had a corrugated metal roof and was painted yellow and white with an inviting-looking screened porch that appeared to run the entire circumference of the house.

Trev slowed the motorcycle and they rolled to a stop by the steps to the porch. He turned the engine off, dismounted, and helped her off, then pulled a tarp lying on the stairs up and over the bike. Catching her elbow, he guided her up the stairs and through a screen door onto the porch.

The silence after the motorcycle's roar emphasized the steady rain on the metal roof. The porch was built of polished wood. Rattan loveseats and chairs sat in comfortable groupings with chintz coverings in peony floral pattern. Potted palms swayed in the breeze through the screens. Trev's grip on her elbow urged her to the main door and inside. She toed off her sandals and he took off his muddy shoes.

She blinked because the lighting was dim, though rain-dimmed natural light came through expansive windows on the far side of the house. They looked out on greening fields and, farther away across the fields, what looked like the construction area she'd noticed from the highway the other day. Loaded trucks were dumping rock and soil that cascaded down into the edge of the gleaming rice field.

She pulled her gaze back and let her eyes adjust to the house's interior. A great room held a comfortable leather couch and chairs. A heavy wooden dining room table sat in a corner by the windows. A kitchen island divided the kitchen apparatus from the dining and living area. On the walls hung paintings of men and women clad in red jackets, riding long-legged horses across an English countryside.

She blinked and did a slow scan of the room again. Comfortable, yes, but not at all what she'd expect in this part of the world. This was an English cottage plopped into the Cambodian countryside.

"You look surprised," Trev said as he stripped off his rain gear.

She pulled her poncho over her head. "I am, I guess. I thought you'd have some of your wonderful photographs hanging. They're such striking images."

He sniffed and shook his head. "This is home. This is me."

He swung his hands wide as if exposing himself to her, but all she could see was the construction site across the fields and the fact there was nothing—exactly nothing—of Cambodia or the Cambodian people inside. Considering the lovely silks she'd seen and hand-made baskets and woodcarvings, she'd expect to see some appreciation of the

Cambodian aesthetic here. The nearest she could see were the ferns on the porch.

"It's very nice. Large, though." She shoved down her disquiet. "You live here alone?"

He nodded. "There are extra bedrooms for visitors when foreign donors come to see our work. It saves on hotel bills." He motioned to a hallway that led off the main room. "Speaking of which, let's get you some towels and dry clothes."

He ushered her down the hallway to a guest bedroom with adjoining bathroom replete with white marble counters that matched those in the kitchen. "Make yourself at home. Here." He pulled open a closet door and offered her a plush white bathrobe like she'd seen in pictures of expensive spas. "You can dry off. I have a small propane clothes drier so we can at least dry your clothes."

He left her then, closing the door to the bedroom behind him.

Geez Louise. She wasn't sure how she felt about doffing her clothes in a strange man's home, let alone a man she suspected of murder, but in for a penny, in for a pound. She crept to the bedroom door and pulled it slightly open. He was back in the great room kitchen and was on the phone.

"How did it go?" Trev asked, his voice somehow different from that she knew. This Trev's voice was sharp, as if he brooked no nonsense. He hmm-mmmed at the phone a few times.

"And the old man?" He filled a kettle at the kitchen sink, the running water masking his words.

"Bloody hell! You were supposed to distract him; stop his little enquiries." He listened again. "I don't care whether he's surrounded by the US Marines. Things are too delicate right now. We can't afford more questions—or allegations. Now do something before he ruins everything!"

He slammed down the phone and swore.

Phoebe eased the door closed and leaned against it for a second. Footsteps sounded in the hall and she raced across to the bathroom, closed and locked the door, and turned on the shower. Then she sank down on the toilet and began to shudder. She couldn't seem to catch her breath. Had Trev been talking about Leng? He was older and had been making enquiries.

She pulled out her phone, dug the Blue Lotus Guesthouse business card out of her daypack and dialled. Jorani's familiar voice came over the line.

"Jorani, hi. It's Phoebe Clay. Have you heard from Chan? He took me out to the temples, but he left me high and dry at Preah Khan. I had to walk back to Angkor Wat and call Trevor Morgan to pick me up."

"Miss Clay, Phoebe. I am so sorry. This thing should not happen. Please accept my sincere apology."

"No! No, Jorani. I'm not mad. I'm worried. Have you heard from Chan? Is he okay? And his family?" Please, please, please, let her be wrong. Let Chan's disappearance be a matter of coincidence. Confusion about where and when she was to meet him.

Jorani paused. "Chan is well the last I heard, but there has been a fire. His uncle's home has burned. Chan and his family may be there to help him."

Leng.

"So the uncle—is okay?" Better not to let anyone know how familiar she was with Leng. If word got back to Trev that she'd been talking to him…

Unless he already knew…

She glanced at the closed bathroom door and felt her plans crumbling around her. If Trev knew about Leng, he very possibly knew of her connection to him. What had she landed herself in by calling Trev? The man she'd just heard on the phone wasn't anyone she'd want to cross.

The bathroom steamed and she couldn't very well just sit here letting his water run out. He'd get a tad suspicious if she used all his hot water and hadn't even had a shower.

"Jorani, can you please give me Chan's phone number?"

Jorani did and Phoebe signed off.

She forced herself to strip off her wet clothes and stepped into the shower. The quaking shudders ran through her in waves that even the heat couldn't dispel. She stepped out quickly, though she still wasn't warm. She simply couldn't bring herself to stand naked in this man's home.

She dressed in her bra and panties, but even with the robe, she felt vulnerable. She quickly rinsed the worst of the dust and mud off her clothes, ran a brush from her daypack through her hair, and studied herself in the mirror. She looked pale. Felt pale, too. She certainly didn't look like any kind of threat, that was for sure. If only she could convince Trev of that and still find out what had happened to Sokha.

Taking a deep breath, she left the bathroom with her wet clothes in a ball.

"Where's your drier?" she called out when she stepped into the hall.

"Here," he called from the kitchen.

He stood beyond the kitchen island, a welcoming smile on his face, a freshly brewed pot of tea and two cups on the counter before him, all in an old country rose pattern. "I hope the shower warmed you up a little from the outside in. The tea's to warm you from the inside out." He grinned.

"Thank you. The shower was lovely." Though she doubted whether she'd ever be warm again.

He pulled open a cupboard door and there was a small washer-drier combination like she'd seen on old trips to Europe. She opened the front latch and tossed her wrung-out clothes inside. Trev reached over her shoulder and tapped the keypad and the small machine began rotating.

"There we go, shouldn't take longer than thirty minutes and you'll be good as new. Just enough time for tea."

He poured them each a cup and she climbed onto a leather stool on her side of the counter. "That shower was amazing," she said because she couldn't think of much beyond that to say other than "where have you hidden Sokha."

He nodded. "When I moved here, I recognized that I would be doing without my friends and a lot of the creature comforts of home, so I vowed that creature comforts would be allowed. I had to be comfortable. So I had this place built. Actually, the villagers built it for me in thanks for all I've done for them. They'd still send in a woman to cook and clean for me, but I'm a big boy. I can take care of myself."

She hid her incredulity behind the rim of her teacup. She could believe Trev Morgan vacuumed and dusted his house about as far as she could throw him…

"You're smiling. Why? Don't you believe I can take care of myself?"

She set her cup down and smiled openly at him. "I can totally believe it. I just had a mental image of you with apron and feather duster."

"Now there's a mental picture I'd not like to encourage anyone to have." He grinned and sipped his tea. "So what have you seen of the temples? Maybe I can point out some high points you've missed. Banteay Srei?"

A safe topic, thankfully.

"Oh! Yes. That's the one out all by itself in the jungle. The women's temple, right?"

He nodded. "What did you think of it?"

Her mind raced trying to reclaim her impressions of the place. She remembered the trip out, the lovely stop at the shadow puppet place, and the manic race trying to escape the person on the yellow motorcycle, but of the temple itself, she recalled very little.

"Intimate," she said. "Different from the other temples because they're much larger and seemed to have formed an alliance with the jungle to create something more, something greater. Banteay Srei, though. There isn't any great jungle around it, more like just brush. So it's more like a small jewel in the landscape with its lily pad moat and all those amazing carvings. It's small, but I think that's a good thing because all those carvings could overwhelm you. I experienced that in India at some of the temples. You get so overloaded that you simply don't see anymore. If I was going to describe Banteay Srei, I'd say it was a space where small silences dwell."

Where the heck that had come from, she didn't know. "I guess the bad road and the small size keep a lot of the large tour buses away." Which was a good thing.

Trev inclined his head slightly. "The road is poor, but there are plans to broaden it to two paved lanes. The larger tours will finally be able to come. It will give lots of opportunity for economic development for the villages along the way."

"Really?" She took another sip of tea and hoped he didn't see the slight tremor in her hands. "What kind of development?" Get him talking. Maybe he'd give something away.

"Oh. Well. There are opportunities for the villages. They can open restaurants, perhaps guesthouses—not everyone likes to be in the center of town. People can make and sell locally made wares. They can reintroduce traditional Khmer arts. Theatre, perhaps. Shadow puppets. Dance. They have done that in Phnom Penh and it is well attended by tourists and foreigners alike."

"It sounds wonderful. I never realized that a road could offer such prosperity." She thought a moment. "Won't it take a lot of money to do things like that? The people I've seen in villages aren't rich… They're farmers." When she thought about it, along the road to the women's temple there, she hadn't seen many villages, either. Of course, that didn't mean that there weren't some.

Trev shook his head, then nodded at her tea. "You should drink up. You're still shivering."

So he *had* seen. God, she had to be careful. Obediently, she picked up her cup. Sipped and warmed her hands around the rose-painted sides.

"Money. Yes. Filthy lucre as they call it. The root of all evil. That's where *Cambodia Prosperous* comes in. We can help connect the local people to people with financial means. Together, they can share in the benefits brought by foreign money."

The way he waxed on, she could almost believe that he thought of himself as the people's benefactor.

"It's a wonderful dream to lift these poor people out of poverty. Some that I've seen look like they work ' til they drop. It's not pretty."

The smug smile on his face suggested she'd said the right thing. Maybe she could relax a little. Maybe she could flirt.

As if she even remembered how. And if she couldn't recall how to do it naturally, faking it was going to be a problem.

"I really want to thank you for all you're doing for me. I feel so bad about the other night." She picked up her cup to sip and studied the cloudy liquid rather than meet Trev's gaze. From across the kitchen the clothes dryer buzzed. The thirty minutes were over. Setting her cup down, she slid off the stool. "I should get dressed."

With Trev's help she gathered her clothes now warm and dry and headed for the bedroom. By her watch it was only three o'clock, but she was already dead tired. Fatigue weighted her limbs and fogged her head.

In the bedroom she pulled on her capris and her blouse. Her phone buzzed in her daypack. She fished it out and opened the phone, noticing a text had come in from Alice, her niece, but the phone call was from Chan.

She stabbed talk. "Hello?"

God, even her tongue felt thick. The word sounded like it was a million miles away.

"Miss Phoebe? Where are you? I come for you now."

She slumped down on the edge of the bed. "Chan? You're okay?"

"Fine, Miss Phoebe. Just fine. Uncle's house burned down. Men came. They beat him. I'm so sorry I leave you. I try to send a friend, but he say you were gone."

Leng beaten?

"How is he?" she asked, but the words didn't come out. Instead the room seemed to oscillate around her in waves. They lifted. Lifted higher and then...

The entire room came crashing down and she slid off the bed.

Gone.

18

———————

*B*ecca *sat in a rattan chair in a screened porch before a yellow-and-white house. A blue-and-white vase sat on a glass-topped rattan table. The vase was filled with blue lotus flowers. Unlike the Becca Phoebe knew, this Becca had her hair cut severely over her ears. She had broader shoulders and wore a scowl on her face that was ingrained in deep wrinkles much like the principal at Phoebe's school.*

She shook her head. "I don't know why you're bothering me with your problems. You refused to listen when I warned you. Now you have to pay the price."

She crossed her arms across her chest and gave a disgusted shake of her head. "Typical of you, though. You go running into trouble and then expect others to pick up the pieces."

"But I don't." Phoebe tried to make the statement forceful, but it came out as barely a whisper, quickly stolen by a breeze through the screens. "I don't expect anyone to pick up the pieces. There isn't anyone to do it. Not since you and Alice left."

She wouldn't say abandoned her, because that would suggest she was feeling sorry for herself. But...

"I could use a little help, here."

"You picked the wrong horse, Phoebe. You picked yourself. You

always tell yourself that you don't need anyone and look where that's got you now? You need help, Phoebe. But I've been telling you that for so long that I've given up even hoping you'll listen."

"But I'm alone, now."

Becca turned a disinterested gaze toward her. "Yes. You are."

Phoebe groaned and rubbed her head. Her skin felt tender. So did her brain. Dim light came through her eyelids. Something soft lay under her.

She didn't remember lying down. She remembered…

Having tea with Trevor Morgan.

Oh my God! She struggled up to sitting and the world wobbled around her. She was on a pristine white bed. Cream walls were hung with floral paintings. It was—familiar but she couldn't quite place it. Her head was still full of Becca's face, of Becca's rejection.

What had happened? Where was she? She shook her head and images slowly came flooding back. Preah Khan temple. Being stranded. The storm and sitting at a restaurant table and looking at Trev's business card. Her plan and calling.

There'd been the ride on the motorcycle and then…

A yellow-and-white house.

Had that been reality or the dream with Becca?

She had had a shower and then tea with Trev while she tried to make small talk and mine him for information. The trouble was, she had a feeling that she'd given away more than she'd found out.

Before she passed out?

Because she *had* passed out.

How had that happened?

Had Trev drugged her or was it something natural? If it was natural, she definitely needed to see a doctor.

She stumbled to her feet and crossed to the bedroom door. If it was locked, she was in serious trouble. If it wasn't locked, she was probably still in serious trouble, she just couldn't be sure.

The door knob turned easily and she limped out into the hallway.

The world did a loop-de-loop around her and she clung to the walls, dragged her feet down the hallway to where Trev hummed in the kitchen as he worked.

He must have heard her, because he turned around. "Phoebe! You're up."

It looked like real surprise on his face, but she couldn't be sure.

He glanced at his watch and came around the kitchen counter to her, his expression now one of concern. "You collapsed when you went to change. I picked you up off the floor and left you on the bed to rest. You must have been exhausted. Do you feel better now?"

On the living room coffee table lay her day pack and beside it, her phone. Hadn't she taken the day pack with her when she'd gone to change? She couldn't imagine that she'd left her phone out and exposed, but she really couldn't be sure…

Weren't memory gaps a sign of being drugged? The date-rape drug for example? She scrubbed at her face to hide her alarm.

"I don't know what came over me. I must have been more tired than I thought." And she knew darn well that she hadn't been that tired. She was pretty sure dear Trev had put something in her tea, but she'd woken earlier than he expected.

And that he'd been snooping through her stuff. She tried to take inventory of its contents, but her brain simply wasn't working well enough.

"I've really overstayed your welcome and I should be getting home. I'll give Chan a call so he can come and get me." She headed for her pack.

Trev wiped his hands with a pristine cloth and ran some water into a pot. "That really won't be necessary. I've just put dinner on. At least you can stay for a bite to eat and a glass of wine. Then I can run you home."

The way he said it, she was pretty sure there was no room for disagreement.

"I—I'd really like to get home and have a good night's sleep. Clearly, I've picked up something, given I'm so tired. It must be from going in and out of air-conditioned rooms."

Trev shook his head. "Dinner first. I suspect you haven't eaten much today, correct?" He cocked a brow as if this was simply a social occasion.

Or he was playing with her. Stalling her long enough for something else to happen, like someone to get here. For her.

Because Trev Morgan was the nice English man who lived in an English cottage and ran a wonderful nonprofit charity. He wasn't someone who did the dirty work?

She nodded and glanced down at her pack, but her knees were shaking. She'd had it with her in the bedroom—she remembered that now. So he'd had all the time she'd been asleep to go through her stuff. He could have even unlocked her phone with her fingerprint and read through everything. Not that there was much relating to Sokha's disappearance and Cham Nath's death. But he would have been able to read the flurry of emails between her and Becca reaffirming Becca's determination to have nothing to do with Phoebe as long as she continued "her compulsive investigating and running into danger."

Phoebe had replied with a sarcastic comment about maybe she'd be better in a retirement home. At least they weren't "thought police."

So she truly was alone in this, and regardless of her last text message to Becca, it was doubtful anyone would come looking for her if she disappeared. Of course, Trev would have also seen her last communication to Becca that mentioned Trev's name. He probably wasn't too pleased about that.

It also could explain why he hadn't done anything to her while she was passed out...

He needed her to be somewhere else when the "accident," or whatever, happened.

She needed to get out of here.

She just wasn't sure how.

Trev fussed about in the kitchen and then poured two glasses of wine. He brought hers to her as if he wasn't planning to have her killed, and settled on the couch.

"We just need to wait for the rice to cook."

Outside, the light was fading and the newly planted rice rippled in the fields. The construction site had gone silent, the earth movers hunkered like beasts threatening the landscape. A single snowy egret, abandoning the countryside toward the lake, caught a lone beam of the sunlight through the still-falling rain.

She eyed the wine goblet Trev had handed her. She didn't trust it—not when she seriously suspected he'd drugged her tea. She pretended to sip, barely letting the liquid touch her lips and set the glass down on the coffee table.

"So what's under construction there?" she asked, nodding at the burgeoning pile of earth across the field and edged closer to her pack and phone.

"Eventually? A hotel and golf course. It will provide excellent jobs for the villagers."

"I see. A very ambitious plan." And a lie. There was no way uneducated villagers could operate a hotel except at the menial level. The well-paying jobs would go to educated people brought in from elsewhere, perhaps even from other countries. The locals would become the cleaners. Gardeners, perhaps. From being farmers who owned and worked their own land, to being landless, all so some pasty-skinned foreigner could swing a golf club.

"You look concerned."

She glanced from the darkening view back to Trev. "I was just trying to figure out how you'd build a golf course. There's a lot of good farmland here and people need to eat. Besides, the land floods, doesn't it?"

"The land floods, but we're bringing in fill to raise it above flood levels, and yes, there'll be a few farms lost, but those people will benefit, too."

"How?" She could have kicked herself for how sharply she asked the question.

Both Trev's brows rose and for a moment the twinkle in his blue eyes was obscured by something darker. He set his wine glass down and returned to the kitchen to remove the lid off the rice cooker. He stirred the contents and tasted. "Done. Dinner is just about ready."

She seriously needed to get out of here and she needed to do it now.

He turned on the heat under a wok he had on the stove and opened the lid he had over the contents. Steam filled the air redolent with spices.

"If you're not going to drive me to town, I'll walk." She'd see now whether she could walk out of here, or not.

"Sit down, Phoebe. I'll drive you later—after we've eaten." Though he tried to make his words light, they came out more as an order. The Trev that he'd cultivated with her was wearing off and showing something darker.

Retrieving her daypack and phone from the coffee table, she headed for the door.

Trev was around the counter in a flash. He grabbed her arm and swung her around. "You're not going anywhere."

If she stayed, she was pretty sure no one would ever hear from her again.

"Like hell, I'm not." She stomped down on his instep, jerked loose, and swung her day pack into his head. Hard.

He staggered back. She scrambled for the door and out onto the porch. Leapt off into the muddy open square and set off at a run.

19

Rain immediately soaked her through. Darkness thick enough to smother her enveloped the tiny Cambodian village. Small cook fires glowed, marking the stilted houses. Her sandaled feet sank into the mud as she plunged away from Trev's house. Mud oozed up over her toes and splattered her bare lower legs. Head down the road was the obvious thing to do, but she couldn't afford that. Trev was standing on his porch shouting into a phone. She kept running, past the stilted houses and out of the village, following the road until the light from the house surely didn't reveal her. She cut off the raised road to the right and plunged down the embankment, but the tip of her sandal caught on a stone. She fell, tumbled through tall, sharp grass to splash into deep muddy water. The ditch. She came up spluttering and yanked her pack up, holding it above the surface.

Above her, light filled the road and the roar of a motorcycle engine hurtled toward her. She ducked down behind the grass, for the moment thankful for the cover she'd gained in her fall. The muck she was standing breast deep in was nothing compared to what Trev might do if he caught her.

The motorcycle roared past overhead and she traced the glow of light down the elevated road. But then it slowed.

Stopped.

The headlight beam suddenly panned across the open field. Then the light and the growl of the engine started back toward Phoebe's vantage. More slowly this time.

Trev wasn't stupid. Logic said she couldn't have run so far so fast, so she had to be hiding some place closer to the village. She was pretty sure that her fall had left marks on the bank.

She had to get moving—fast.

Slinging her sodden pack over both shoulders, she turned back toward the village. Hopefully Trev wouldn't expect her to do that. From the village she might be able to reach the construction site and then cut across the fields beyond to the highway. From there it was simply a long walk to home.

With a bit of luck she could do this.

The rumble of the motorcycle set her struggling faster through the murky water. Her body cut a deep V through reeds that filled the ditch in places. Low bushes, invisible in the dark, caught at her hair and shirt. Something slithered over her outstretched hand. Her stifled scream came out as a moan.

If she got out of this alive, she was going to listen to Becca. This was the last time she let herself interfere in matters that were none of her business.

The dark water dragged at her limbs, but she kept going. A glance over her shoulder showed that Trev was almost back to the spot where she'd fallen. She splashed forward more quickly, counting on the sound of the engine to mask her noise. The motorcycle came to a stop just as the ditch she was in reached the edge of the village and curved away to her left. She looked up at the stilted houses. Maybe she could get help if she climbed up. Or she could steal a bicycle. But there was just as good a chance that Trev would catch her there. Better, actually.

Stay in the ditch and head for the construction site? She glanced back the way she'd come. Through a screen of reeds and branches, she could see Trev's silhouette easing its way down the bank. He was not going to be happy having to come after her like this.

She turned back to her dilemma. If she was going to go up to the village, this was the time to go. She could follow the road to the construction site faster than she could get there this way.

Decided, she shoved in amongst the reeds and grabbed low-hanging branches to haul herself up and out of the water. An oath and a splash behind her made her scrambled faster. If Trev caught up to her now, she wasn't sure what he'd do, but it wouldn't be pretty. The swearing floating down the ditch made her certain. Her sandals slid in the muck from the rain. Her hands arms and legs were slicked with the greasy stuff.

She just prayed she could get out of the village before he figured out that she'd doubled back.

A last giant heave brought her up over the edge of the ditch and she lay gasping for breath, then pulled her knees under her. She squatted between two stilted houses. The low fires she'd seen still burned and something stirred in the murky darkness. She caught a glimpse of a face turned ruddy by the fire glow. Chan had said people slept below their houses for the cool. Clearly that was the case and the people couldn't help but have seen her.

She scrambled up and prayed they wouldn't raise the alarm.

No sound came from them. It was as if they didn't exist. Maybe, in Trev's village, they almost didn't. She crept between the houses and reached the road. The motorcycle still idled at the side of the road, its headlight shattering the falling raindrops. Trev's curses carried through the downpour's quiet thrum. He hadn't reached the village yet, but it wouldn't be long if he figured out that she'd headed back this way. Or did he think she could have carried on toward the road?

Wherever she went, she needed to ensure Trev couldn't track her movements.

She looked down at her feet. She wore heavy-soled sports sandals with tire treads. That would stand out in the muddy road like a signpost —infuriating western woman that direction.

With a sigh, she slipped them off and attached the Velcro closures to her pack. She wiggled her toes in the slimy mud and set off down the road, the rain sluicing some of the worst mud from her skin. Her tracks still might stand out because of the narrow shape of her feet, but she didn't figure Trev for a tracker of any kind.

The motorcycle engine roared before she'd passed Trev's home. She started to run, but the motorcycle was coming for her fast. Staying on the road was the best way to be seen. Back to the ditch? She had to think he would guess what she planned if she stayed in the ditch.

That meant...

She threw herself between two houses on the opposite side of the village, just as the motorcycle's headlight beam cut through the village's darkness and illuminated the old ruins and the serene Buddha's face in the center of the village.

From where she was, there was no way to reach the construction site, and the main road that would take her to the highway was too dangerous. That left only one choice.

She slipped-slid between the houses to the line of brush that separated the village from the fields. Then she sat and slid down the edge of the berm into the paddy field. Soft mud enveloped her lower body.

Black night pulsed around her. Rain slicked down her face. The motorcycle's roar came closer. The beam of the headlight pierced the heart of the dark. The air smelled of muck and manure and growing things and Phoebe was pretty sure she was sitting straddle-legged in all those things, but terror had left her afraid to move.

A rice paddy. One of the ones she'd seen earlier where the people were planting the young stalks of rice. The motorcycle roared to a stop in the village and she pulled her legs in toward her chest, preparing to run. She hoped she hadn't damaged the paddy too much. Planting had looked like back-breaking work.

Overhead, the headlight's beam cut a swath through the rain. The motorcycle engine revved noisily. Then Trev barked something in Khmer. An order? A question?

Either way, the people would likely tell him that they'd seen and he'd be after her. She needed to get going. She shoved to her feet—the mud was only as deep as her shins—and set off barefoot along the edge of the field trying to keep her splashing to a minimum and duck down behind each of the houses. Somewhere along here, if she followed the field, there had to be an adjoining dike that divided growing areas. If she could find it, they usually had paths along the top that could lead her to the other side of the field. From there, she could find her way to the Banteay Srei road and then to the highway and home.

She could do this. She could, though her stomach was regretting not eating Trev's excellent-smelling food. It was a long time since breakfast.

She found moving slowly was actually the best way to make progress. Trying to move quickly like her fear demanded just tired her out. She eased her feet through the mud, trying not to think about what floated, swam, crawled or slithered in the oozing liquid. Trying not to consider her fate if Trev caught her.

From the village came raised voices, then Trev's voice in the tone of an order. Then there were smaller beams of light slashing through the darkness. God, he'd got up a search party. She was doomed.

But the flashlights didn't splash out over the rice paddy. In fact none seemed to turn in her direction at all.

The village fell behind her, and she glanced over her shoulder. There were flickers of light between the silhouettes of the village houses, but none were turned in her direction.

How could that be? She knew villagers had seen her climbing out of the ditch and there was little doubt in her mind that someone had been aware of her slide into the rice paddy.

Were the villagers helping her?

It seemed farfetched, but perhaps it was possible that even the villagers who lived here weren't happy with Trev's arrangement or the changes coming.

She quickened her pace, learning that long, swooping strides without raising her legs out of the water seemed to let her go faster. She hoped.

The village voices diminished. The motorcycle engine faded along the road toward the construction. Trev meant for the villagers to drive her toward him and then she could believe she'd meet with an unfortunate accident. Such things were easily possible with construction equipment.

Tamping down her terror, she fought to slow her breathing. Slowly in, slowly out. Move her legs slowly.

Above, the rains slowed and the clouds parted, exposing a sea of stars. She'd think they were beautiful if she had time to admire them. Instead, there was only the darkness between them that had bled down and filled this landscape. She could barely see her hand before her face, but then something stepped out of the blackness toward her.

Man-shaped. She stumbled back, slipped, and fell on her rear. Mud sucked at her lower body. Her daypack splashed in the water behind her shoulders.

She scrambled to her knees, then her feet, preparing to run straight out into the paddy.

The man-figure hadn't moved. Then it did, advancing a step and she fell back again, but held her feet.

"Who are you? What do you want?"

"Please." Heavily accented English, with the kind of tremor that comes with age.

She saw a flash of what she thought were white palms and he stepped forward again. This time she didn't move.

"Dara. I Dara." That white flash of palm again, but this time she saw it touch the figure's chest, though she still couldn't make out his face.

"Hello, Dara." She nodded. The night air cooled her sodden clothes. The bushes rustled at the edge of the field. She touched her chest with her palm. "Phoebe."

She glanced over her shoulder, fully expecting to see the motorcycle headlight coming her way. Instead there was only the breeze.

"Man bad," Dara said. That white palm came up again and waved toward the village. She could imagine which man he was referring to.

"Trev. Trevor Morgan. Bad," she said.

She thought she saw a nod through the darkness.

"You run. I help," Dara said softly. "Come."

She hesitated to trust him, but what harm would it do given he knew exactly where she was? Almost silently, he turned away and motioned her to follow along the edge of the field. It was only a little farther before a mud dike she'd been seeking rose out of the water and he climbed to the top, then offered her a hand to help her up the slippery surface.

His grasp was dry and rough, the hands of a man used to hard manual labor. She clasped it in thanks as she came up beside him. She caught a glimpse of hollow cheeks and sharp cheekbones and hollow eyes. There was little flesh on this man, yet he used what energy he had to help her.

"Thank you," she said and half bowed.

He patted her hands and turned to motion along the top of the path. Grass grew ankle high, but starlight seemed to catch on the hard-packed earth that followed the top of the dike. He led off, like a sure-footed mountain goat, while she slipped and slid barefoot behind him.

They hurried along the path, with Phoebe only slipping into the paddy once. Then they reached another dike that paralleled the village road. Dara pointed her the way she should go and she thanked him and turned to go, but then she stopped.

Her own escape was one thing. This man had helped her with that. Might he know where Sokha was being held?

She caught his hands. "There is a girl. Sokha is her name. Mr. Yong's daughter. Do you know her?"

His gaze was invisible from the dark hollows of his eyes. He shook his head.

"Girl. Sokha. Where?" She squeezed his hand. "Please." Let him understand how important this was.

He shook his head and danced around a little as he spoke to her in rapid, indecipherable Khmer, but two words caught her attention because he kept saying them over and over. "*Sbek Toch.*"

She thought she recognized them, but couldn't place it.

Frustrated, but realizing the futility of trying to communicate when their languages were so different and the darkness made body language all but impossible to read, Phoebe thanked Dara again and turned the way he had pointed. A dike trail faintly snaked away in the direction she wanted to go, dark muddy water reflected the stars to either side.

She started out, but turned back to see him wave. Then he hurried back the way they'd come. Across the field, the village was still in darkness, save for the glow of Trev's modern home. Whether the people still searched the ditch and fields beyond she didn't know and didn't have time to care. She needed to get far enough away that Trev couldn't find her.

She hurried away, her bare toes slipping in the slick mud, her arms out for balance, her pack banging between her shoulders. How she'd managed to keep it through her battle with Trev, her run, and her numerous falls, she didn't know.

Thankfully, there was no moon to light the landscape so she was harder to see. Unfortunately, it made it harder for her to see, too. The wind rippled the rice fields around her and chilled her muddy clothes. The air carried a scent of moisture that made her think more rain was coming. Overhead, the thickening number of towering clouds said that she'd need to find shelter soon. Night insects set up an incessant thrum and frogs groaned and chirped a chorus.

She almost missed the engine's rumble. Not the motorcycle, thank goodness, but double headlights flared along the road toward the village. She slid down the far side of the dike into the muddy rice paddy. Something small squealed and splashed away from her presence.

The backwash of headlight allowed her to see the car—likely whoever Trev had called to come and take care of her when he drugged her. The car looked older, she thought, though she couldn't be sure. It drove slowly, easing its way over the worst of the potholes. The jarring rattle of car parts reached where she hid. Older, yes. She took a chance and peered over the dike's rim again.

There was something familiar about the car.

It looked like the car that had sat outside her hotel after she'd had her scare at the restaurant. The two men who had watched her had been in that car and were likely here, now. She'd forgotten them because she'd thought Yong had sent them because she was asking questions.

She glanced back at the village. Had it been Trev all along? But how had he known she had spoken to Yong?

Davuth? Had her guide been working for Trev?

That was a bit too great a coincidence wasn't it? No, it was more likely that Trev had had someone watching Yong.

The car rattled past and on to the village, its headlight beams illuminating the weather-silvered wood of the stilt houses and their sad repair. At least sad compared to all the mod cons of Trev's home.

She waited for the car to get a little farther away and then slip-scrambled up to the path on the dike and hurried toward the Banteay Srei Road. If anything, the night grew darker as the clouds once more ate up the sky.

Through the darkness, a line of trees grew up to block her way. The scent of jasmine wafted on the wind along with something pungent and gaggingly unpleasant.

Stifling a need to retch, she covered her nose with her hand. It didn't help much, but the stench reminded her of where she was. She had to be getting close to the main road to Banteay Srei. This was the horrible stench of the tanning factory.

She hauled a scarf out of her bag and wound it around her head and over her nose. It helped—a little. She kept going, the path heading for the trees, but she could see the bulk of the building off to her left. God, how could anyone stand to work there? She'd been told at the puppet school that preparing the skins for tanning involved urine and lime to soften the skins and allow the blood and gore to be removed. But then, in a country with one of the lowest incomes in the world, any source of income would be treasured.

She eyed the building. If it was here, so close to Trev's village, was Trev involved? He could practically order people to work there, given *Cambodia Prosperous* or *Cambodia Prosperity Lands* owned practically everything of value in their lives.

The dike rose under her as the trees neared. Their leaves rustled comfortingly in the night breeze, but even the wind couldn't dispel the effluent stink. The dike ended and she stepped up onto a path between the tall, leafed trees. Pausing long enough to pull her sandals on over her filthy feet, she headed for the road. She really needed to quit getting in situations that involved mud.

The road's damp surface was pale in the night. To the left lay the way to the puppet school and Banteay Srei. Visiting them had been a highlight of her trip, until the motorcycle had come after them. She turned from that direction toward the highway. The next leg of her escape was in sight. Just head for the highway and get home and help. Or she could call the police now.

She decided not to, given the strong possibility Trev could have spies there. She could call Chan, too, but figured he had enough to worry about to keep his family safe. At least get back to the guesthouse. From there she could call Chan and Leng. They, at least, she thought would help her.

She stepped out on the road but something stopped her. She turned around and looked into the dark distance toward Banteay Srei. The road disappeared northward into darkness. Around her the trees creaked in a burst of damp wind that whipped at her hair and clutched at her clothes.

The puppet school.

She swayed and grabbed a tree trunk to hang on. It had been too long since she'd eaten, or maybe it was something else. The world swung around her and she remembered Arun, the young man who worked at the school. He had been telling her about the puppets. There were three styles. *Sbek Thom*, the large ornate puppets she had loved, the painted *Sbek Por*, and small articulated *Sbek Toch*.

The word Dara had been using.

She opened her eyes and stared out into the night. That couldn't be right.

Arun had been such a nice young man and the children had seemed so happy…

But had they been, really? There'd been a sense of desperation, too, though she hadn't seen it at the time. They *needed* to sell those puppets. Was there some darker alternative to working there if they didn't?

She looked at the dark bulk of the tannery and had one possible answer.

No! Arun had been nice. He's been very open with her and she hadn't seen anything wrong.

Like she hadn't with Trev?

No! She'd had a very nice conversation with Arun. He'd told her about the puppets and the orphan or impoverished children and how they came to learn a trade and at the same time save the cultural traditions of the Cambodian people.

And how the puppet school survived regardless of the threats by none other than Mr. Yong.

Her knees gave and she sank down on her heels.

Arun had been the only person who had echoed the tone of Trev's stories about Yong. Davuth and Chan had all been afraid, but it seemed their fear was more about disrespecting a Big Man. Leng, the women in the market and the monks had all told a different story.

And now, when questioned about Sokha, Dara had said the puppet names. If Arun was working with Trev, they could be holding Sokha there. It was close enough to be convenient for Trev, but far enough away he could deny all knowledge…

She glanced once more toward the highway and the journey home —back to Siem Reap, back to civilization and Canada where Becca and Alice waited. If Phoebe could capitulate to Becca's demands, there could be fence mending between them.

Then she thought of the young girl she'd met on the ferry. So young, with all of her life in front of her. And then there was her father, who must be frantic. If he loved her as much as Phoebe thought he did, then he'd probably do about anything to get her back, including sell out his people.

She couldn't allow him to be put in that position. There were too many people here who needed him.

With a sigh, she shoved back to her feet and futilely wiped at the drying mud on her clothes.

"I'm sorry, Becca. I'm doing it again."

She turned away from the highway and started down the road.

20

She soon left the worst of the tannery stench behind, though every now and again the wind would bring a fetid reminder. For the moment, the rain had stopped and the solid gravel road was a welcome change from the slippery dike paths. She thought she made pretty good time hurrying through the darkness. The air smelled of rain on parched earth and carried the promise of more rain. She wondered what this road would be like when the downpour came, but she didn't have time to worry about it. To either side lay the dry fields with their twisted crop of dragon fruit cactus that loomed like fairy tale monsters out of the dark.

Her feet hurt from the time walking barefoot and from the gravel stones that repeatedly got into her sandals. Her skin itched from the mud and her stomach growled rebelliously. Otherwise she was in a lot better shape than other times she'd been in this kind of trouble. And she had reclaimed her phone from Trevor's coffee table, though she wasn't sure how the phone could help her. She could almost see Becca throwing up her hands in frustration.

"Call the damn police," she'd be saying. "That's what they're there for!"

Which was true in Canada and had even been true in India. But here? Trev had urged her to stay away from them. Leng hadn't liked the idea of going to them, either. That suggested she should be careful about calling in the authorities.

A gust of wind sent her staggering sideways.

But if she couldn't call the police, she could still call for help, Becca would say.

And it wasn't a bad idea.

Another wind gust sent a fetid blast of tannery scent into her face. She blinked, coughed, and yanked her scarf back up over half her face against the smell.

Hadn't she yelled at the detectives on too many TV shows who failed to call for backup when they walked into the bad guy's lair?

She kept walking, head down against the growing wind. The smell ended, but if anything, the gusts were increasing both in strength and frequency. She chanced a look up, and ahead, through the darkness, was a wind-tossed copse of tall trees on the right side of the road. Across from it lay a ramshackle greater darkness.

The shadow puppet school.

She stepped off the road into bushes that should help mask the light from her phone. She hauled it out of the pack and pressed the unlock button. The screen sprang to life but there was barely twenty percent battery left. Trev had spent a long time reviewing her phone's contents. Thank God she didn't keep much personal information on the phone.

A text message from Becca flashed on her screen.

Call me. I'm worried.

Phoebe didn't have time to respond, though she was a little surprised. She punched in Chan's number—bless her good memory for numbers—and hit call.

The line buzzed. Buzzed again and again.

Was that someone moving around the puppet factory? She ducked back, further into the bushes, certain that she saw the red glow of a cigarette. She used her palm to mask the glowing phone screen.

She was about to give up on Chan when the line clicked.

"Hello," said a sleepy voice.

"Chan?" she said, keeping her voice low. "Chan, I need your help."

"Miss Phoebe?" He was suddenly awake. "I call the Blue Lotus but no one know where you are!"

His voice sounded too loud and she turned down the volume so no one else could hear.

"Chan, is your uncle with you? Leng? Is he there?"

"Uncle? Yes, he here. His house and everything burn. My mother say he push his nose into too many people's business and now his house all gone and all of their secrets, but uncle laugh and call her old-fashioned. You okay, Miss Phoebe?"

"I'm fine, Chan, but I need to speak to Leng. I think I may have found the girl, but I think I'm going to need some help."

"Very good! Tell me and I will come help."

She closed her eyes momentarily. That was exactly what she was afraid of.

There it was again! That small red glow. Yes, there was definitely someone out there by the puppet school.

"Chan, please put Leng on the phone. I need him to do something for me. Please hurry. My phone battery is low."

She heard the sound of footfall and then, barely heard over the growing wind around Phoebe, "Uncle? Uncle?"

"What? What?" The disoriented sound of Leng waking. The background voices of others waking. She'd disturbed Chan's whole household.

"It is Miss Phoebe. She wishes to talk to you."

The phone changed hands and then the older man came on the phone.

"Phoebe? You are well?" All trace of slumber had erased from his voice.

Wind whipped the bush's branches into her face. She didn't want to burden him with the story of her day. "I think I've found Sokha. The trouble is, I think there are people guarding her. I need help, but I wasn't sure whether to call the police. I thought—I thought perhaps you could get a call through to Yong and tell him where I am and what I'm doing. He might send help."

"Where are you?"

For a moment she hesitated. She might be wrong. She could be causing the puppet school and Mr. Yong a whole lot of trouble for nothing, but from everything she knew, it made sense. Holding Sokha here would keep her close to Trev at a location few would suspect.

"The puppet school on the road to the Banteay Srei. Chan knows it. He brought me here."

"Everyone knows it, Phoebe. It is quite famous. But how do you know the girl is there?"

Quickly she sketched out her information. A few fat drops of rain hit her head and face.

Leng was quiet a moment. "You are a very good investigator, Phoebe. I am impressed. Wait where you are and I will call Yong for help." He hung up.

She slipped her phone into her pocket and sank down in the bushes. The rain increased into a steady pat-pat-pat around her. Enough rain and she might be able to wash off this mud. She was ever the optimist, but the sound of a distant vehicle engine from behind her brought her up to her feet. She couldn't tell whether the vehicle was coming toward her or away, but someone was driving down the road she stood on and there hadn't been enough time for help to arrive.

That meant that either Dara had told someone what he'd done, or else Trev had determined that she wasn't in the construction site or around the village. Hopefully, the vehicle was driving the route to the highway and into town to try to find her there.

Gradually the vehicle engine receded so she breathed a sigh of relief. She was safe for the moment. Increasingly wet, but safe. But then another engine sound came from behind her. This one had the higher-pitched whine of a motorcycle.

Trev.

It had to be, and she was pretty sure he wouldn't retrace the route his men were taking. Which meant he was likely coming here.

To move Sokha?

She couldn't see that happening on a motorcycle.

To get rid of her?

A jolt ran through her because the idea felt too right. He'd had nothing but issues to deal with ever since he took the girl and he couldn't afford to be caught with her. The worst part was it was Phoebe's fault that he'd been pushed into this corner.

No. She was not going to wear any blame for his misdeeds.

What she needed to do was use what little time she had to get Sokha out of harm's way.

The gusts of wind rocked the bushes around her. Down the road, she watched the red arc as the cigarette was thrown away. A figure detached itself from the greater darkness of the puppet school and began pacing up and down the road.

Phoebe watched a moment, counting the number of paces, and used the interval where his back was turned to dash across the road.

She crept through the brush at the side of the road until suddenly something stabbed the arm she used to push the brush aside. She yanked her arm back and gingerly tried again. The weeping limb of a dragon-fruit cactus hung just beyond the line of brush demarking the road.

She eased past and found herself in a field with long rows of cactus, their mop-top gaggle of limbs drooping down under a profusion of white flowers. Even the gusts of wind couldn't dispel their heady, sweet perfume. She inhaled deeply, taking full advantage to rid herself of the tannery stench that still seemed to lay across the back of her tongue. She listened, and through the wind, rain, and the sigh of the trees, she was pretty sure the motorcycle was coming closer.

She had to move, and fast. Unless she was entirely wrong.

No. She had to trust herself. Most of the time her instincts were good.

She followed the line of brush that demarked the field and reached the corner where she stepped among the bushes that separated the dragon fruit from the puppet school. The rain fell harder in large fat drops that splatted on her head and ran down her forehead and into her eyes.

Peering through the branches, she made out the low hump of the corrugated building. Except that there were two.

Of course. She remembered that there had been two buildings.

Arun had run the boys' puppet carving school, but he'd said that there was a silk weaving program for girls, except it was closed at the moment. It would be the perfect place to hold Sokha.

She studied the road, but in the dark, with the rain now falling in earnest, she couldn't spot the person she'd seen earlier. He'd likely retreated to shelter.

The question was, where.

From what she recalled from her brief glance at the "weaving school" the other day, though the building was smaller, it was structured similar to the puppet school, with open areas that faced the road and a more enclosed area on the story above. In the open area there had been looms with half-finished lengths of patterned silk. It would be a good place to stand guard while waiting out the storm.

If the guard was there, it would make her plan harder. And she couldn't for the life of her remember where there might have been stairs or a ladder to the upper level. She'd have to get closer to discover how things were configured and the sound of the motorcycle through the rain said that if she was going to do this, she had better go now.

Easing out from behind her masking bushes, she crept toward the building. Thankfully, the night rain also worked to her advantage by making her harder to see. Praying the guard was busy peering at the road, she chanced a hurried scuttle to the rear of the building and ducked behind a low wall that separated the area under the building from the empty field behind it.

Rain soaked through her clothes and sluiced down her arms and legs, taking some of the caked mud with it. Through the hiss of rain, the sound of the motorcycle came closer.

She chanced a peek over the top of the wall and smelled the acrid scent of cigarette smoke. She chanced a second look and spotted the guard leaning silhouetted against the road. He was watching for the motorcycle.

She quickly surveyed the lower level and spotted the stairs to the upper level. They'd been right there at the side of the building between this one and the puppet school, but she simply hadn't noticed. Bent over to remain hidden by the half wall, she made it to the stairs. They faced the open field and led up into the dark, so she only had to worry about making a sound or the guard turning and seeing her.

Praying the rain would mask any sound the stairs made, she kept her feet to the sides of the risers and quickly climbed up. She was pretty sure the guard couldn't see her even if he turned when she came to the closed door. Locked? Would it squeal if she managed to open it?

There was no knob on the door when she felt for one. Instead there was a two-by-four piece of wood slotted across the door to hold it closed.

She placed her hands under the wood and it lifted easily. Too easily?

More like it was never intended as something to hold in a prisoner. She stepped down a step and allowed the door to swing open and, still holding the board as a weapon, stepped into the dark.

The darkness was total, but the movement of air suggested that she stood in a single large room. The rain pounding the metal roof meant she could no longer hear the motorcycle and not much beyond her own pulse and breathing. She took another step inside.

The air smelled fetid and a urine scent permeated the room.

"Sokha?" she whispered. But if the girl was here, she made no sound.

"Sohka?" Phoebe spoke a little louder.

A small sound. A moan? Came from off to the side. Phoebe followed the sound and banged her shins on something metal. She stopped, listening for a response from the guard.

Nothing.

The moans persisted. She pulled her phone from her pocket and woke it up to allow the light from the screen to show her what she faced and expose who she was.

Sokha lay bound and gagged on what appeared to be an old metal bed frame, though where they might have gotten such a thing was beyond Phoebe at the moment, given most people in Cambodia slept on bamboo mats. Sokha still wore a white blouse and sarong, much as the last time Phoebe had seen her, but the girl's arms and legs were each tied to a corner post with rope. A filthy rag had been stuffed in her mouth. Phoebe felt ill. She'd driven right past the girl twice.

At first Sokha turned her head away from the light. Then she looked up at Phoebe and her gaze went wide in recognition.

Phoebe leaned in close to Sokha's head. "You speak English don't you?"

The girl nodded.

"I'm going to pull off your gag, but don't speak. There's a guard downstairs. You understand me, right?"

Sokha nodded again.

Phoebe untied the knot on the gag and pulled the filthy thing out of Sokha's mouth. Then she dug in her pack for her trusty Swiss army knife and set to work cutting the ropes. It was taking too long. Overhead the rain lessened and through it came the drone of the motorcycle engine. It was close. Too close.

But she couldn't leave Sokha here. Not after all the girl had been through. She kept doggedly sawing, freeing one hand, then the other. She set to work on one ankle while Sokha sat up and picked at the knot tethering her other foot.

The dual attack worked. The knot gave to Sokha's teasing just as Phoebe's knife cut through the last of the rope.

Triumphant, Sokha swung her legs off the bed and went to stand. Her legs failed her and she collapsed back on the bed. She turned a horrified gaze on Phoebe.

The poor kid needed water and Phoebe had a bottle in the pack on her back, but outside, the motorcycle had arrived. The engine cut off.

Water would have to wait.

Phoebe jammed her phone in her pocket and in the resulting darkness slung her arm under Sokha's shoulders to help her off the bed.

The girl grunted, hissed in a breath, but stood. She trembled in Phoebe's hands.

"It's okay," Phoebe said. "We can do this."

Sokha nodded. Phoebe handed her the wooden two-by-four—they couldn't afford to lose their only weapon—and together they limped toward the door.

No good. The male voices downstairs were on the move. Phoebe stopped her retreat to the stairs. There was no way they could make it past the men now. They couldn't even lock the door and call Sokha's father. Sokha's voice on the phone would surely bring him running if Leng's call hadn't done the trick.

"Is there anything else in this room we might use a weapon?" Phoebe asked the girl.

"There are only sleeping mats for the girls that they sent away when they brought me here."

Sleeping mats were made of woven bamboo. Even rolled up they weren't much of a weapon…

But Trev and his crony didn't know she was here. They didn't know Sokha was no longer a prisoner.

"How are you feeling?" Phoebe whispered.

"I can stand on my own." As if to prove it, Sokha slipped free of Phoebe's arm.

"Are you well enough to swing that board?"

"I—I think so."

"Good. Get to one side of the door. Use that board on whoever comes up those stairs."

Phoebe left her to get into position and searched the room until she found a sleeping mat that had, thankfully, already been rolled. She picked it up just as she heard the first footfall on the stairs. Overhead, the tin roof thundered with a sudden deluge.

A beam of light flickered across the ceiling as she turned around. Its backwash caught Sokha pressed against the wall, the board gripped in her hands. The steps up the stairs stopped. There was a brief, but loud conversation in Khmer. Then the footfall rushed up the stairs. No time for Phoebe to get into position on the other side of the door. Instead, gripping one end of the bamboo mat and pointing the other in front of her like a battering ram, she ran for the stairs.

The light filled the room. Darkness filled the stairs. She aimed for the space she guessed was the chest.

The end of the rolled bamboo mat slammed into the man. The

flashlight fell. A figure staggered back. Trev caught in the rolling flashlight's glare. He stumbled back into the man behind him.

For a moment it looked like that might stop their fall, but then their momentum sent them down the stairs in a tangle of swearing, furious men.

"Come on!" She grabbed Sokha and together they leapt down the stairs. Trev was still on the ground, shaking his head. The guard had just about regained his feet. Sokha swung the board and caught him at the side of the head. He went down hard.

She looked like she was going to hit him again, but Phoebe grabbed her hand and the two of them leapt out into the night. The rains had begun again, this time in earnest, instantly soaking them through when they left the building's cover. Sokha turned toward the road. Trev's motorcycle was there, but Phoebe couldn't believe he'd leave his keys there and she didn't know how to operate a motorcycle anyway.

"This way," Phoebe yelled and they headed back the way she had come, through the brush hedge to the dragon fruit forest of twisted trees.

Figuring Trev and the guard would be after them, Phoebe headed back between the cactus rows. The air was still sweet with their blossoms. The parched earth had turned to mud that splashed up Phoebe's legs, even as the rain sluiced the worst of the dried mud from her upper body. Her hair stuck to her skull and falling white dragon fruit petals stuck to her skin.

They reached the end of the field and both of them paused, panting.

"Okay?" Phoebe asked and fished in the pack for the bottle of water. She handed it to Sokha and the girl drank deeply.

"I—I think so. I've not had much to eat or drink since I've been hostage."

Hostage. Phoebe hadn't thought of her as such, but that was indeed what the girl was—a hostage to be traded for the rights of the people to their land. She nodded.

"How did you find me?" Sokha asked. "Why even come looking? I barely spoke to you on the ferry. I pretended to not speak English and basically ignored you."

Phoebe smiled in the darkness, even though there was no way that Sokha could see. "You reach a certain age and you get used to being ignored. But I thought you were charming and got worried when I saw you with Yong. I thought you looked scared and then when Cham Nath was killed and I saw your barrette by his hand, I started asking questions. It didn't make me too popular with anyone."

"Well, thank you. My father must have been frantic, but we long ago agreed that if one of us was taken, we would not give in to the conglomerate."

"*Cambodia Prosperity Lands,*" Phoebe said, the pieces coming together.

"You know it?"

Phoebe scanned the darkness back toward the road. A light had pushed through the brush and was illuminating the trees in spectral shapes. Two figures traced the line of brush along the road.

"We need to keep moving." Trev wasn't stupid. She'd done the unexpected once before. He wouldn't be fooled again. And dammit, where were Leng and Yong and Chan? Where was anyone to help them? She'd even be happy to see the police.

She and Sokha shoved through the brush at the rear of the field into an area of scrub grass and low bushes. It was harder going, picking their way across rough ground, the grass sharp against any exposed skin as they struggled to put as much distance between them and the field as possible. Through the sheets of rain, Phoebe thought there was a line of larger trees ahead, but she couldn't be sure.

Behind came a shout and a glaring flash of light when she glanced over her shoulder. For a moment she was blind, but she had no doubt they'd been seen.

"Run!" she yelled.

Sokha hiked up her sarong and ran. With her much older legs, Phoebe was hard-pressed to keep up.

The light from behind bobbed around her, not letting her disappear into the darkness. Her foot caught on a root and her ankle twisted, but she ignored the pain and limped on. Lightning snaked through the sky. The immediate roll of thunder told her just how close it was. It might not be safe under the trees, but it wasn't any safer out here with Trev on her heels. She kept running but the pain in her ankle surged up her leg.

Sokha disappeared amongst the trees just as a hand fell on Phoebe's shoulder.

21

———————

The hand was a lead weight on Phoebe's shoulder.

She tore away but strong fingers caught the pack on her back and swung her around so fast her legs tangled under her. She went down in the mess of sharp-edged grass and pointed branches, her daypack half off. Mud squelched through her fingers and the air was full of the stench of trampled growing things.

"You stupid bitch. I should have known better than to talk to you. Western women are only trouble." She looked up in time to see Trev's furious face as his flashlight fell toward her head. She blocked the blow with her forearm and felt something give. She slumped forward, moaning.

Then she regrouped and glared up at him. Beyond him stood a second man also with a flashlight. Keep them here. Give Sokha a chance to escape.

"Why did you even talk to me on the ferry? Why arrange to meet Sokha on the ferry and then sabotage the meeting?"

"Stupid cow." He kicked her legs and the rain pummeled her head. "You think I wanted that meeting? Yong insisted we have it there. He'd called in Cham Nath to negotiate and give the meeting credibility. So I gave in. When it didn't work out because of you, it allowed me to suggest a second meeting—at a location that would allow me to secure more leverage in our negotiations."

So Phoebe's presence had set in motion a man's murder and Sokha's abduction. She felt sick to her stomach. Keep him talking. Just keep him talking…

"Why kill Cham Nath?"

Trev went still. "First of all, I have killed no one. As for why Cham Nath died, he was gaining influence in the Lands Bureau and had been advocating policies that were not supportive of our development projects. At least not the role of foreign investors. And then he had the affront to try to mediate a local disagreement. We could read the writing on the wall. He had already made his decision when he climbed on that ferry. A pronouncement could not be allowed."

She shook her head. "I don't understand. Why are you doing any of this?"

He glared down at her through the rain. The flashlight's backwash and the rain painted eerie, shifting shadows on his face. "That's what Yong can't seem to understand. I'm helping Cambodia build its future. *Cambodia Prosperous* is helping villages and villagers. There will be more jobs that will help the economy. A stronger economy means the government will have more income to support the services the people need. If a few villages have to lose their land tenure to make that happen, isn't it still a reasonable cost? I'm bringing progress to a country that has been held back for decades. Cambodia has one of the lowest average family incomes in the world and on the prosperity index ranks in the worst five countries in the Asia Pacific. These people work hard. They should benefit."

"But you and your cronies will benefit more, am I right?"

His backhand came out of the night so fast it sent her reeling into the mud. Trev glanced at his man, the burly, bald man from the restaurant that night. "If she moves, hurt her."

Trev set his flashlight beam on the line of trees. The guard loomed over her. The white glow of the tree trunks through the darkness and rain said these were huge Tetrameles trees like those she'd seen at the Angkor temples.

Trev turned back to her. "She's in there, isn't she?"

Phoebe said nothing. *Please just let Sokha run and keep running.*

He grabbed Phoebe by the hair and hauled her to her feet. Her daypack slid off her shoulder, but she managed to catch it on her elbow. Pain screamed in her scalp and tears ran down her face.

"Isn't she?" he spat.

She shook her head. "In the darkness, I couldn't tell where she went."

He shoved her into his partner's hands. The man's clothes smelled of temple incense, but his grip was rough with calluses. Her wrist throbbed painfully, but she was more worried about Sokha than anything.

If Trev caught her…

Trev stomped off through the rain, his flashlight playing over the trees and the ground in front of him. He disappeared into a gap between the tree trunks that suggested a path. His flashlight flickered dimly and went out as he put more trees between them.

Phoebe stood in the man's grip as the rain increased, trying not to move and increase the pain. Her guard muttered as the wind brought rain in sheets. He shifted as if torn between retreating back to the cover of the weaving school or obeying orders. Phoebe stayed rock-still, waiting. If she didn't move, he wouldn't expect it when she did.

The grip on her arm eased slightly, but she wasn't sure it was enough. He could catch her in a heartbeat unless he was distracted.

She waited. And waited. There was nothing but the thunder of the rain on the leaves and the sound of their breathing, her pulse pounding in her ears.

But then she heard it. Distant, but clear through the sound of the rain, a car engine came closer down the road.

Straining to hear, she didn't move. Was it simply the return of the car Trev had sent to find her? Dare she hope it was it rescue?

From the trees came the alarmed call of a bird. Then another and another. A flock of something winged burst from the trees. Birds wheeled above her and then returned to the forest. Something had happened beyond the wall of trees, but the rain had swallowed any sound.

But the sound of the vehicle engine increased. It was almost here.

Her guard looked toward the road. She heard a car door close. And another. And another. And another.

It couldn't be the search car unless they'd brought reinforcements.

But the way the guard shifted on his feet suggested he didn't think that was the case. He was nervous.

Silently, she focused on his fingers around her arm.

From the direction of the road, voices started calling. She thought she recognized Chan.

The rescue had come, but they didn't know where she was. Or Sokha.

Her phone trilled in her pocket and the guard jerked and swore. His fingers loosened slightly.

She stomped on his instep with all her power.

His grip tightened.

She wheeled in his grasp, kneed him in the crotch, and yanked. He froze, then sank to his knees, his hand releasing her. Then he roared and lunged for her. She turned, screamed, and bolted toward the trees clutching her daypack as she ran.

Please let them hear her. Please.

Lightning flashed overhead and thunder rumbled.

Fearing the guard's wrath, she found wings for her feet and injured ankle. She leapt small bushes, clumps of grass, and was at the tree line. Huge roots snaked out into the grass. She leapt them, too, and bolted under the canopy of leaves, too scared to look back.

But a headlong run could send her right into Trev. She needed to be careful and cautious. And what was it Davuth had said? There were still landmines in some areas?

Slowing slightly, she kept going. She didn't have any choice.

Leaves slapped against her face and arms. A huge vine smacked her shoulder. She ducked under and then leapt behind a trunk to check behind.

There was no one there. Either she'd outrun the guard or he'd given up. Which meant that she could either head back to whoever was at the car, or find Sokha.

She'd been looking for the girl for so long, she wasn't about to lose her now.

Cradling her injured arm against her, she kept going through the trees and realized that the footing under her had changed. No longer just muddy soil, now the footing was harder, though there were still roots and brush to trip her up. Another flash of lightning cut through the darkness. A huge face stared down at her. She stumbled back and almost screamed as the darkness once more engulfed her and the air rumbled. Then she realized what she's seen.

Old ruins. The ruins of Angkor spread for miles across the flat land around the central temples. This was some of them, though clearly not yet available to the tour buses. Because it was dangerous? She didn't want to think about it. Half blind from the lightning, she crept toward the temple. It would make sense that Sokha would hide there. There would be plenty of nooks and crannies for a girl her size to hide in. She just prayed Trev hadn't found her.

Phoebe picked her way over the stones, watching for the flickering light that would betray Trev's location. She stood amongst half-collapsed walls, trees growing up out of the litter of blocks, long roots like ropes draped over openings that opened on each side. In the dark she chose the way that had the fewest roots blocking it and picked her way up and over huge tumbles of stone to the doorway.

The inside smelled of bat guano and mold and she was glad she didn't have a light to see whatever it was twittering over her head. She ducked down and crept forward, stumbling on chunks of stone that had crumbled from the roof, toward a lesser darkness ahead. Hopefully, it was a doorway.

A flash of light fell across the opening.

She froze.

She sought around herself for a weapon, her hand closing on a fist-sized chunk of stone.

The stone by itself wasn't worth much as a weapon, but…

She unslung her daypack. She'd carried the thing for so long it was like a part of her. Now she was going to put it to a different use.

The light flashed across fallen, moss-covered stone and brush beyond the opening.

She quickly dumped the pack's contents on the damp stone and filled it with rock.

"Well, well, well. What have we here?" Trev's voice carried through the rain. Phoebe stopped moving. Had he seen her?

A squeal of pain and then the sounds of struggle came from ahead. Clearly, he'd found Sokha and that couldn't be good. He'd be likely to kill the girl just to be rid of her and he could still blackmail Yong because Yong wouldn't know his daughter was dead.

Phoebe hefted the pack. It was heavy, but suitable to her needs. She hoped.

She crept for the opening and peered out into the sheeting rain. The flashlight had fallen, placing a glittering chiaroscuro kaleidoscope of light and shadow across an ancient courtyard. The light caught on apsara faces amongst vines. A huge, fallen Khmer head lay on its side and two figures struggled beside it. Beyond them was only darkness.

Trev had Sokha by the neck, pressed up against the ancient face. The girl kicked and clawed at him, but couldn't get free and clearly her efforts were weakening.

Stone and vines littered the courtyard floor, but somehow, limping, Phoebe crossed it in just a few strides. Trev's attention was on his victim, but at the last moment he saw her. He turned toward her just as Phoebe swung the pack.

It smashed into his face, but he still held Sokha. Phoebe brought the pack back again and swung it down on his head. The crack of bone reverberated in the small courtyard and Trev screamed.

Phoebe swung the pack again and again. Finally, Trev slumped against Sokha.

The girl shoved him away and he fell to his knees, blood-covered hands covering his ruined face.

Sokha leapt away from him, into Phoebe's arms.

"Phoebe! Miss Phoebe!" A familiar voice traveled through the ruins.

"Here!" she yelled. "In the central courtyard!"

And then there were lights in the dark, illuminating the trees beyond the courtyard where she and Sokha waited. It was roughly square, with four-sided faces above a door on each side except where the head had fallen from the gate behind her. She turned back to Trev.

He wasn't there.

Probably escaped through the gate gaping darkly behind where he'd knelt.

Light streamed through the dark gap that Phoebe had come through and was followed by a stream of people crawling through the gate. There was Chan, blessed Chan. And Leng. Pushing past them came Yong, who took his daughter in his arms, stroking her head, her back, her hair, tears and rain streaming down his face.

Then he looked at Phoebe and nodded. "Thank you."

It was then that the explosion rocked the forest behind the temple.

22

The warm water was a blessing as it sluiced down Phoebe's body and she hummed as she washed, reveling again in the feel of clean. The sandalwood of her soap filled the steamy room as she held her face up to the stream of water. Good. So good, but even three days after Sokha's rescue, she couldn't rid herself of the feel of dried mud on her skin, nor get used to the dead weight of the cast on her left arm or the tensor bandage around her ankle. At the moment the tensor bandage was off—her ankle was only a sprain—and her cast was wrapped in a dark green plastic garbage bag to keep from getting wet.

She finished rinsing and turned off the water to towel off. Today was the big day—the only reason she was still in Siem Reap. Otherwise she'd be back in Thailand, deciding where to go next. Becca might have texted, but she hadn't taken the call when Phoebe phoned. Instead, Phoebe had left a message that she was fine. There'd been no other communication and that hurt more than anything.

Sooo… she'd heard Bali was lovely. Penang in Malaysia was supposed to be good, too, and she'd also heard great things about Vietnam. She could go wherever she chose.

Finished drying off, with a sigh she slipped a comb through her blonde hair and then retreated to her bedroom.

The trouble was, she couldn't seem to get excited about visiting any of them when in the past the prospect of travel had always sent a tingle up her back.

The fans turned lazily above the two beds. On one, Stoney-the-pack lay open, most of her belongings already packed away and ready for more travel. She'd booked a direct flight from Siem Reap to Bangkok the next morning.

Changing into white capris that were ridiculously inappropriate for most activities in this dusty or muddy part of the world, and a robin's-egg blue linen top with three-quarter sleeves that skimmed away from her body, she regretted that all she had for shoes were the athletic sandals that she'd hosed off after her time in the rice paddies and fields.

Sliding her feet into the worn footbeds brought that fateful night right back to her. After all that she and Sokha had been through, the aftermath of the explosion had been worse. First had been the horror of forest matter raining down on them. There'd been the rush of wings as the trees had emptied of their denizens. Then came the male screaming that rose higher and higher, piercing the night.

Phoebe, Chan, and Yong's men had darted through the ruined courtyard gateway, but Yong's men had grabbed Phoebe and held her and the others back. Mines. Someone had stepped on one, and where there was one, there were usually others. They would not let her go and they would not go themselves. Instead they called in the army, and who knew how long that would take?

Too long for the man in the forest.

Phoebe and Sokha were leaving for the hospital in the back of Yong's car when a green truck and soldiers finally arrived. By then the screaming had stopped and dawn glimmered red on the horizon, the clouds and the rains having moved on northward over the jungle-clad mountains of Laos.

She suspected it was Trev who had died, but still didn't know for sure. The guard had also been running. But the military, the police, and even Leng weren't releasing the information to the public and she was no more than a tourist and had no right to know.

Still tired, but ready to face the day, she headed down to the lobby to wait for her ride, but Jorani nodded her to the road. A sleek gray Audi sedan purred waiting. With a wave at Jorani, she headed for the car, but a beaming Chan leapt out of the front seat to hold the rear door for her. Today his usually dusty jeans and t-shirt had been replaced by neatly pressed black trousers and a white, long-sleeved shirt.

"Miss Phoebe! I come, too!" He looked as excited as a kid as he ushered her inside.

Waiting for her was none other than Leng. The older man's scraggly hair was neatly combed and pomaded to hold it in place. He was dressed like Chan so that he looked like a businessman instead of a reporter. Or a reporter in North America.

"Leng," She gave him a hug as Chan thunked the door shut behind her. "It's so good to see you and to have a chance to thank you again for bringing help that night." Thinking of what could have happened tightened her chest. If they hadn't come when they did…

Chan climbed in the front and the driver started out.

Leng patted her back and set her away. "I simply did what had to be done. There was no question of 'if.' I am honored that you trusted me enough to call for help."

Not caring whether he liked it or not, she clutched his hand. "I'm glad you both are here today. It was a team effort that got Sokha free."

"I believe her freedom may have more to do with you than me or Chan. And I believe there are other outcomes as well."

She frowned. The vehicle cruised past the broad driveway of the fancy hotel where Trev had taken her, and gradually the road opened up to highway. They picked up speed and passed the Angkor turnoff, the temples and Khmer faces hidden amongst the trees.

She thought of the fallen Khmer head in the temple ruins, of the placid face while Sokha was strangled by a foreign man. The odd thing was, in the jungle that night, the expressive faces hadn't felt like they showed condemnation for her history. Instead they'd seemed benign —and sad.

She swallowed. "Was it Trev we heard?" she asked softly and glanced at Leng.

"That is state information. It cannot be reported on," he said with his gaze straight ahead, but his chin dipped once in a nod. "I have heard *Cambodia Prosperous* is seeking a new director."

The car turned off the highway onto a gravel road, but this one was newly graded so there was only a slight vibration as they sped between greening rice fields. Ahead lay the decrepit village she had seen, and the winding road to the hilltop. This morning, however, a truck was at the side of the road in the village, the rear filled with lumber that men were unloading. Other young men were repairing roofs and the siding on the houses.

The car swept past and onto the curved road to the hilltop.

This time the iron gates weren't closed. The car swept in and onto the broad circular driveway where Chan had once reluctantly driven his motorcycle taxi. The car stopped by the stairs to the front door and the door swung open. Vitthu ran down the stairs to open the door for her as Chan climbed out and Leng climbed out on his side.

"Welcome! Welcome! Please come with me, Mr. Yong is waiting," Vitthu said, more effusive than Phoebe had seen him. Today he was clad in pristine white trousers and shirt, a gold sash tied around his waist. "We are so honored to have you visit us again."

"I'm thrilled to be invited instead of pushing in where I'm not wanted," Phoebe said.

Color seeped into Vitthu's face. "That was—most unfortunate."

"It was, but you were still most hospitable, Vitthu." He beamed when she smiled and as she introduced Leng and Chan.

With Chan and Leng trailing, Vitthu led them through the house once more to the atrium at the rear. This time, though, he led them through that room as well and out to a terrace shaded by trees that overlooked the pool. A wonderful breeze came off Tonle Sap Lake, whose blue waters glittered in the sun. The breeze ruffled Mr. Yong's dark hair and the plaid sarong he wore when he stood to greet them, though he also wore a long-sleeved white shirt. Beside him waited Sokha, her long hair like an ebony curtain shifting at her movements. She also wore a sarong, this one with blue flowers on it reminiscent of the barrette she had worn that first morning.

"My fine guests," Mr. Yong said and shook their hands. "You have given me the greatest gift possible—my lovely eldest daughter, my family complete once again." He nodded down by the pool where a younger girl dabbled her feet in the blue water. Yong leaned forward conspiratorially. "That is Neary. She wants to go swimming and pouts because I tell her we must honor our guests first. I am too doting as a father."

He motioned them to chairs, and they settled together, Sokha close at her father's right hand. She chatted lightly with Chan while Yong and Leng and Phoebe spoke of the view. Soon Vitthu appeared with tall glasses of lemonade and a pot of tea for those who preferred. Sokha poured and they sipped their drinks. Vitthu nodded and murmured something to Yong in Khmer.

"I saw changes happening in the village at the base of the hill," Phoebe said.

Yong nodded. "They approached me and asked for my help. Already the news travels that something has happened to Trevor Morgan. The villagers no longer wish to associate with *Combodia Prosperity Lands*. It is too soon to say what will happen, but my lawyers are examining the documentation to see if the villagers may reclaim their tenure. At this moment, that company appears to be in disarray. Over the past few days when my people approached them, they cannot seem to find a spokesman. It is not a good thing when it becomes known that you kidnap your enemy's child. They know this. Knowledge of their actions would destroy their reputations and their prospects." He smiled softly, clearly relishing the power he now wielded.

"Together, you three have changed the prospects of many, many people. You have given hope back when all hope seemed lost." He reached over and caught Sokha's hand in his, twining his fingers through hers. Neary gave up her pout and joined her father. She was a pretty child of perhaps eight, with delicate features even more refined than Sokha's. Yong looped his arm around her shoulders. "We have been especially close since I lost my wife four years ago."

The action caught Phoebe's breath in her chest. Once she'd held

Becca's hand like that. And she'd draped her arm over Alice's shoulders. Together they had been family, just as Yong, Neary, and Sokha were family. She wondered whether the two sisters were close, but then relationships changed over the years.

"I'm sorry for your loss," she said. She'd given him back his family, but at what cost to her own? Why hadn't Becca called her back after Phoebe left her message? She'd texted Alice that all was well and had received a happy face emoji in reply. But then, she would never tell Alice all she had been through here. She glanced at Chan and Leng. Chan might be speaking with Sokha while Leng watched the view, but the way they glanced at each other from time to time, there was clearly a connection between them, too.

Family.

Missing hers felt like a gaping wound in her chest. She'd felt this way in India when Becca had left her. She'd thought she'd set the feeling away—had healed enough to go on more adventures.

Alone.

"You look troubled, Miss Clay," Yong interrupted her thoughts.

She shook her head. "A little, perhaps. Seeing you with your girls reminds me that I am a long way from my family."

"Ah," he said. "You have children?"

"Not of my own, no. I never had the opportunity. I have a sister and niece who I love deeply, but we have taken a bit of a break from each other." She sighed, though she hadn't intended to.

Yong's gaze narrowed slightly. Then he released his daughters and stood. "Come. Walk with me for a bit. Lunch will be served in a few minutes."

They left Chan and Leng with Sokha and Neary, while Yong led Phoebe across the terrace to a narrow path that led down amongst a grove of palms, papaya heavy with fruit, and a tall Tetrameles tree that sent a smooth trunk twisting into the sky. The breeze was cool here, the air tinged with the scent of growing things and jasmine that grew in profusion along the wall downslope from where they were.

"You know that I thought you worked with *Cambodia Prosperous* when you first visited here?" Yong said, glancing at her.

She shook her head, surprised. "I didn't. I was just a nosy tourist."

"Sokha had mentioned that Trevor Morgan was bringing a woman to Siem Reap. I wish to apologize, but I had to know what dangers you brought to my people—especially after Sokha was kidnapped. I had you researched. You have an interesting past, Phoebe Clay." He stopped beside a pond that was filled by a small man-made waterfall that tinkled down the hill. In the dark water, dappled orange and white koi drifted languidly—until Yong pulled pellets from a small hollow gourd in a niche beside the waterfall and tossed them on the pool. The water roiled as the fish fed.

He met her gaze. "You have tried to help people—at your school and elsewhere. The last time in India, I believe."

She frowned. "How do you know about that?"

He tipped a brow at her. "A man grows his status through his connections. My business dealings have created connections many places in the world. Plus the detective I hired in Canada happened to speak to your sister." He smiled. "She seems to think you help everyone except yourself. From what I have seen, I think perhaps that is true."

Phoebe looked away, uncomfortable with the conversation and the fact that he was likely right. Her throat felt thick. She nodded so she didn't have to speak.

"I am indebted to you for saving my daughter. My people had searched for her, but no one thought to look there. It was almost as if she was held in the open and was invisible. It took you to see."

Of course Becca said Phoebe could see everything except the trouble she was in with her determination to always meddle in dangerous situations.

"I had no idea things were going to turn out as they did. I simply met a lovely young girl on the ferry and wanted to make sure she was safe. Things just happened." Just as they had at the school, in Johnstone Strait, and in Kochi. "I wish they hadn't..."

Yong raised his brows at her in question.

"Well, I wish I hadn't been put in the situation where I felt it was necessary to ask questions, but in each case I stopped people from being hurt. Isn't that worth something?"

He nodded. "I think perhaps the question is whether it is worth hurting yourself—both risking yourself physically and tearing yourself apart inside. Can you afford to lose those dearest to you? Is that not too high a price?" He caught her hand and squeezed. "For myself, I would pay any price to keep my family safely with me."

She met his gaze; the turmoil had died out in the pond but surged in her mind. "Maybe they're safer without me."

"But are you?" He released her hand and reached into his pants pocket to pull out a folded piece of paper. He handed it to her.

Phoebe unfolded it and looked up at him, puzzled. "I don't understand."

"It is a travel voucher. It will take you wherever you wish to go in the world for as long as you live. I hope you will return to Siem Reap over the years so that we can build our friendship. Perhaps you will bring your sister and niece with you on occasion. Your first flight is booked. You have first class tickets from Bangkok to Vancouver the day after tomorrow."

"What?" Phoebe couldn't believe what she was hearing. "I can't accept this. It's too much!" She tried to hand him back the paper. Besides, where she was going was her decision.

Instead he caught her shoulders and held her to face him. "Miss Clay, it is my gift to you for risking your life to protect one of the two people most precious to me. Now it is time for me to help you regain those who are most precious to you. Please. You need to do this. No matter where you go, you must know that you always have those who love and wait for you at home."

Darn it, all the tears she'd held in place since Becca and Alice had left her started to flow. She squeezed her eyes shut but couldn't stop the gaping ache in her chest. "Thank you," she managed. "Thank you so much."

"Good then. It is settled. Your sister did not think you would do it. Stiff-necked, I believe, was how she described you. Now I have one final thing I must do." He caught her hand and turned her around to face back the way they had come. Vitthu came down the path she had followed with Yong, followed by a blonde woman in a broad-brimmed straw hat, floral blouse, and white capris."

Tall, blonde. Clearly western, and then she recognized the swing of the stride and the shoulder-length bob of the hair.

"Becca?" She almost couldn't get the word out, her chest was so full. "Becca!" And then she was sprinting up the path. Vitthu stepped aside and Phoebe threw her arms around her sister.

Warm arms came around her, hugging as if they would never let her go.

"Oh my God, Becca! How did you know to come? What are you doing here?" Phoebe pulled back to palm her tears away.

Becca nodded over Phoebe's shoulder, a stern look on her face. "It's all his fault I'm so far from home again."

Phoebe's stomach dropped.

Then Becca grinned. "Like he could have kept me away. Alice would have been here, too, except she had an important interview for an advanced photography course she's dying to get into. She was devastated she had to make a choice, but I assured her you'd understand."

Phoebe nodded and Becca caught her hand, squeezed. Her gaze searched Phoebe's. "I've been an idiot, Phoebe. Holding onto my mad when you're my sister. We're family. And it *was* my fault that I was a suspect in Kochi and had to be saved. You just did what you always did when I was a kid—tried to keep me safe. Will you forgive me?"

"Apparently the text message you sent concerned her. She was already packed and had a reservation to come here when my people contacted her about coming. So I arranged an upgrade on a earlier flight." Yong dipped his head as if to say, here she was.

Vitthu spoke softly to his employer and Yong smiled. "It seems lunch is waiting for us if we would care to return to the terrace."

Holding Becca's hand, Phoebe followed Vitthu and Yong back toward the house and Yong regaled them with his hopes for his country and for the people around Siem Reap. Laughter drifted down to them from the terrace. Sokha saw them and waved.

Yong ushered them up across the pool pavers, the sunlight coruscating bright lights into Phoebe's eyes. Then Phoebe introduced Chan, Leng, Sokha and Neary to Becca. She slung her arm around Becca's shoulders.

"And this is Becca, my one and only very special sister."

The others seemed thrilled to meet her and drew her into conversation.

Phoebe sat back, marveling at Becca's presence. Soon they'd be on a plane to Bangkok and the flight home to Alice. The flight would give them a chance to talk, to truly mend things between them. Then she really could get on with her life.

She could hardly wait.

TO MY READERS

1. Thank you for reading *Within Angkor Shadows*. I hope you enjoyed it. If you did, (and even if you didn't) it would be immensely helpful if you would leave a review on Goodreads or your favourite online retailer. Reviews help other readers find my books.

2. Sign up for my newsletter and receive a free novel, a novella and an award-nominated short story. To receive your FREE eBOOKS, go to my website at www.karenlabrahamson.com.

3. While you're there, check out my website for more books, my adventures and extra content.

4. For more links or to chat with me, check out www.facebook.com/karenlabrahamson, or www.instagram.com/karenlabrahamson.

CHEERS!

WATCH FOR: INSIDE FOREST FOG

Book Four of the Phoebe Clay Mysteries.
Coming September 2022

ABOUT THE AUTHOR

Author of the well-regarded Detective Kazakov Mysteries and the Phoebe Clay Mysteries, K.L. Abrahamson writes fantasy and romance as Karen L. Abrahamson and mysteries as K.L. Abrahamson. Her best known books are the unique Cartographer series in which secret agents of the American Geological Society use their powers to take on the purveyors of dark magic. Her romantic suspense and mysteries take readers on adventures to dangerous locations around the world.

Her short fiction has appeared in numerous magazines and anthologies, including Ellery Queen Mystery Magazine, Black Cat Mystery Magazine and Strange Horizons; her short story "With One Shoe" was nominated for a Crime Writers of Canada Award of Excellence.

Karen's background includes time as a police officer, corrections officer, and probation/parole officer.

To find out more about her and her writing, visit www.karenlabrahamson.com

MYSTERY, FANTASY AND ROMANCE
FROM TWISTED ROOT BOOKS

If you enjoyed this book, you might enjoy other titles available from
Twisted Root Publishing in your local bookstore or wherever e-books
are sold.

www.twistedrootpublishing.com or
www.karenlabrahamson.com

*After Yekaterina: A lone-wolf detective must chose between
justice and revenge when murder gets personal in this gritty
novel filled with mystery and adventure. Find it at http://www.
karenlabrahamson.com/books/after-yekaterina/*

AFTERBURN: Vallon Drake, agent of the American Geological Survey, the secret arm of Homeland Security that protects America from illicit changes to its landscapes, discovers her partner smothering in a wall. Now someone is rewriting the Seattle maps and killing AGS agents. Their actions threaten the safety of the entire Northwest and only rogue agent Vallon can stop it.Find it at http://www.karenlabrahamson.com/books/ afterburn/

SHADOW PLAY: Star reporter Kaitlin Blackwood arrives in Cambodia and lands right in the case of her missing father. When men try to abduct her, the wrong man rescues her: B.J. McCallum, ex-man of her dreams, who comes with his own heap of trouble. The two must put aside their differences long enough to solve the case—and maybe save themselves in the process. Find it at http://www.karenlabrahamson.com/books/shadow-play/

www.ingramcontent.com/pod-product-compliance
Lightning Source LLC
Chambersburg PA
CBHW020755190726
48285CB00006B/2042